Once Upon a Christmas

Mistletoe Falls Series, Book #2

Tara Baisden

Sterling Ridge Press LLC

Copyright

Once Upon a Christmas © 2025 by Tara Baisden

This is a work of fiction. Names, characters, places, and incidents either are the product of the author's imagination or are used fictiously. Any resemblance to actual persons, living or dead, events, or locales is entirely coincidental.

Cover designed by Sterling Ridge Press LLC

Published by: Sterling Ridge Press, LLC www.sterlingridgepress.com

ISBN: 978-1-966093-37-4 Printed in the United States of America

First Edition: September 2025

For permissions, contact: tara@tarabaisden.com or visit www.tarabaisden.com

Dedication

For the teachers, the librarians, and the wise Aunt Lilys of the world
who see the story inside us, even when we can't see it ourselves.
And to anyone who needs a second chance—at love, at life, at a happy
ending. This one's for you.

With mistletoe and magic,

Tara

Contents

Chapter 1

"**M**iss Emma! Miss Emma!"

Eight-year-old Lucy Kenmore practically vibrated with excitement near the children's corner of Once Upon a Time Bookshop, her small hands pressed against the curved arm of the reading chair as if she might launch herself into the air at any moment. Her dark eyes sparkled with the kind of pure anticipation that only children possessed—the certainty that wonderful things were always just about to happen.

"My mom said you're writing a new book!" The words tumbled out in a breathless rush. "Is it done yet? Does it have a dragon? Or maybe a princess who saves everybody? Ooh—what if the princess has to teach him how to build snowmen so he won't be lonely in winter anymore?"

Emma Sullivan set down the stack of picture books she'd been shelving and crouched to Lucy's eye level, smoothing the soft cashmere of her burgundy cardigan—one of the last birthday gifts her mother had chosen for her. The child's enthusiasm reminded her why she'd fallen in love with storytelling in the first place.

"Well, sweetie," Emma managed, "I'm still working on it. Sometimes the very best stories take longer to tell."

"But you always make the best stories," Lucy insisted, leaning closer with the conspiratorial air of someone sharing a precious secret. "That one about the girl who talks to snowflakes and learns they each have names? That's my most favoritest. I read it to my baby brother Tommy every single night before bed, and when I get to the part where the snowflake teaches her to dance, he claps his hands and makes squeaking sounds."

The praise wrapped around Emma's heart like a warm shawl, even as it pressed against the tender wound of her current struggle. Six months. It had been six months since her mother's funeral, since the words had simply... stopped coming to her. Six months since she'd been able to write anything more meaningful than grocery lists and thank-you notes.

From across the shop, Emma caught the subtle exchange of glances between Cora Franklin and Molly Carter. Cora, tall and elegant with her ash-blonde hair swept into its signature low ponytail, offered the kind of gentle, supportive nod that had steadied Emma through countless difficult days. Beside her, Molly's chestnut curls caught the morning light streaming through the front windows as she turned from the coffee bar, her hazel eyes soft with understanding. They were more than employees—they were family, the ones who kept Once Upon a Time running smoothly when Emma couldn't quite manage to keep herself steady.

"You know what, Lucy?" Emma said, rising slowly. "The very best stories are like my Aunt Lily's famous apple butter. They need time to simmer and bubble and develop all their flavors before they're ready to be shared with the world."

Lucy's forehead wrinkled in concentration, the expression so earnest it made Emma's heart squeeze. "So... if you taste it too early, it's all burnt-tongue and no good?"

"Exactly like that," Emma laughed. "But I promise—pinky promise, super-duper forever promise—you'll be the very first person I tell when the new book is ready."

"Promise, promise?" Lucy held up her tiny pinky with the solemnity of someone sealing a sacred pact.

Emma wrapped her finger around Lucy's, marveling at how small and trusting it felt. "Promise, promise."

What if there is never a story this time? The thought whispered through her mind like cold wind through bare branches, but she pushed it away as Lucy skipped toward the picture book section, already distracted by a display of winter tales Emma had arranged near the window.

The bookshop settled back into its familiar rhythm around her—the gentle background of soft instrumental music Molly had chosen for the morning, the whisper-soft sound of pages turning as customers browsed, and the comforting hiss and gurgle of the espresso machine where Cora was crafting someone's perfect cup of coffee. Emma moved toward the front of the store, drawn by the November light filtering through the large windows that faced Mistletoe Lane.

The morning carried the crisp promise of winter, and she could see the town square beginning its magical transformation into the Christmas wonderland that drew visitors from across Tennessee and beyond. Pete Morrison balanced on a ladder near the Victorian gazebo, his teenage daughter Katie steadying it while he carefully wove strands of white lights through the intricate woodwork. Their easy laughter drifted across the square, and Emma watched Katie hand her father sections of lights with the practiced efficiency that spoke of years of shared holiday preparations.

The bell above the front door chimed its cheerful welcome, and a small family stepped inside, bringing with them a swirl of chilly air. Emma's attention was immediately caught by the father—tall and broad-shouldered, with kind eyes that crinkled at the corners and the sort of patient presence that seemed to slow time around him. His dark hair showed traces of silver at the temples, and when he smiled down at his children, something about the gentleness of his expression made Emma's heart flutter with unexpected longing.

"Alright, team," the father said. "What's our mission today?"

"Find the perfect-est book for Grandma's birthday!" the little girl announced, then immediately pressed her face against her father's leg with sudden shyness.

"And we need a truck book too," the boy added quickly. "A really big truck. With wheels that can crush stuff and maybe go really fast, but—" He paused, his expression growing serious with the weight of an important clarification. "But it has to be a good story. Bad stories don't count for anything, right, Daddy?"

"You're absolutely right, buddy. Stories do have to be good to count. What makes a story good, do you think?"

Both children scrunched their brows in concentration, the question clearly requiring their most careful consideration.

"It has to make you feel happy inside," the little girl said finally, her words slightly muffled by the way she'd tucked her face against her father's leg. "Or maybe scared, but the good kind of scared. Not the kind that makes you hide under your blanket."

"And it has to be funny," the boy declared with authority. "But not fake funny like when grown-ups pretend vegetables taste good. Real funny that makes you laugh until your tummy hurts."

Their father chuckled as he ruffled his son's hair with obvious affection. "Not fake funny like vegetables. I'll definitely remember that important distinction. Come on, let's see if we can find some really funny stories."

"Good morning," Emma said. "It sounds like you're on a very important mission today."

"We're looking for the perfect book for my mother-in-law's seventy-fifth birthday," he explained. "She reads to these two every Sunday after dinner. We want to find something special—something that will make her smile and maybe remind her how much joy she's given all of us."

"I have just the thing," she said, leading them toward a carefully curated display she'd arranged near the stone fireplace.

"This entire section features intergenerational stories," she explained, selecting a beautifully illustrated hardcover with gilt edges and embossed lettering. "Tales about the special bonds between grandparents and grandchildren, the wisdom that passes between generations, and the adventures that can happen when you believe in magic. But this one," she opened the book to reveal watercolor illustrations that seemed to glow with their own inner light, "is about a grandmother who teaches her granddaughter that the most powerful magic in the world happens when stories are shared aloud and when voices carry love from one heart to another."

The father's eyes lit up as he accepted the book, and Emma watched his children immediately cluster around him, small hands reaching to turn pages as he read the first few lines. The scene created an ache in Emma's chest that was part longing and part recognition.

She wanted to be part of moments like this. She wanted to share stories and laughter and quiet Sunday afternoons that built memories, creating something solid and enduring. She wanted someone who understood that her love of creating children's books wasn't just a career choice but a calling that lived in her bones, someone who would read her stories aloud with the same gentle reverence this father brought to the book in his hands.

"This is perfect," he said after reading the first few pages.

As Emma rang up their purchase at the counter, she found herself studying the details that spoke to the father's character—the way he automatically steadied his daughter when she swayed against his leg, the patient attention he gave his son's excited chatter, and the genuine gratitude in his smile when she included bookmarks featuring characters from her own published series.

"These are from books I wrote," she explained, watching his expression shift to pleased surprise.

"You're an author?" He examined the bookmarks more closely. "What kind of stories do you create?"

"Stories about children who discover they're braver than they thought," Emma said. "Tales about finding magic in everyday moments."

"That sounds exactly like the kind of books the world needs more of," he said, and something in his tone made her believe he truly meant it.

"Say thank you to Miss Emma," he prompted his children as they prepared to leave.

"Thank you, Miss Emma!" they chorused in unison, and the little girl added with the earnest solemnity that only children possessed, "Your bookshop smells the bestest... like books and cookies."

Emma's heart swelled at the compliment. "That might be the most wonderful thing anyone has ever said about my store," she told the girl, meaning every word.

She watched as the family made their way outside and across the square; the father walking slowly to match his children's shorter strides. Occasionally, he stopped to point out something interesting or to listen to one of their rapid-fire observations about the world around them. The sight filled her with a bittersweet mixture of hope and yearning that lingered even after they'd disappeared around the corner toward Pine Street.

Emma remained at the counter, one hand resting on the polished wood that had been worn smooth by years of books and conversations and countless small moments of human connection. Around her, Once Upon a Time hummed with its familiar gentle energy—the sound of soft music and the whispered conversations between customers sharing book recommendations. The scents of fresh coffee and a light sugar cookie fragrance from the candle burning nearby created an atmosphere that regular customers often described as "calming and peaceful."

"That was lovely," Molly said, appearing at Emma's elbow with a steaming mug of coffee. "The way that father included both children in choosing the book, making sure they both felt important to the decision. You can always tell the really good ones by how they treat their kids."

Emma accepted the coffee gratefully, wrapping her fingers around the warm ceramic and inhaling the rich aroma of the medium roast blend Cora special-ordered from a local roaster. "He reminded me of why I fell in love with writing in the first place. There's something magical about parents who truly understand the power of stories, who know that the right book at the right moment can change a child's entire world."

"Speaking of writing," Cora said, joining them with the kind of gentle directness that made her such an excellent manager—firm but never harsh, honest but always kind, "how is the new manuscript progressing? You've been unusually quiet about it lately, and that's not like you."

Emma's fingers tightened around her coffee mug.

"It's been... more challenging than usual," Emma said finally, choosing her words with the care of someone walking across thin ice. "I think I'm still trying to find a new rhythm in my life. Everything feels different now since I lost Mom, like I'm learning to write all over again."

Her mother's death six months ago had shaken more than just her personal foundation—it had rattled the very core of her creative identity.

"Well," Molly said with determined brightness, "whenever you're ready to share your new book, we'll be here with eager hearts and honest feedback. Just like always."

Emma managed a smile, though it felt as fragile as spun glass around the edges. "Just like always," she agreed, then excused herself to tend to the afternoon's tasks upstairs.

The transition from the bookstore's bustling warmth to the quieter atmosphere of her apartment felt like moving between two different worlds. The narrow wooden staircase creaked familiar greetings under her feet as she climbed, each step taking her further from the comforting sounds of commerce and community toward the more challenging territory of solitude and creative responsibility.

She paused on the small landing to gaze through the tall window that offered one of her favorite views of Mistletoe Falls. From here, the town square unfolded like the opening scene of a cherished storybook. Massive elm trees, their bare branches stretching like cathedral arches, waited patiently for the thousands of twinkling lights that would soon drape them in holiday splendor. The Victorian gazebo stood proudly at the square's heart, its gingerbread trim dusted with early frost and its weathered shingles whispering of generations who had gathered beneath it for concerts, marriage proposals, and candlelit caroling.

Her eyes drifted toward Mistletoe Lane, the broad road that circled the square like a protective ribbon. Beyond it stretched the brick-paved sidewalks, busy with neighbors, visitors, and couples strolling hand in hand, their breath rising in delicate puffs into the crisp mountain air, while children dashed ahead, tugging at mittens and scarves as though even the cold couldn't catch them. The storefronts that lined the street each seemed to radiate their own personality. Windows sparkled with holiday displays—towering gingerbread houses dusted with fake snow, mannequins wrapped in red velvet scarves, and displays of sweet treats ready to be devoured. Painted doors in shades of hunter green, cranberry red, and buttercream yellow offered cheerful welcomes, while strands of twinkling lights framed each entryway, their glow casting pockets of warmth into the crisp mountain morning. Mistletoe Falls in winter was the kind of place that belonged on greeting cards, a place so enchanting that even the most practical hearts might pause and believe in the magic of Christmas and the possibility of wishes coming true.

If only she could find the words to capture that magic again.

Shaking off her thoughts, Emma continued up the stairs to her apartment. Her writing office occupied the front corner, perfectly positioned to catch both the morning light and her beloved view of Mistletoe Falls. She had arranged the space with deliberate care: built-in bookshelves lined with children's classics and writing references, a comfortable reading chair in sage green velvet where she often puzzled through stubborn plot problems, and her grandmother's antique desk angled just so, so it caught the shifting light throughout the day.

But today, like so many days before, the space felt more like a battleground than a sanctuary.

She settled into her desk chair; the leather creaking softly as she faced the computer screen where the cursor blinked with mechanical patience. Her deadline loomed with increasing urgency—January 31st, just over two months away. Sophia Dillard, her usually patient editor, had begun sending emails with subject lines like "Manuscript Status Update" and "Contract Obligations Timeline," each message a little more pointed than the last.

Twenty successful books had established Emma as a reliable voice in children's literature. She was someone her publisher could count on for quality storytelling and dependable delivery schedules. That reputation felt meaningless now, when every attempt to write felt like trying to draw water from a well that had mysteriously run dry.

She was more than creatively blocked—she was paralyzed, trapped in a space where inspiration used to flow as naturally as breathing.

The blank document stared back at her from the screen, as empty and unforgiving as it had been for weeks. Emma closed her eyes and reached deep inside herself, searching for the narrative voice that had once emerged so effortlessly—the storyteller who could weave magic from ordinary moments, who could help children believe they were brave enough for any adventure and worthy of any dream.

But the voice that had sustained her through years of successful writing, that had been nurtured and encouraged by her mother's unwavering faith in her talent, remained frustratingly silent.

Emma opened her eyes and let her gaze drift around the space, taking in the shelves lined with children's books—classics that had shaped her childhood, contemporary works that inspired her professional development, and her own published stories arranged in chronological order like a visual timeline of her career. At the center of her desk, positioned where she could see it easily while working, sat a framed photograph of her mother taken just two months before the cancer diagnosis—Loretta Sullivan laughing at something Emma had said, her eyes bright with the kind of joy that had defined their relationship.

Her mother, who had read to her every single night throughout her childhood and had celebrated her daughter's first published story with tears of pure pride. She had been her first reader, her most trusted critic, and the person who believed most fiercely that Emma's words could make a meaningful difference in children's lives.

"I don't know how to do this without you, Mom," Emma whispered. "I don't know how to find the magic when it feels like it disappeared with you."

The words hung in the air like a prayer, or perhaps a confession. Because that was the truth she'd been avoiding for months—the growing fear that her creative gift had been so deeply intertwined with her mother's love and encouragement that losing one had meant losing the other forever.

Emma's fingers moved to the keyboard, hovering over the keys as they had countless times before, trembling with the weight of possibility and failure in equal measure. Maybe today would be different if she tried a little harder. Maybe today the words would come flowing back like water returning to a river that had been temporarily dammed, bringing with them all the stories that had been waiting patiently for their chance to be born.

She began to type, *"Once upon a time, in a place where winter lasted just long enough to make spring feel like a miracle..."*

Then stopped.

The opening felt forced, artificial, like trying to wear clothes that no longer fit properly. Emma stared at the words for a long moment, then selected and deleted them with sharp, decisive keystrokes.

She tried again: *"In a small mountain town where Christmas magic lingered year-round, there lived a little girl who could hear the stories that snowflakes told as they fell..."*

Delete.

"There once was a dragon who was afraid of his own fire and a princess who taught him that the things we fear about ourselves..."

Delete.

Each attempt felt more hollow than the last, more evidence that whatever spark had made her a storyteller might have been buried alongside her mother on that gray morning in May. The day the world had suddenly become a much quieter, less colorful place. The cursor blinked accusingly at her from the empty screen, marking time with mechanical precision while her creativity remained frozen in place.

Emma pushed back from her desk with enough force to send her chair rolling across the hardwood floor. She stood and walked to the window, pressing her forehead against the cool glass, watching the town continue its gentle rhythm of daily life below. People walked their dogs along the brick sidewalks, chatted with friends, and carried packages that might contain perfect gifts for people they loved.

In just a few weeks, this view would be transformed by even more elaborate Christmas decorations and thousands of twinkling lights. Children would press their noses to shop windows, couples would share hot chocolate and stolen kisses under the mistletoe that gave the town its name, and families would create memories that would be treasured for generations.

The irony wasn't lost on her that she lived in a place literally famous for Christmas magic. Yet she couldn't seem to find her way back to the wonder and hope that had once made writing feel as natural and essential as breathing.

Emma turned back to her computer, studying the empty document that seemed to mock her. For a moment, she considered forcing herself to continue, to sit in that chair and type words—any words—until something resembling a story emerged from the stubborn blankness.

Instead, she closed the document without saving it. Not because she was surrendering, but because forcing inspiration had never worked for her before, and it wouldn't work now. Whatever came next—whether it was finding her creative voice again or discovering that her path as a storyteller needed to take an entirely different direction—it would happen in its own time, through its own mysterious process.

Tomorrow she would try again, and the day after that, and every day after that, until either the words returned like migrating birds coming home or she found peace with their absence.

Today, she would simply go back downstairs and be present in her bookshop, helping people find the stories they needed, trusting that sometimes the most important thing a storyteller could do was remember why stories mattered at all.

Chapter 2

Nathan Reid paused in the empty hallway outside the library, his hand resting on the cool brass handle as he studied Mrs. Dorothy Benson through the glass panel. Her posture sent a flutter of concern through his chest—the careful way she held her shoulders, deliberately straight despite what looked like discomfort, and the slow, measured turning of pages in the thick planning binder spread across her desk like evidence of a problem she was trying to solve alone.

The late November afternoon had settled into that particular quiet that belonged only to schools after dismissal, when the last sneaker had squeaked down the corridor toward waiting buses and the final backpack had been zipped with the satisfied finality of another day completed. Nathan had always found this time of day both peaceful and melancholy—peaceful because the building could finally breathe after containing the boundless energy of four hundred children, melancholy because the silence reminded him how much life and purpose these walls held only when filled with young voices and dreams.

He knocked gently on the library door, then stepped inside, immediately enveloped by the familiar atmosphere Mrs. Benson had cultivated over her twenty-five years of service. The scent of well-loved books mingled with the lingering sweetness of apple-cinnamon from the potpourri bowl she kept near the reading corner. Late afternoon light streamed through the tall windows, warming the colorful reading corner and creating gentle shadows between the aisles of books that made the library feel like a sanctuary from the world outside.

"Afternoon, Dorothy," Nathan said.

Mrs. Benson looked up from her planning binder, and Nathan caught the flash of pain that crossed her weathered features before she managed her usual warm smile. Her silver hair was pulled back in its customary neat bun, but wisps had escaped around her face in a way that spoke of a long day. Most telling were her hands—the way her fingers moved with deliberate care as she closed the binder, each motion calculated to minimize the obvious stiffness in her joints.

"Oh, Nathan, it's so good to see you," she said. "Are you ready to chat about the Christmas play preparations? There are some things we need to discuss."

The slight hesitation before her final sentence made Nathan's administrative instincts sharpen. In three years of working together, Mrs. Benson had never hedged around difficult conversations—her directness was one of the qualities he most respected about her leadership style.

Nathan settled into one of the small wooden chairs across from her desk, his long frame folding awkwardly into furniture designed for much shorter occupants. His knees nearly touched his chest. He'd sat in these same chairs for countless meetings over the years, planning everything from literacy initiatives to the annual spring carnival that had become a cornerstone of Mistletoe Falls' community calendar.

"The fourth-graders are buzzing with excitement about play practice beginning next week," he said, pulling out his phone to check the notes he'd made during lunch duty. "Aaron's already started working with them on the musical numbers during their weekly classes, and the parent volunteer sign-up sheet has been getting enthusiastic responses for everything from costume construction to prop building. Mary Phillips even volunteered to coordinate the PTA refreshments for opening night."

"Yes, that's..." Mrs. Benson paused, flexing her fingers in a way that made Nathan's chest tighten with understanding. "Nathan, I need to be completely honest with you about something that's been weighing on my mind."

The careful formality in her tone made him set his phone aside and give her his complete attention. Whatever she needed to discuss clearly required more than casual conversation. "What's troubling you, Dorothy?"

She remained quiet for a long moment; her gaze drifting to the windows where the first hints of winter were already painting the mountains that cradled their small town. When she finally spoke, her words came slowly, as if each one had been carefully weighed against alternatives that felt equally difficult to voice.

"I've been directing our Christmas play for twenty-five years," she said. "Twenty-five years of watching shy children discover they could be brave enough to speak in front of an audience, creative enough to become someone else entirely for an evening, and confident enough to sing their hearts out for their families and friends."

Nathan nodded. Her Christmas plays had become more than school events—they were community celebrations that former students, now adults with children of their own, still talked about with fond nostalgia. She somehow managed to give every child a meaningful role while weaving together traditional holiday themes with lessons about kindness, courage, and the magic that happened when communities came together.

"It's been one of the greatest joys of my career," Mrs. Benson continued, and Nathan heard the wistfulness that had crept into her voice. "Watching children grow into themselves through the magic of storytelling and performance. But this year..."

She lifted her hands, and Nathan saw clearly what he'd been noticing in fragments in the past—the subtle swelling in her knuckles, the way she'd been favoring her left wrist when reaching for books on high shelves, and the momentary winces she'd been trying to hide when she thought no one was watching.

"My arthritis has gotten significantly worse," she admitted, the words coming out with the exhaustion of someone who'd been carrying a burden alone for too long. "My doctor says it's going to be progressive now, and I need to start making realistic adjustments to activities that require fine motor control and extended periods of physical demands."

A knot of understanding and dread formed in Nathan's stomach as the implications of her confession became clear.

"You already know I've submitted my notice that I'll be retiring at the end of the year. But I think—" Mrs. Benson stopped, took a careful breath, then tried again. "I think I need significant help directing the Christmas play this year. I can still work with the children on their lines and character development, but I need someone else to handle the more physically demanding aspects—the costume fittings that require precision work, the set construction that involves hours of detailed building, the late rehearsals where we're constantly moving props and adjusting lighting, and, let's just be honest... chasing fourth-graders around the multipurpose room."

The silence that followed felt heavy with the weight of tradition hanging in the balance. Nathan understood, perhaps better than Mrs. Benson realized, what it cost her to make this admission. She'd built the Christmas play program from nothing, transforming what had once been a simple holiday assembly into an elaborate production that families planned their entire December schedule around.

"We'll figure this out," Nathan said firmly, though his mind was already racing through the limited options available to them in a town of six thousand people where most residents were either already volunteering for multiple community organizations or working demanding jobs that left little time for additional commitments. "There has to be someone in this community who could step in and provide the support you need."

Mrs. Benson's smile carried both gratitude and worry in equal measure. "I've been thinking about this for weeks, Nathan, lying awake at night making mental lists and weighing possibilities. It needs to be someone who genuinely understands children—not just tolerates them, but truly enjoys their energy and creativity. Someone with enough artistic background to help bring the vision to life, and someone who has both the time and energy to commit to six weeks of intensive, often chaotic rehearsals that can stretch into the evening hours as we get closer to performance time."

Nathan leaned back in the small chair, his mind automatically scrolling through what he privately called his "community resource database"—the mental catalog of parents, volunteers, and residents he'd cultivated since taking the principal position. The list was short, and most of the names on it belonged to people who were already stretched thin with other commitments.

"What about Felicia Nethers?" he suggested, grasping for the most obvious candidate. "She helped coordinate costumes last year, and she has a theater background from her college years."

"Felicia's expecting her third baby in January," Mrs. Benson reminded him gently, her tone carrying the patient knowledge of someone who'd already exhausted the obvious possibilities. "She's barely managing her current volunteer obligations. And Bill Peterson's been traveling for work more frequently since his promotion to regional manager. His wife mentioned at the last PTA meeting that he's gone three weeks out of every month now."

Nathan felt his optimism deflating slightly. "Margaret Foster might have the available time now that her youngest started high school. She's always been supportive of school programs."

"Margaret's wonderful, but she's never worked with children in a creative capacity," Mrs. Benson said thoughtfully. "I worry about the learning curve, especially with such a compressed timeline. The Christmas play requires someone who can think on their feet when children forget their lines or when costumes rip during dress rehearsal or when parents have strong opinions about their child's role assignment."

Nathan rubbed his temples, feeling responsibility settling on his shoulders like a well-worn coat.

"We're not going to let this tradition fail on my watch," he said with quiet determination, meeting Mrs. Benson's worried gaze directly. "The Christmas play means too much to this community, and it means far too much to you personally. I'll find someone who can learn from your expertise quickly and help carry this legacy forward."

Mrs. Benson's eyes brightened with relief, and what Nathan recognized as pride in his response. "I knew you'd step up to the plate and see to this matter quickly. I've always admired your leadership,

Nathan—your understanding that some things are infinitely more important than curriculum standards and budget constraints. You never lose sight of why we're really here."

Nathan felt his cheeks warm at the unexpected praise. Mrs. Benson had been an invaluable mentor since his first day on the job, offering the kind of institutional wisdom and practical guidance that couldn't be learned from education courses or administrative manuals. Her respect meant more to him than any formal evaluation.

"I'll start making calls right away," he promised, already mentally organizing his approach. "And I'll mention this at tomorrow morning's faculty meeting. There has to be someone out there with the right combination of time, understanding, and commitment who would be willing to step into this role."

"Time, understanding, and commitment," Mrs. Benson repeated thoughtfully. "You know, Nathan, those are precisely the same qualities that make for successful partnerships in general. Not just professional collaborations, but personal ones as well."

Nathan raised an eyebrow at the subtle but unmistakable shift in conversational direction. "Dorothy..."

"Oh, hush now. I'm simply saying that finding someone to share important work with—work that truly matters to you—well, that's not so different from finding someone to share the other meaningful aspects of your life with. You spend far too many evenings alone in that beautiful house of yours, and too many weekends working in your office instead of getting out and enjoying life."

Nathan stood up from the small chair, suddenly needing the advantage of his full height to maintain some dignity in the face of Mrs. Benson's well-intentioned but persistent matchmaking efforts. The woman had been subtly hinting about his solitary lifestyle for months, her concern growing more direct with each conversation.

"My personal life is just fine, thank you very much," he said with a slight smile, though his attempt at lighthearted deflection only made Mrs. Benson's knowing look more pronounced.

"Is it really? When was the last time you shared dinner with someone besides Aaron Morgan or a stack of budget reports? When was the last time you had exciting news to share with someone who would be genuinely thrilled about your successes because they care about your happiness?" The questions came gently but relentlessly, each one landing with uncomfortable accuracy. "When was the last time you had someone to talk through a difficult decision with other than the faculty, someone whose opinion you valued not because of their professional expertise but because you trusted their heart?"

The questions hung in the air between them like morning mist, each one settling into spaces Nathan had been carefully avoiding for the past three years. He loved his job with genuine passion, believed deeply in the importance of education and community building, and found real satisfaction in watching children grow and discover their capabilities. But Mrs. Benson's gentle interrogation forced him to acknowledge what he'd been avoiding—the growing awareness that professional fulfillment, while meaningful and necessary, wasn't quite the same thing as a complete life.

"Finding the right person to help with the Christmas play is my immediate priority," he said carefully, choosing his words like someone navigating around dangerous terrain. "Everything else can wait until after I've solved this more pressing problem."

"Of course. The play comes first—it has to. But Nathan?" She paused until he met her knowing gaze. "Just keep an open mind, dear. Sometimes life has a way of working things out better than we planned."

Nathan wasn't entirely sure what that meant, but something in Mrs. Benson's tone suggested it was worth filing away for later consideration. Her instincts about people and situations had proven remarkably accurate over the years.

"I should head back to my office," he said, glancing at his watch. "I want to put together a list of potential volunteers before I go home tonight."

"Of course," Mrs. Benson agreed, rising from her chair with careful movements. "And Nathan? Thank you. For not even entertaining the possibility of scaling back or canceling the play this year. For understanding that some traditions are worth fighting for, even when the path forward isn't immediately clear."

Nathan paused at the library door, his hand on the handle as he looked back at the woman who'd shaped not just his understanding of elementary education but also his appreciation for the quiet dedication that made communities stronger.

"Twenty-five years is far too important a legacy to abandon without exploring every possible solution," he said. "I'll find someone to help us."

"I have complete faith you will."

Nathan made his way through the empty hallways toward his office, his footsteps echoing off the polished floors and colorful bulletin boards that lined the corridors like a gallery of childhood achievement and creativity. The school possessed a different energy after hours—peaceful in a way that reminded him why he'd fallen in love with education in the first place. During regular hours, these halls buzzed with the irrepressible energy of four hundred children learning and growing and discovering new possibilities for themselves and their world. But in quiet moments like this, he could almost sense the accumulated weight of dreams and hopes and futures that moved through these spaces every single day.

His office, located at the end of the main corridor, felt both familiar and slightly lonely as he settled behind his desk. The space reflected his practical approach to leadership—organized but not sterile, professional but welcoming, with photographs of school events and student achievements sharing wall space with his education degrees and administrative certifications.

Nathan opened his laptop and created a new document titled "Christmas Play Co-Director—Potential Candidates." He stared at the blank page for a moment, then began typing the essential qualifications: experience working with children, creative background or artistic inclination, available for six weeks of play rehearsals, understanding of the importance of community traditions, and patience with the controlled chaos that defined elementary school productions.

As he worked, Nathan's thoughts drifted back to Mrs. Benson's pointed comments. He'd been deliberately avoiding romantic relationships since his divorce three years ago, telling himself he needed to focus on establishing his professional reputation. Sure, he'd had a few random dates here and there, but none had ever amounted to anything.

His ex-wife Jennifer's accusation about being "married to his job" had cut so deeply because it contained an uncomfortable grain of truth. He did care passionately about his work and found genuine meaning and purpose in serving his students and the broader community. The question that haunted his quieter moments was whether caring deeply about his professional calling meant he was fundamentally incapable of caring equally about a romantic partner or whether he simply hadn't found someone who understood that his dedication to education wasn't a barrier to love but an essential part of who he was as a person.

Nathan saved the document he was working on and closed his laptop. He gathered his things and prepared to head home but paused at his office window for a moment to look out at the school parking lot, where a few cars remained—teachers staying late for lesson planning and custodial staff going about their cleaning duties. Beyond the parking lot, the mountains that surrounded Mistletoe Falls were already showing the first hints of winter. Their peaks touched with snow that would soon blanket the entire valley in the kind of pristine beauty that made their town a tourist destination for celebrating everything Christmas.

The Christmas play was an integral part of that celebration—not just entertainment, but a cherished tradition that connected past and present, that gave children confidence and families joy, and that reminded everyone why communities like Mistletoe Falls were worth preserving and protecting.

The tradition would continue. Whatever it took, however many calls he needed to make or meetings he needed to arrange, he would find the right person to help Mrs. Benson.

Somewhere in this town was exactly the person they needed. He could feel it.

Chapter 3

Nathan stepped out of Mistletoe Mercantile, the cheerful jingle of door chimes behind him sounding like mockery. Disappointment settled heavily in his chest. Three hours of going door to door among businesses in downtown Mistletoe Falls, and he still didn't have anyone willing to help Mrs. Benson with the Christmas play.

His methodical approach—the same systematic problem-solving that worked so well with budget crises and parent conferences—was yielding exactly nothing.

The afternoon sun stretched long shadows across the brick sidewalks along Mistletoe Lane as Nathan paused to check his phone, scrolling through the list he'd been building since yesterday's conversation in the library. Each business owner's name now had a note beside it: Claire—too busy with holiday orders; Margaret—mother's health issues; Natalie—brother's wedding.

Sugarplum Bakery had been his first stop an hour ago, where Claire Whitfield had listened with genuine sympathy while kneading bread dough, her flour-dusted hands never pausing in their practiced rhythm.

"Oh, Nathan, I wish I could help," she'd said, her voice carrying the kind of regret that told him she truly meant it. "But between the holiday orders ramping up and organizing the tree lighting ceremony, I'm barely sleeping. Have you tried Margaret at the tearoom?"

But Margaret Finley at The Copper Kettle had been equally sympathetic and equally unavailable, explaining apologetically that her elderly mother in Knoxville was having health issues requiring frequent visits. And Natalie Collins here at the Mercantile had just shaken her head before he'd even finished explaining the situation.

"My brother's wedding is December fifteenth," she'd said, gesturing toward a thick planning binder that sat open behind the cash register, sticky notes sprouting from it like colorful confetti. "I'm the maid of honor, which apparently means I'm also the wedding coordinator, florist, and amateur family therapist. I can barely keep up with everything right now, let alone take on a six-week commitment."

Nathan tucked his phone back into his jacket pocket and looked at the town square, where Pete Morrison and his crew were placing more holiday decorations. The sight should've been comforting—evidence of a community preparing for its favorite season, traditions being lovingly maintained by people who understood their importance. Instead, it reminded him of everything at stake if he couldn't find Mrs. Benson the help she needed.

He started walking toward the Once Upon a Time Bookshop, his pace steady but purposeful. Nathan knew Emma Sullivan by reputation, of course—successful children's book author and beloved local business owner. But they'd never had more than passing greetings at community events and the kind of polite exchanges that happened when you lived in a small town.

The bookshop's windows displayed a carefully curated selection of seasonal books alongside holiday decorations and locally crafted seasonal pottery that spoke of Emma's commitment to supporting the broader artistic community. Through the glass, Nathan could see customers browsing among tall shelves, someone behind the coffee bar steaming milk, and the general bustle of a business that had become as much a community gathering place as a retail establishment.

Christmas garland and twinkle lights were wrapped around the doorframe, and the scent of fresh coffee drifted out when he pushed open the heavy wooden door. The warmth hit him immediately—not just the physical warmth of a heated space, but that indefinable coziness that seemed to emanate from walls lined floor-to-ceiling with books, from the soft country music playing in the background, and from the way the lighting made everything feel welcoming and intimate.

"Good afternoon! May I help you find something?"

Nathan turned toward the voice and felt his step falter. Emma Sullivan looked up from the display table she'd been arranging, her striking blue eyes reflecting a genuine interest in his answer rather than the polite-but-distracted attention of someone going through customer service motions. She was prettier than he'd realized during their brief encounters at community events—not in a flashy way that demanded attention, but in the kind of understated, authentic way that made you want to keep looking.

"Actually, I'm hoping you might be able to help with something a little unusual," Nathan said, stepping closer to the display where Emma had been arranging a collection of holiday books for children. "I'm Nathan Reid—"

"The principal at the elementary school," Emma finished, her smile brightening with recognition. The transformation was remarkable, warming her whole face. "Mrs. Benson talks about you all the time when she comes in. She thinks you're single-handedly keeping the joy in education, which is quite a compliment coming from someone who's devoted her life to it."

Nathan's cheeks warmed at the unexpected praise, though he was struck by how naturally Emma spoke about Mrs. Benson, as if the librarian was someone she genuinely cared about rather than simply a customer who happened to buy books. "Actually, she's part of why I'm here today."

Emma's expression shifted to one of gentle concern. "Is everything okay?"

Nathan lowered his voice, not wanting to broadcast Mrs. Benson's struggles to the entire bookshop. "Mrs. Benson is struggling health-wise; her arthritis is getting worse. She can't direct this year's Christmas play alone. I'm searching for a volunteer—someone who can work with her, learn from her, and help with the physical demands of six weeks of rehearsals and performance preparation."

Emma's eyes widened with immediate understanding and sympathy. "Oh, poor Dorothy. She must be heartbroken. The Christmas play means everything to her."

The tightness in Nathan's chest eased slightly at Emma's response. "It does, but she's handling it with her typical grace," he said. "The thought of canceling the play is out of the question. Honestly, it'd be a real loss for the whole community. The kids start looking forward to the Christmas play from the moment they enter kindergarten."

Emma nodded, her fingers absentmindedly straightening the books on the display table as she processed what he'd told her. Nathan watched her face, noting the way her brow furrowed slightly as she considered the problem and the way she worried her lower lip between her teeth.

"What exactly would this person need to do?"

Nathan's pulse quickened with cautious optimism. "Help with costume fittings, coordinate prop construction with parent volunteers, assist with staging and choreography, and be available for rehearsals." He mentally checked off items from the list he'd been refining all morning. "Mrs. Benson needs someone who can manage the physical aspects of the play."

"Someone with time and enough energy to keep up with excited children for six weeks," Emma said.

"Yes. It'd be a big time commitment, but Mrs. Benson's an incredible mentor. Anyone working with her would learn more about bringing stories to life than most people pick up in years of theater experience."

Emma was quiet for a long moment, her gaze moving past Nathan toward the front windows. Nathan could practically see her mind working, weighing considerations he couldn't begin to guess at. The silence stretched just long enough to make him wonder if he was about to add another name to his list of well-meaning but unavailable volunteers.

"I'll do it," she said suddenly, the words coming out in a rush.

Nathan blinked, certain he'd misheard. "I'm sorry?"

"I'll help Mrs. Benson with the Christmas play," Emma repeated. "I mean, if you think I'd be suitable. I don't have formal theater experience, but I understand storytelling, and I love working with children, and—" She paused, seeming to catch herself. "Yes. I'd like to volunteer."

Nathan stared at her, trying to process the sudden shift from desperate searching to unexpected solution. In all his mental preparation for this conversation, he'd anticipated having to make a case for why someone should consider taking on such a demanding volunteer role.

He'd prepared arguments about community service and the importance of supporting education and the incredible learning opportunity that working with Mrs. Benson would provide.

He had not prepared for someone to simply say yes.

"Are you sure?" he asked, the question slipping out before he could stop it. "It really is a large time commitment. We start play practices next week."

Emma's smile was rueful but determined. "I'm sure. If Dorothy's willing to teach me, I'm willing to learn." She tucked a strand of hair behind her ear, a gesture that seemed somehow endearing. "Sometimes the best decisions are the quick ones you make before you have time to talk yourself out of them, don't you agree?"

"Absolutely," Nathan said. "Mrs. Benson's going to be thrilled... and relieved."

"Well... I hope I don't disappoint her. Or you. Or the children."

"You won't. I can already tell you will be perfect for this."

Emma's cheeks flushed pink, and Nathan realized he was staring at her pretty face like a lovesick teenager.

"Would you like to have dinner tonight?" The question emerged before Nathan had fully formed the thought, propelled by the sudden realization that he didn't want this conversation to end. There were things about Emma Sullivan he wanted to learn more about that went beyond her qualifications for helping with the Christmas play. "To discuss the details, I mean. The play logistics... of course."

Emma's eyebrows rose slightly, and Nathan caught a glimmer of what might've been amusement dancing in her eyes. "Dinner would be lovely," she said. "For discussing play logistics, of course."

"Seven o'clock?" he asked, trying to ignore the way his pulse had picked up. "The Fireside Diner... maybe, if that's okay with you."

"Seven's perfect," Emma said. "And I love The Fireside."

Nathan noticed that their conversation had attracted the attention of her employees, who were making a valiant effort to appear busy while clearly monitoring the interaction with interest. The blonde woman was now wiping down the espresso machine with suspicious thoroughness, while the younger woman had moved on to straightening the magazine display, her head tilted at an angle that suggested acute eavesdropping.

Nathan shook his head and grinned. "Thank you. I mean it. You have no idea how much this means to me and to the whole school community."

Emma's smile was warm and slightly self-deprecating. "Ask me again in six weeks, when we're trying to convince a stage full of fourth-graders to remember their lines while wearing angel wings and tinsel halos."

Nathan laughed, surprised by the genuine pleasure the mental image brought him. He could picture it perfectly—Emma kneeling at a child's level, her voice patient and encouraging as she helped them adjust a crooked halo, her natural warmth putting nervous young performers at ease. "I have a feeling you're going to handle that challenge better than you think."

"We'll find out," Emma said. "See you at seven, Principal Reid."

"Nathan," he corrected. "Let's just drop the formalities."

"Nathan," Emma repeated, and the way she said his name—warmly, as if she were trying it out and finding it to her liking—made him realize he was in serious danger of staying longer in her bookshop than needed, grinning like an idiot instead of gracefully making his exit.

"Seven o'clock," he confirmed, then forced himself to turn toward the door before he could find another excuse to extend their conversation.

The bell chimed softly as he stepped back onto Mistletoe Lane, and Nathan paused for a moment to collect his thoughts. The crisis that had been weighing on him for the past day had been resolved, solved by a woman who'd volunteered without hesitation.

Nathan started walking toward his truck, trying to convince himself that his anticipation for seven o'clock had everything to do with the relief of finding Mrs. Benson a volunteer and nothing to do with the way Emma Sullivan had looked at him when she'd said his name.

He was only partially successful.

Chapter 4

E mma stood frozen, staring at the spot where Nathan had been standing moments before, her mind cycling through the same panicked thought: What have I just done?

The question ricocheted through her mind with increasing urgency. She'd just volunteered to help direct the elementary school's Christmas play. Her. The woman who couldn't even finish a children's book manuscript right now.

"Well," Cora's voice cut through her spiral of second-guessing, warm and practical as always, "that was interesting."

Emma turned to find both her employees watching her with expressions of barely contained delight.

"I can't believe I just did that. I don't know anything about directing plays. What if I mess up? What if Mrs. Benson realizes I'm completely unqualified and—"

"Emma." Cora's voice carried the gentle firmness she used to redirect customers who were spiraling into book-selection panic. "Breathe."

Emma drew a shaky breath, then another. "What have I done?"

Molly planted her hands on her hips. "Well, from what I heard, you just volunteered to help with the Christmas play at the school. You'll be fine. You're great with kids. What are you worried about?"

Emma shook her head, pushing a strand of hair behind her ear with nervous fingers. "Writing for children is entirely different from helping direct a play. I write alone in my office, where I can revise and edit and make everything perfect before anyone else sees it."

"Emma. You lead story hour here in the store several times a week," Cora pointed out. "The children who come hang on your every word. You become different characters, you use voices, and you make them laugh and gasp and believe in magic. You are the play for all those children."

The observation stopped Emma short. She loved story time and had been doing it since she had opened the bookshop a few years ago. She transformed the children's corner into whatever world the featured book of the week required—a pirate ship, a fairy garden, or a dragon's cave.

"That's... different," she said.

"Is it?" Molly challenged. "Because from where I stand, it looks exactly like what Mrs. Benson and Principal Reid need. Someone who understands kids, someone who can bring stories to life, and someone who cares enough to make it special."

Emma leaned against the counter, feeling some of the panic begin to ebb. "I suppose I do know how to work with children. And I do understand storytelling."

"Plus," Cora added with the kind of practical wisdom that made her such an excellent manager, "Mrs. Benson has been directing this play for twenty-five years. She's not going to throw you into the deep end without guidance. She needs a partner, not a replacement."

"You're right," Emma said. "This could actually be good for me too… help me get back out in the world and begin to enjoy life again."

She thought about the past six months, the way grief had shrunk her universe to the boundaries of her apartment and office, the bookshop serving as her only real connection to the community she'd always loved. Maybe what she needed wasn't more solitude to wrestle with her creative block, but the opposite—engagement, collaboration, and the kind of meaningful work that reminded her why stories mattered in the first place.

"Exactly," Molly said, her eyes bright with enthusiasm. "You need something different, something that gets you out of your head and back into the world. And working with kids—that's where all the best stories come from anyway… right?"

Emma felt a stirring of something she hadn't experienced in months—anticipation. Not the anxious dread that had accompanied thoughts of her writing deadline, but genuine curiosity about what this new challenge might bring. "The children will probably teach me more than I teach them."

"They always do," Cora agreed. "Principal Reid is a very nice man, by the way… and handsome."

Heat flooded Emma's cheeks so quickly she pressed her palms to her face, earning delighted laughter from both employees. "We're just collaborating on the play."

"Mmm-hmm," Molly hummed, clearly unconvinced. "Is that why you said yes and volunteered so quickly?"

"I said yes because Mrs. Benson needs help, and I care about her," Emma protested.

"Of course," Cora said. "And it has nothing to do with the fact that Nathan Reid is one of the kindest, most dedicated, and single men in town."

"Wait, you know him personally?" Emma asked, then immediately regretted the question when both women exchanged knowing looks.

"Everyone knows him, Emma," Molly said. "He's been the elementary principal for three years, and in that time, he's transformed the school. The teachers adore him, the parents respect him, and the kids light up when they see him in the hallways. He's a highly respected man."

"He volunteers at the food bank every once in a while as well," Cora added. "Never makes a big deal about it, just shows up and works."

"And remember when the Martin family's house flooded last spring?" Molly continued. "He organized the whole school community to help—not just collecting donations, but actually showing up with tools to help with the cleanup. Janet Martin still tears up when she talks about it."

Emma listened to this catalog of Nathan's virtues. She'd sensed his genuine kindness during their brief conversation and had noticed the way he'd spoken about Mrs. Benson and the children with real affection rather than professional obligation.

"He's a good man, Emma," Cora said softly, her expression growing serious. "The kind who shows up, who keeps his word, and who puts others first without keeping score. In my experience, those are rare qualities worth paying attention to."

"I'm sure he's a wonderful person," Emma said, hoping her voice sounded steadier than she felt. "But I'm volunteering for the play because I want to help Dorothy, not because of... anything else."

Both women nodded with the exaggerated understanding of people who clearly didn't believe a word she was saying but were kind enough not to press the point.

Emma glanced at the clock above the coffee bar again and felt a little flutter of anticipation. Four-thirty. In two and a half hours, she'd be sitting across from Nathan at The Fireside Diner.

"You're thinking about dinner, aren't you?" Molly asked with the kind of knowing smile that suggested Emma's face was more transparent than she'd hoped.

"I'm thinking about the play and how I'll have to rearrange my schedule," Emma protested.

"Of course you are," Cora said dryly. "And I'm sure that's why you've checked the clock three times in the past ten minutes."

Emma opened her mouth to deny this, then realized it was probably true.

"It's been a long time since you've looked forward to anything that wasn't directly related to this bookshop," Molly said. "It's nice to see you a little rattled about something new."

Emma considered this. When was the last time she'd genuinely looked forward to an upcoming social interaction? When had she last found herself curious about spending time with someone she didn't know well, interested in learning more about their thoughts and perspectives?

"I'm looking forward to the conversation. Nathan seems like someone who genuinely cares about the children and Mrs. Benson and preserving traditions that matter. It'll be refreshing to speak with someone who understands that some things are worth working hard to protect."

"Absolutely," Molly agreed. "And if he happens to be handsome and single and exactly the kind of steady, caring man who would appreciate a woman who builds her life around books and stories and helping children believe in magic, well, that's just a happy coincidence."

Emma laughed, shaking her head. "You're impossible."

"I'm hopeful," Molly corrected. "There's a difference. You've been so focused on taking care of everyone else—the customers, the bookshop, making sure you meet your writing deadlines even when the words won't come—that you've forgotten to leave room for yourself."

The observation hit closer to home than Emma was prepared for.

"Well," Emma said, smoothing her hands over her cardigan. "I suppose we'll see what happens. For now, I should probably focus on not making a complete fool of myself during dinner."

"Just be yourself," Cora advised.

Emma glanced at the clock again—4:35—and felt that flutter of anticipation intensify. She had just over two hours to finish the afternoon's bookshop tasks, help close up for the day, and figure out what to wear to dinner.

"I should get back to work," Emma said, though she made no immediate move.

"You should," Cora agreed. "Emma. Don't overthink this. Sometimes the best things happen when we stop analyzing and start trusting our instincts."

Emma nodded, feeling the nervous energy that had been building since Nathan's departure settle into anticipation. She was committed to helping with the Christmas play, and she was having dinner with a man who'd impressed her. It was as simple as that.

Chapter 5

Emma pushed through the heavy wooden door of The Fireside Diner, the familiar warmth enveloping her like a well-worn sweater. The scent of pot roast and fresh-baked rolls mingled with the distinct aroma of fresh coffee. She unwound her cream-colored scarf, her eyes scanning the bustling restaurant until she spotted Nathan in the corner booth she'd always considered the best table in the restaurant.

He was studying the laminated menu with the focused attention she'd noticed during their brief encounter at the bookshop, his dark brow slightly furrowed as he considered his options. When he looked up and saw her approaching, his face transformed with a smile so genuine it sent an unexpected flutter through her chest.

"Emma," he said, rising from his seat in a gesture that felt both old-fashioned and entirely natural. "Perfect timing. I was just trying to decide between Carter's famous pot roast that everyone talks about constantly and the chicken and dumplings."

"The pot roast," she said without hesitation, sliding into the booth across from him. "Trust me on this one."

Nathan chuckled, closing his menu with a decisive snap. "Pot roast it is, then. I've learned to trust local expertise."

Vicky Henley, the diner's longtime waitress with silver hair pulled back in a practical bun and laugh lines that spoke of decades serving comfort food to comfort-seeking people, appeared at their table with two steaming mugs of coffee and a knowing smile.

"Well, well," she said, "Emma Sullivan and our elementary principal. Now, this is a nice surprise. The usual for you, honey?"

"Please," Emma said. "And Nathan's having the pot roast as well."

"Excellent choice," Vicky said, jotting on her pad. "Two pot roasts coming up. And might I say, you two make a lovely pair. It's about time our Emma had someone nice to share dinner with."

Heat bloomed across Emma's cheeks as Vicky bustled away, and she focused intently on adding cream to her coffee, stirring with unnecessary concentration.

"Don't mind Vicky," she said, risking a glance at Nathan. "She's been trying to marry off every single person in town for years now."

"I don't mind at all... it's just a unique aspect of small-town life," Nathan said.

Emma took a sip of coffee, using the moment to gather her thoughts. This was supposed to be a professional meeting about the Christmas play, yet sitting across from Nathan in the intimate lighting of their corner booth, she found herself acutely aware of details that had nothing to do with elementary theater—the way his gray sweater brought out the blue in his eyes, how his hands looked strong and capable wrapped around his coffee mug, and the fact that he'd chosen the same booth she would have selected.

"Thank you for agreeing to dinner on such short notice," Nathan said. "I imagine Friday nights are probably busy at the bookshop."

"Actually, Friday evenings are usually pretty quiet," Emma said, grateful for the easy opening. "Most people are either cooking dinner or settling in for the weekend. It's one of my favorite times to catch up on paperwork or just enjoy the shop when it's peaceful."

Nathan's eyebrows rose slightly. "You typically spend Friday evenings at the bookshop?"

"Usually. I live above the store, so it's hard to walk away from work sometimes. And I love the shop when it's quiet—there's something peaceful about being surrounded by all those stories, knowing each book is waiting to find its way to exactly the right reader."

"That sounds incredibly restful, actually."

"What about you? How do you spend Friday evenings when you're not recruiting volunteers for Christmas plays?"

Nathan's laugh was warm and self-deprecating. "Usually answering emails or planning the following week's meetings. Occasionally I'll work on a project in my workshop—I do some woodworking when I need to think through problems with my hands instead of my head."

"What kind of woodworking?"

"Mostly practical stuff. Bookshelves, toy chests for the kindergarten classroom, birdhouses for the community garden." He shrugged. "Nothing fancy, but I like the process of taking raw materials and turning them into something useful."

Emma found herself picturing Nathan in a workshop, sleeves rolled up, hands steady as he shaped wood into beautiful, functional pieces. There was something appealing about a man who worked with his hands, who understood the satisfaction of creating things that lasted.

"I've always admired people who can build things. I can barely hang a picture frame straight."

"It's really just patience and practice," he said. "Though I suppose writing requires the same qualities—taking scattered thoughts and shaping them into something that connects with people."

Emma's chest tightened at the mention of her writing, the automatic reminder of the creative struggles that had been shadowing her for months.

"So," Nathan said, leaning forward slightly, "tell me about the bookshop. How long have you been running it?"

"Four years this January," Emma replied, grateful for safe territory. "It started as a dream I'd been harboring since college—this idea of creating a space that was more than just a retail bookstore. I wanted a place that felt like everyone's favorite reading nook."

"And the writing career? I've heard you've published several children's books."

Emma nodded. "Twenty books so far," she said. "Though I have to admit, the twenty-first is giving me some trouble."

"Writer's block?"

"Something like that," she said quietly. "It's been a challenging year."

Nathan didn't push for details, didn't offer platitudes about creativity being cyclical, or suggest she just needed to power through. He simply nodded, his expression conveying the kind of empathy that suggested he understood how it felt when something you'd always relied on suddenly felt uncertain.

"Well," he said, "maybe working on the Christmas play will shake something loose. Being around kids and their boundless imagination—it tends to be contagious."

Vicky appeared with their dinner plates, the pot roast arriving in generous portions with carrots and potatoes roasted to caramelized perfection. Sprigs of parsley were placed around the edges of the plate, adding splashes of color. Steam rose from the gravy-covered meat, and Emma inhaled appreciatively.

"Vicky, you've outdone yourself again," she said.

"Oh, honey, Carter did all the real work. I just prettied the plates up and carried them out here," Vicky replied. "You two enjoy. I'll be back to check on you in a few."

Nathan cut into his pot roast, took a bite, and his eyebrows rose in obvious appreciation. "This is incredible."

"Comfort food at its finest," Emma agreed, savoring her own first bite. "I actually used to come here as a child with my mom after our Saturday library trips. I'd always have a list of books Mrs. Benson recommended, we'd check them out, and then Mom would bring me here for grilled cheese and chocolate milk."

"You've known Mrs. Benson for a long time, then?"

"Years," Emma said, smiling at the memory. "She was already the elementary librarian when I started school. I was this painfully shy little girl who preferred books to people, and she never made me feel like that was something I needed to change. She'd set aside new books as soon as they arrived that she thought I'd enjoy. She let me help with small tasks like organizing picture books or straightening the reading corner cushions in the library too."

Nathan's expression grew thoughtful. "She has that gift—seeing what individual children need and meeting them exactly where they are. I've watched her work with kids who struggle with reading, kids who are too advanced for their grade level, and kids dealing with difficulties at home. She adapts her approach for each one."

"She does," Emma said, touched by his observation. "She saw that I needed books to be my bridge to feeling confident in the world. And when I started writing, she was the first adult outside my family who treated my stories as real literature worth discussing seriously."

"She mentioned you've done story time at the school before."

"A few guest author sessions over the years. One year I read to the first graders during National Library Week. I remember all those six-year-olds sitting criss-cross applesauce on the reading carpet in the library, completely absorbed in a story about a little mouse who learned to be brave. It was... magical."

Nathan smiled. "That's what I love most about working in elementary education. Those moments when you watch a child learn something new about themselves or the world. It never gets old."

"Is that why you became a principal? For those moments?"

"Partially." Nathan considered the question as he cut another piece of meat. "I taught third grade for five years before moving into administration. I loved the classroom, but I kept seeing systemic things that could be better—ways to support teachers more effectively or programs that could benefit more students. I wanted to have a broader impact."

Emma studied his face as he spoke, noting the passion that animated his features when he discussed his work. This wasn't someone who'd fallen into education as a fallback career; he genuinely believed in what he did.

"What about you?" he asked. "Was writing always the plan?"

"Always," Emma said without hesitation. "I wrote my first story when I was seven—a masterpiece about a dragon who was afraid of his own fire. Mrs. Benson helped me bind it with construction paper and yarn, and I was convinced I was already a published author." She laughed at the memory. "I never stopped writing after that. Stories were how I made sense of the world."

"And now you help other children make sense of their worlds through your books."

"I hope so. I try to write stories that acknowledge real feelings—loneliness, fear, uncertainty—but always end with the message that those feelings don't have to be permanent."

"That's beautiful."

"So... the play. What exactly will I be doing?" Emma asked. "Beyond keeping track of fourth-graders in costumes and making sure they remember their lines?"

Nathan's laugh was warm and entirely free of condescension. "Well, that's actually about sixty percent of the job right there. The rest involves helping Mrs. Benson transform her creative vision into something that can be performed on a multipurpose room stage by children whose attention spans are directly correlated to their blood sugar levels."

"You make it sound like a cross between theater directing and lion taming," Emma said, grinning at his description.

"That's not entirely inaccurate," Nathan admitted. "Though lions are probably more predictable than nine-year-olds."

Emma laughed more easily than she had in weeks, charmed by Nathan's ability to find humor in the challenges of working with children.

"What's your favorite part about these annual Christmas plays?" she asked.

Nathan was quiet for a moment, his fork paused halfway to his mouth as he considered the question. "The moment during dress rehearsal when it all comes together. When the kids stop worrying about their lines and their costumes and just become part of the story. There's this shift that happens, where they stop performing and start believing."

Emma's pulse quickened at the obvious affection in Nathan's voice, the way his face had softened as he described that moment of transformation. This was a man who understood that the real magic happened not in the polished performance but in the process of helping children discover their capabilities.

"That sounds incredible," she said softly. "I can't wait to see it happen."

"You will," Nathan said with confidence. "And you'll probably be amazed by how much you contribute to making it happen."

Emma felt a flutter of anticipation that had nothing to do with nervousness and everything to do with genuine excitement. "How many children are we working with?"

"Forty-six fourth-graders. Mrs. Benson's already done some preliminary casting based on the kids' personalities and comfort levels. Some are natural performers who'll thrive in larger roles; others prefer being part of the ensemble."

"When do you need me to start helping?"

"Monday after school, if that works for you," Nathan said. "Mrs. Benson's planning to walk you through twenty-five years of Christmas play evolution. And fair warning—she's been compiling notes for weeks on ideas for this year's production, and she has opinions about everything from costume construction to the optimal spacing for angels on stage risers."

"I love that she cares that much about getting it right," Emma said. "There's something beautiful about someone who's been perfecting their craft for twenty-five years and still approaches each new project with fresh enthusiasm."

Nathan nodded. "It's rare to find people who care that deeply about their work, who understand that excellence comes from combining experience with a continued willingness to learn and grow."

"What about parent involvement?"

"Enthusiastic but manageable," Nathan said with a grin. "We get volunteers for costumes, set construction, and refreshments for the performance night. The key is giving everyone specific tasks, so they feel included without overwhelming them."

"And the performance itself?"

"December seventeenth, one o'clock in the multipurpose room. The entire community is welcome to attend. We usually have a crowded room."

Emma nodded, picturing the scene. A room full of proud parents and grandparents, children in handmade costumes bringing a story to life, and Mrs. Benson beaming. It sounded lovely.

"I think," she said slowly, "this is going to be fun."

Nathan's smile was brilliant. "I think so too."

"I have a feeling," she said, "that working with you and Mrs. Benson is going to remind me why I fell in love with writing for children in the first place."

"I hope so. And I hope you'll find that the Christmas play gives you the same thing it gives the kids—a chance to discover capabilities you didn't know you had."

They finished dinner talking about everything from Emma's favorite children's books to Nathan's thoughts on the importance of preserving small-town traditions, their conversation flowing with an ease that surprised Emma.

By the time Nathan walked her the short distance down Mistletoe Lane toward her bookshop, Emma realized the nervous anticipation she'd felt earlier had transformed into genuine excitement.

"We should probably exchange phone numbers," Nathan said as they paused beneath the warm circle of light from the streetlight in front of Once Upon a Time. "Just in case."

"Of course," Emma said, pulling out her phone and trying to ignore the little flutter in her chest. There was an odd excitement in watching him type her number into his contacts.

"There," he said, sending her a quick text, so she'd have his number. "Now you can reach me anytime you need to."

Emma's phone buzzed softly, and she glanced down to see Nathan's message: *Looking forward to working with you.—Nathan.* The simple text made her smile more than it probably should have.

"Thank you for dinner," she said.

"Thank you for saying yes to helping with the play," Nathan replied.

"I'll see you Monday afternoon? At the school?"

"I'll be there," Nathan said. "Probably taking notes while Mrs. Benson explains the finer points of angel wing construction and the impact of proper lighting."

Emma laughed, already looking forward to witnessing Mrs. Benson's legendary attention to detail. "I can't wait."

As she climbed the narrow stairs to her apartment above the bookshop, Emma replayed moments from their dinner conversation. Nathan's understanding of her creative struggles, his obvious affection for Mrs. Benson, and the way his face had lit up when he talked about watching children discover their capabilities. She'd gone to dinner expecting to discuss practical details about the Christmas play logistics, but instead she'd discovered that Nathan Reid was someone who understood that the most important work happened in small moments of connection between adults and children.

More than that, she'd discovered that Nathan was someone whose company she genuinely enjoyed, whose thoughts and perspectives she wanted to understand better. The anticipation she felt about Monday's meeting had as much to do with seeing Nathan again as it did with beginning her collaboration with Mrs. Benson.

For the first time in months, Emma was looking forward to something new and excited about possibilities she couldn't yet fully envision.

Chapter 6

Emma kicked off her shoes and curled up in the corner of her sofa, pulling the soft chenille throw around her shoulders. Her apartment felt especially cozy tonight, with warm lamplight creating intimate pools of brightness throughout the familiar space filled with books and photographs and the accumulated comfort of three years of making this place truly home.

She should probably tackle some bookkeeping, review next week's shipment orders, or attempt once again to coax words onto the page for her upcoming book. Instead, she reached for her phone, scrolling to Aunt Lily's number with the sudden need to share the day's unexpected developments with the one person who'd understand both her excitement and her underlying nervousness about what she'd committed to.

The phone rang twice before Aunt Lily answered. "Emma, sweetheart! What a lovely surprise! I was just thinking about you while finishing up some quilting. How is your Friday evening going?"

Emma smiled at the familiar comfort of her aunt's greeting, the way Lily always managed to sound as if Emma's call was exactly what she'd been hoping for. "It was... unexpectedly eventful. I may have done something slightly impulsive today."

"Oh?" Aunt Lily's voice carried a note of intrigued amusement. "Do tell. It's been far too long since you've called with news of anything impulsive."

Emma laughed, recognizing the gentle truth in Lily's observation. When had she last done anything truly spontaneous, anything that wasn't carefully planned and thoroughly considered from every possible angle?

"I volunteered to help direct the elementary school's Christmas play," Emma said, the words coming out in a rush. "Mrs. Benson's arthritis has gotten worse, and she needs someone to work with her. Principal Reid came into the bookshop this afternoon searching for a volunteer, and I just... said yes. Without thinking it through or making a list of pros and cons or considering whether I'm remotely qualified for this."

The silence that followed held what Emma recognized as Aunt Lily processing this information, probably trying to decide whether to be concerned about Emma's sudden departure from her usual careful decision-making or delighted that she'd finally done something impulsive.

"Mrs. Benson," Lily said finally. "She must be heartbroken about not being able to manage the play alone. That woman has poured her heart into these productions for years."

"Twenty-five years," Emma confirmed. "Nathan—Principal Reid—was desperate to find someone who could help her."

"Nathan Reid," Aunt Lily repeated thoughtfully. "I've heard his name before but never met him."

"We had dinner tonight to discuss the details."

"Dinner," Lily said with obvious delight. "How lovely. Where did you go?"

"The Fireside Diner."

"And what did you think of him?"

Emma tucked her feet under her, trying to find words for the unexpected compatibility she'd discovered during their dinner conversation. "He's... thoughtful. Excellent at listening. He understands why traditions like the Christmas play matter, not just for the children but for the whole community. And he talks about Mrs. Benson with such genuine affection—you can tell he really respects her."

"That speaks well of his character," Lily observed. "A man who appreciates the guidance of experienced women is usually someone worth knowing better. Emma, sweetheart, you sound more animated than you have in months. There's a lightness in your voice that I haven't heard since before your mother got sick."

Emma paused, considering this observation. It was true; she felt more energized tonight than she had in quite some time. But was that because of the Christmas play opportunity itself or because of the man who'd presented it to her with such obvious hope and gratitude?

"I think," Emma said slowly, "that I've been stuck in the same patterns for too long. Going through the motions of life without really engaging with anything new or challenging. Maybe volunteering for this play is exactly what I need to shake things up."

"Maybe," Aunt Lily agreed. "Or perhaps what you need is to remember that there are still good people in the world who share your values and appreciate your gifts. People who might help you see yourself the way others see you—as someone with talents worth sharing and a heart worth knowing."

"Aunt Lily, this is about helping Mrs. Benson. It's not about... whatever you're suggesting."

"I'm not suggesting anything specific. I'm just observing that you sound happier talking about this evening than you have about anything in quite a while. And if some of that happiness happens to be connected to spending time with a man that you find interesting, well, that would be perfectly natural."

Emma opened her mouth to protest, then closed it again. There had been something appealing about Nathan's company that had made the evening feel significant beyond their shared commitment to helping Mrs. Benson.

"He's easy to talk to," Emma admitted. "I didn't expect that. I thought we'd spend the evening going over play schedules and budget constraints, but instead we ended up talking about all sorts of things. He has a way of asking questions that makes you want to give honest answers instead of polite responses. And he listened to me as if he were genuinely interested in what I had to say."

"That's a rare quality," Lily said warmly. "Most people are so busy waiting for their turn to speak that they never really listen to the answers they receive. A man who knows how to ask the right questions and then actually hear what you tell him—that's someone worth getting to know better."

Emma smiled at her aunt's assessment, recognizing the truth in it. Nathan had made her feel genuinely heard during their dinner conversation, as if her thoughts mattered to him.

"I'm probably overthinking this," Emma said, though she wasn't entirely sure what "this," was. "It's been so long since I've had a real conversation with someone new, someone who wasn't either a customer at the bookshop or someone I've known for years. Maybe I'm just out of practice with... getting to know new people."

"There's nothing wrong with being excited about this, Emma. Your mother always said that the best things in life usually came disguised as opportunities."

Emma's throat tightened at the mention of her mother.

"She would have loved hearing about my evening," Emma said softly.

"She would have," Aunt Lily agreed.

Emma's phone buzzed softly against her ear, indicating an incoming text message. "Hold on a second. I'm getting a message."

She pulled the phone away from her ear and saw Nathan's name on the screen. Her pulse quickened slightly as she opened the text: *Emma, hope you don't mind me texting so late. Was wondering if you'd like to meet at the school tomorrow around 9 AM? I could give you a quick tour of the multipurpose room and show you where we keep the costume storage and set pieces. Might help us get a jump-start before Monday's meeting with Mrs. Benson. Let me know if that works for you.—Nathan.*

Emma stared at the message, aware that her heart was beating a little faster. Nathan was being thoughtful and efficient, making sure she felt prepared for Monday's official planning session. It was exactly the kind of considerate gesture that spoke well of his character and his commitment to making their collaboration successful.

So why was she having trouble focusing on anything other than the prospect of seeing him again in less than twelve hours?

"Emma?" Aunt Lily's voice called her back to their conversation. "Everything okay?"

"It's Nathan," Emma said, returning the phone to her ear. "He's asking if I want to meet at the school tomorrow morning for a tour before Monday's meeting with Mrs. Benson."

"How thoughtful of him," Lily said, and Emma could hear the smile in her voice.

Emma typed back quickly: *That sounds great. 9 AM works perfectly. Thank you for thinking of that. See you tomorrow.—Emma.*

"I said yes. It makes sense to get oriented before we start making detailed plans."

"It makes perfect sense," Aunt Lily agreed. "And Emma? It's perfectly all right to be excited about tomorrow. About the Christmas play, about working with Mrs. Benson, about getting to know Nathan better. You've been so careful about protecting your heart since your mother died that you've almost forgotten how to let good things in. Maybe it's time to remember that opening yourself up to new experiences doesn't mean you're being disloyal to your grief."

Emma felt a shift in her chest at her aunt's gentle wisdom, a recognition that she had indeed been holding herself apart from possibilities for connection and growth. Not intentionally, but as a way of maintaining control in a world that had already proven it could change unexpectedly.

"I miss her so much, Lily," Emma said quietly. "Sometimes I feel guilty about being excited about anything, like happiness means I'm forgetting how much losing her hurt."

"Oh, sweetheart. Your mother's greatest joy was seeing you happy and fulfilled. She'd want you to embrace every opportunity to feel good again. Grief doesn't heal by avoiding life—it heals by slowly learning to carry love forward into new experiences."

Emma wiped away her tears, grateful for her aunt's ability to offer both comfort and challenge in exactly the right proportions. "Thank you. For listening, for understanding, for reminding me that it's okay to look forward to tomorrow."

"Always. Now, what are you planning to wear tomorrow?"

Emma laughed, caught off guard by the practical question. "I hadn't thought about it. Something comfortable, I suppose."

"Wear something that makes you feel confident and young and attractive."

"Lily," Emma protested, though she was smiling. "It's a tour of school facilities, not a…"

"Not a what?" her aunt asked innocently.

Emma realized she'd been about to say "not a date," but actually speaking those words aloud felt unnecessarily defensive.

"Not a fashion show," Emma finished lamely.

"Of course not," Aunt Lily agreed. "But there's nothing wrong with looking your best while spending time with someone whose company you enjoy."

Emma considered her closet, mentally reviewing options that would strike the right balance between competence and… what? Approachability? Attractiveness? The realization that she was actually thinking about what might appeal to Nathan made her feel both nervous and oddly excited.

"I should probably get some sleep," Emma said.

"Emma? I'm proud of you for saying yes to helping with this play. Your mother would be too. Sometimes the best decisions are the ones we make with our hearts before our heads can talk us out of them."

"I love you, Lily. Thank you for always knowing exactly what I need to hear."

"I love you too, sweetheart. Enjoy your tour tomorrow and remember—it's perfectly all right to be excited about new things."

After they hung up, Emma remained curled up on her sofa for several more minutes. Tomorrow she'd walk through the elementary school where she'd spent some of her happiest childhood years, where Mrs. Benson had first encouraged her love of storytelling.

For the first time in months, Emma was genuinely looking forward to something new, something that had nothing to do with her bookstore or writing obligations. Tomorrow represented possibility—creative collaboration, meaningful work, and maybe, if she was honest with herself, the chance to explore the unexpected connection she'd felt with a man who seemed to understand that the most important work happened when people chose to care about things bigger than themselves.

Chapter 7

Nathan adjusted the stack of planning folders in his arms and glanced at his watch again. Emma would be here any minute, and he'd been pacing the main hallway of Mistletoe Falls Elementary like a teenager waiting for his first date.

Get it together, Reid.

The front door's familiar squeak made his pulse kick up a notch.

Emma stepped inside, pausing just past the threshold as if the building had caught her in some kind of spell. The November morning light followed her in, highlighting the rich brown of her hair and the soft green of her cardigan. But it was the expression on her face that made Nathan's chest tighten—pure wonder, like she'd just walked into a favorite childhood memory.

"Emma?"

She turned toward his voice, and Nathan smiled.

"Hey, Nathan. Sorry if I'm a couple of minutes late. I got distracted by the gorgeous garden boxes out front. Mrs. Phillips would absolutely love seeing how beautiful the landscaping looks now."

Nathan smiled, charmed that Emma remembered details like that. "She actually comes by every fall to help the third-graders plant the autumn mums. Says retirement doesn't mean you stop caring about the important stuff."

"That's so sweet." Emma's gaze wandered appreciatively around the hallway, taking in the bulletin boards bursting with student artwork and the display cases showcasing everything from science fair projects to poetry anthologies. "This feels exactly as I remember it, but somehow brighter. More... I don't know, more welcoming? You've really done something special here."

Warmth spread through his chest. The improvements she'd noticed—the updated lighting, the carefully curated displays, the general sense of pride that seemed to hum through the building—represented three years of thoughtful work. Having Emma recognize those efforts felt surprisingly meaningful.

"Want to start with the multipurpose room?" He asked, gesturing down the hallway. "That's where all the Christmas play magic happens."

"Lead the way." Emma fell into step beside him, her footsteps light on the polished floor. "Fair warning though—I'm feeling pretty nostalgic right now. This building holds a lot of happy memories."

Nathan slowed their pace, partly to give Emma time to soak in the surroundings and partly because he was enjoying watching her face light up with recognition. "What's one of your favorite school memories?"

Emma paused beside the library windows, her smile turning decidedly mischievous. "When I was in second grade, I convinced Mrs. Hicks to let me put on a puppet show for the kindergarteners during indoor recess."

"Of course you did." Nathan grinned.

"I'd written this elaborate story about a princess who was afraid of butterflies. Made all the puppets out of socks and felt, built a whole cardboard castle..." Emma's hands moved expressively as she talked, bringing the memory to life. "But when showtime came, I got so caught up in the storytelling that I completely forgot the princess was supposed to be scared. Instead, I had her chase the butterflies all around the stage while all the kindergarteners cheered like it was the best thing they'd ever seen."

"Please tell me there's more."

"Mrs. Hicks was laughing so hard she could barely help me untangle the puppet strings when everything got twisted together during the finale. But you know what? Every single kid in that room was smiling." Emma's expression grew thoughtful. "It was the first time I realized that making children laugh was one of my favorite feelings in the world."

Nathan felt something shift in his chest as he watched Emma remember that moment. The connection between her childhood joy in storytelling and her adult calling as a children's author was beautiful, and it made her current creative struggles feel even more significant.

They resumed walking down the hallway, their footsteps echoing softly in the quiet building, until Nathan stopped in front of a set of double doors that led to the multipurpose room.

"Here we are," he said, pushing them open. "Home of Christmas play magic."

Emma stepped into the large space and immediately gravitated toward the stage area at the far end. Nathan watched as she took in the folded chairs stacked along the walls, the portable sound system Aaron used for musical numbers, and the storage areas where costumes and props waited for their December resurrection.

"This is perfect," she said, climbing the three steps onto the stage and turning to face the empty room. "I can already picture it—families filling every seat, kids in homemade costumes, and Mrs. Benson directing everything with that wonderful attention to detail she's known for."

Nathan joined her on the stage, close enough to catch the faint scent of vanilla and something floral that seemed to follow her everywhere. "Twenty-five years of Christmas magic have happened right here. Mrs. Benson's transformed this space into everything from Bethlehem to the North Pole to enchanted forests where woodland creatures sing Christmas carols."

"And now I get to help continue that legacy. It's overwhelming."

"You're going to be spectacular at this," he said.

Emma turned to look at him, and he found himself mesmerized by her. They were standing close enough that he could see the way the overhead lights brought out warm highlights in her hair and notice a small scar above her left eyebrow that spoke of childhood adventures.

"Thank you," she said simply. "For trusting me with this."

"Thank you for saying yes when we needed help."

The moment stretched between them, comfortable and charged at the same time, until Nathan forced himself to step back and gesture toward the storage areas. "Want to see where Mrs. Benson keeps all her organizational stuff?"

They spent the next hour exploring the rest of the relevant spaces—the costume storage area, the props and various stage sets that had been used over the years, and the sound booth where Aaron Morgan coordinated musical elements. Throughout the tour, Nathan was drawn in by Emma's reactions as he explained the logistics she'd need to know.

She asked smart questions about sight lines and acoustics, made notes about storage systems, and demonstrated an intuitive understanding of how to balance creative vision with practical constraints. But more than her growing competence, Nathan was drawn to how naturally she fit into the school environment, the way she seemed to belong in spaces designed for nurturing children's growth and creativity.

"I think Mrs. Benson's storage system is more organized than my store's entire back room storage area," Emma said as they finished examining the props that had been accumulating for decades. "Everything's labeled by size, season, or character type. This is inspiring and slightly terrifying."

"She believes chaos in the preparation leads to chaos in the performance," Nathan said, leading Emma back toward the main hallway. "Though she also says some of the best moments happen when plans fall apart and everyone has to improvise together."

"Controlled chaos with room for magic." Emma nodded thoughtfully. "I can definitely work with that philosophy."

As they walked back through the school toward the main entrance, Nathan was reluctant to end their morning together. The tour had accomplished its purpose—Emma now knew where everything was located and had a clear picture of the space where play practices and eventually the play itself would unfold.

"I should probably let you get back to your Saturday," Nathan said as they reached the front entrance, though everything in him wanted to suggest coffee or lunch or any excuse to keep talking.

Emma paused with her hand on the doorknob and looked up at him. "I needed this. I feel so much more prepared now. And seeing the actual space where everything will happen... it makes the whole project feel real and exciting instead of overwhelming."

Nathan nodded, trying to focus on what she was saying instead of the way her enthusiasm made her entire face light up. "Well, I thank you again for stepping up to volunteer. Mrs. Benson is so grateful that you're willing to help, and I'm confident you'll bring this year's play to life in ways we haven't even imagined yet."

"I hope so." Emma smiled with the kind of warmth that made Nathan wonder what it would be like to be the recipient of that smile every day. "Thanks again for taking the time to do this. I know Saturday mornings are probably precious when you spend all week managing four hundred kids and their teachers."

"It was my pleasure. Really. It's been nice seeing the school through fresh eyes, remembering what it felt like when I first started working here and everything seemed full of possibility."

Emma tilted her head slightly, studying his face. "You love it, don't you? The work, the kids, being part of something important."

"I do. Even on the hard days, even when budget cuts and administrative red tape make everything more complicated than it needs to be. Working with children, being part of their growth and discovery... it never stops feeling like a privilege."

"Mrs. Benson was right about you."

"What do you mean?"

"She told me once that you understand the joy in education, that you never forget why you chose to work with kids in the first place." Emma's voice softened. "I can see what she means."

Nathan's breath caught slightly at her words. When was the last time someone had seen his work that way—not as an obstacle to overcome, but as something worthy of respect? He found himself caring about Emma's opinion more than he probably should.

"I'll walk you out," he said, pushing open the front door and stepping into the November morning that had grown warmer while they'd been inside.

"Monday afternoon can't come soon enough," he said as they walked toward the parking lot. "I hope you're ready for Mrs. Benson's crash course in Christmas plays."

Emma laughed, and Nathan realized he was already looking forward to hearing that laugh again. "I'll be ready for whatever she wants to teach me. Though I have a feeling, this is going to feel like I'm trying to learn a new language overnight."

"The language of organized chaos and creative problem-solving. You'll be fluent before you know it."

"I hope so. See ya Monday afternoon, Nathan. Thanks again for this morning."

Nathan watched as Emma walked to her car and then drove toward town.

He stood on the sidewalk long after her car had disappeared around the corner. He thought about the way she'd looked standing on the stage in the multipurpose room. The enthusiasm in her voice when she'd talked about being part of Mrs. Benson's legacy and the comfortable way she'd moved through spaces designed for nurturing young minds.

Emma's warmth, her obvious care for others, and her ability to find joy in opportunities to contribute—all of it had Nathan wanting to know more about her thoughts and dreams and the stories that had shaped Emma into the woman she was today. The enchanting woman who had made a simple school tour feel like the highlight of his weekend.

Chapter 8

Emma opened the door to the Sugarplum Bakery; the scent of cinnamon and vanilla mixed with fresh yeast and fresh-roasted coffee made her smile.

Then she saw him.

Nathan sat at a corner table near the front window, completely absorbed in a stack of papers he was reading. He wore a navy sweater and dark jeans that made him look less like a school administrator and more like... well, like someone she wouldn't mind running into on a typical Sunday morning.

He glanced up from his papers, and his face transformed with the kind of genuine surprise that made her stomach flutter. "Emma." He raised his hand in a small wave. "What're the odds?"

"Pretty good, actually." She said as she approached his table, aware that several locals were watching their interaction. "Considering we live in a small town. I come here every Sunday for my weekly dose of the best coffee in town."

"Want to join me?" Nathan gestured to the empty chair across from him, already gathering his papers into a neat stack. "I was trying to make budget reports more interesting, but I think your company would be much better."

"I'd love to." Emma settled into the chair, noting how Nathan immediately gave her his full attention, papers forgotten. "Fair warning though—I'm pretty particular about my coffee order. Some people think I'm a little... extra."

Nathan's eyebrows rose, amusement dancing in his blue eyes. "Extra how?"

Heat crept up Emma's neck. Why had she brought this up? "Well, I order my coffee with fresh cream, sugar, a shot of French vanilla, and a shot of hazelnut flavoring, and I always ask to have my mug warmed up first, so it stays hot longer." She tucked a strand of hair behind her ear. "Most people think that's overthinking a simple cup of coffee."

"And how exactly do you know what most people think about your coffee habits?" Nathan leaned back in his chair, his tone curious rather than teasing.

"My ex used to give me grief about it," Emma admitted, then immediately wondered why she'd shared that. "He said I was the only person he knew who needed an instruction manual to order coffee. What about you?"

"Black, no sugar, and strong enough to strip paint. I've been drinking it the same way since my college all-nighters."

Emma stared at him in mock horror. "That's not coffee—that's liquid punishment. How do you taste anything besides bitter regret?"

"I happen to like the taste of actual coffee," Nathan said, eyes sparkling with mischief. "Some of us don't need to turn it into liquid dessert."

"I'm not turning it into dessert," Emma protested, with a grin. "I'm enhancing it."

"Mmm-hmm." Nathan clearly wasn't buying it. "I reserve the right to be skeptical."

"Morning, you two." Claire Whitfield appeared beside their table with a coffeepot in hand. "The usual for you, Emma? And Nathan, can I top you off?"

"Please," Emma said, grinning at Nathan. "And Claire, Nathan here thinks my coffee order is liquid dessert. Maybe you could explain to him that there's an art to proper coffee preparation?"

Claire laughed, the sound warm and rich as her cinnamon rolls. "Emma's got excellent taste," she told Nathan with obvious amusement. "She appreciates flavor and complexity; you appreciate simplicity. Sometimes opposites just fit together beautifully, don't you think?"

Emma's cheeks warmed at Claire's observation.

"I'll be right back with your coffee," Claire said, throwing Emma a wink before bustling away.

Nathan shook his head and laughed. "Gotta love a small town. So what else do you do on Sunday mornings besides shock people with your elaborate coffee rituals?"

"It depends on my mood. Sometimes I'll take a walk around town if the weather's good," Emma shrugged. "I might go hiking or visit my Aunt Lily. Sometimes I just enjoy a day of watching old movies. Then, other times I get inspired and find myself writing the day away, though lately that hasn't happened much. Sunday is the one day a week when the bookshop is closed. I try to treat Sundays like a gift to myself, free of all store obligations."

"I tend to fill weekends with catch-up work or house projects. I enjoy a good hike now and then as well."

Claire returned with Emma's perfectly prepared coffee, and she wrapped her hands around the warm mug and sighed with pure contentment.

"This perfect cup of coffee is part of the reason I love Sundays," she said, taking her first sip and feeling that familiar comfort of coffee made exactly right. "Sometimes the most important thing a person can do is slow down enough to actually enjoy the simple things in life."

Nathan took a sip of his own coffee and nodded appreciatively. "I'll give you this—Claire makes incredible coffee, even when it's not... enhanced with half a dessert menu."

Emma burst out laughing. "You seem to be getting a lot of enjoyment out of teasing me about my coffee preferences."

"I simply enjoy seeing you smile."

They settled into a conversation that flowed as easily as Claire's coffee—weekend routines, favorite books, and childhood memories of Sunday mornings. Emma was surprised by how natural it felt, how effortlessly they moved between playful banter and deeper topics, and how Nathan's attention never wavered despite the steady stream of customers flowing around them.

"What made you decide to stay here permanently?" Nathan asked as Emma finished the scone she had ordered. "I mean, you could run a bookshop anywhere, and writing isn't exactly location-dependent. What keeps you in Mistletoe Falls?"

Emma looked out the window at the town square. "The people. Everyone here genuinely cares about each other's happiness. Traditions matter, and neighbors show up for each other." She paused. "I grew up here, and I chose to stay because I never found anywhere else that felt like home."

Nathan nodded slowly. "I get that. I moved here from Nashville three years ago."

"Do you miss the city?"

"Sometimes I miss the resources and the cultural stuff," Nathan admitted. "But I don't miss the pace or the politics or that feeling like everything was urgent without necessarily being important. Here, I can focus on what actually matters—helping kids learn and grow and figure out what they're capable of."

Emma smiled, drawn to the passion in Nathan's voice. "My mom used to say the best teachers are the ones who remember their job is helping kids fall in love with learning, not just delivering content."

"That's a beautiful way of thinking about teaching and so true," Nathan said.

"Refills?" Claire appeared with the coffeepot and a warm smile. "You two look like you're solving all the world's problems over here."

"Just debating the philosophy of education and coffee enhancement," Nathan said with the kind of easy humor that made Emma's smile widen.

"Two of life's most important subjects," Claire said with a grin. "Can I get either of you anything else?"

Emma glanced at her watch and was startled to discover they'd been talking for over two hours. The bakery had filled around them while she'd been completely absorbed in Nathan, time disappearing the way it only did when she was truly enjoying herself.

"No thanks, Claire." She looked back at Nathan reluctantly. "I should probably head home. I really need to attempt to do some writing before I have lunch with my aunt this afternoon."

"Working on something new?" Nathan asked.

"No. Today I promised myself I'd try to work on something I started writing before my mom passed. I'm hoping I'll find a little inspiration or a spark of creativity hidden somewhere in those words."

"Your mother would probably be proud of you for not giving up on a story that matters to you," Nathan said gently.

Emma's throat tightened. "Thanks for saying that. Some days I'm not sure if pushing forward is healing or just stubborn pride."

"Maybe it's both," Nathan suggested. "Maybe the best kind of healing happens when we're stubborn enough to keep believing in the things that brought us joy, even when joy feels temporarily out of reach."

Emma studied his face, noting the genuine care in his expression. "I'm really glad we bumped into each other today. I've enjoyed spending time with you," she said, reaching for her purse.

"Emma?" Nathan's voice made her pause. "I'm really looking forward to tomorrow's meeting with Mrs. Benson. Not just the Christmas play stuff, but seeing how you and she work together. I have a feeling it's going to be something special."

Something warm unfurled in Emma's chest at the confidence in Nathan's voice. "I hope I don't disappoint either of you."

"You won't," Nathan said with quiet certainty. "You couldn't."

Chapter 9

Emma paused in the doorway, taking in the scene before her. Dorothy Benson sat surrounded by what looked like a paper explosion—scripts scattered across three tables, color-coded folders stacked in careful piles, and notebooks probably filled with decades of handwritten notes.

"This looks like Christmas play central command," Emma said, stepping inside and letting the door click shut behind her.

Dorothy looked up, her face breaking into the kind of smile that could make anyone feel like they'd just been welcomed home. "Emma, dear! Oh, I'm so excited you're here. I may have gotten a little carried away with the preparation."

Emma moved closer to the tables, marveling at the sheer volume of materials. Each script was labeled in Dorothy's neat handwriting, with sticky notes poking out like colorful bookmarks. Some folders were thick with what appeared to be decades of accumulated wisdom about staging, costumes, and the delicate art of managing fourth-grade performers.

"A little carried away?" Emma laughed, running her finger along the spine of a binder marked 'Angel Wing Construction—Lessons Learned.' "Dorothy, this is incredible. You've documented everything."

"Twenty-five years of trial and error," Dorothy said, flexing her fingers slowly before reaching for another folder. Emma noticed the careful way she moved her hands, as if each motion required thought. "Some years we learned that glitter is the enemy of vacuum cleaners. Other years we discovered that nine-year-old shepherds will always pet the sheep, no matter how many times you tell them it's just a stuffed animal."

The library door opened again, and Nathan appeared carrying a thick binder and wearing an expression that suggested he'd been hurrying. "Sorry I'm late. Aaron needed backup with what he called 'The Great Xylophone Crisis of Tuesday Afternoon.'"

"Do I want to know?" Emma asked.

Nathan grinned, setting his binder on the only clear corner of the nearest table. "Twenty third-graders, one broken xylophone, and a classroom debate about whether hitting it harder would fix the problem or make it worse."

"And?" Dorothy asked, her eyes twinkling with amusement.

"The crisis was resolved diplomatically. The kids organized sheet music while Aaron and I figured out that some problems require adult intervention and possibly a trip to the music store." Nathan pulled out a chair, glancing around at Dorothy's impressive setup. "Wow, Dorothy. This looks like you're planning a Broadway production."

"I like to be thorough," Dorothy said with obvious pride. "Emma, sit, sit. Let me show you what we're working with."

Emma settled into a chair across from Dorothy, immediately drawn into the older woman's enthusiasm. Nathan took the seat beside her, close enough that she caught the faint scent of his cologne.

"These are all twenty-five years of Christmas plays," Dorothy said, gesturing to the scripts spread before them. "Traditional stories, creative adaptations, and some completely original tales that grew out of whatever that year's group of children needed to learn about themselves."

Emma picked up a script titled "The Snow Angel's Gift" and flipped through the pages, noting the careful stage directions and the obvious love that had gone into every character description. "I can see the thought you put into all of this. Every role feels important."

"That's the secret," Dorothy said, her voice warming with memories. "Every child needs to feel like they're the hero of their own story, even if they're only saying three lines or carrying a prop across the stage."

Nathan leaned forward, studying a script. "Which script is your favorite, Dorothy? If you had to pick just one."

Dorothy was quiet for a moment, her gaze moving across the familiar papers as if she were revisiting old friends. "You know, I always said my favorite was whichever group I was working with at the time. But..." She picked up the "Christmas Wish Tree" script, running her fingers gently across the cover. "This one was special. It's about children who find a magical tree that grants wishes, but only wishes that help someone else believe in themselves."

Dorothy turned the script around so Emma could read the opening scene. The story was simple but profound—children discovering that the best magic happened when you used your gifts to lift others up.

"This is beautiful," Emma said softly. "I can see why it's special. Every character gets to be someone else's hero."

"Exactly." Dorothy's eyes lit up. "You understand. It's not really about putting on a show for parents, though they love it. It's about helping kids discover how brave and kind and capable they really are."

Nathan was examining another script, his brow slightly furrowed in concentration. "So what about this year's fourth-graders? What story would work best with their personalities?"

"Oh, Nathan, this year's group is just lovely. They're such a sweet bunch. They really look out for each other, and some of the more confident ones naturally help the shy kids feel included."

"What about this one?" Nathan asked, sliding a script across the table. "'The Christmas Light Keepers.' I like the teamwork aspect, and the message seems perfect for these kids."

Dorothy's hands flew together in delight. "Nathan Reid, you're reading my mind! I was hoping you'd both be drawn to that one."

Emma picked up the script, immediately charmed by the premise as she read the opening scene. "A village where the Christmas lights start going out one by one, and the children have to work together to discover that each person's special gift is needed to keep the light of Christmas alive." She looked up at Dorothy. "I love it!"

"Right?" Dorothy's enthusiasm was contagious. "There are parts for natural performers and parts for children who prefer smaller roles. Musical numbers that'll showcase different talents and plenty of opportunities for creative problem-solving that'll keep everyone engaged."

Nathan nodded approvingly as he skimmed through the script. "And it won't be too complicated to stage. We can make it beautiful without needing advanced carpentry skills."

Dorothy laughed. "Then it's settled. 'The Christmas Light Keepers' it is. Now, let's talk logistics before we get too excited and start planning costumes."

She pulled out a calendar that was already filled with her handwriting. "I was thinking we'd start with a read-through tomorrow afternoon. We'll meet on Tuesdays and Thursdays from two to three—that gives us the last hour of school without disrupting too much class time."

Emma pulled out her phone, already mentally rearranging her bookshop schedule. "Cora and Molly can handle the shop those afternoons. They're practically bouncing off the walls with excitement about my doing this."

"I'm excited about you being involved too," Nathan said, and something in his tone made Emma glance up from her phone.

Dorothy's eyes moved between them with obvious satisfaction, though she said nothing about the undercurrent of interest she'd noticed.

"Six weeks should give us plenty of time before the December seventeenth performance," Dorothy continued. "And Emma, dear, I can't tell you how grateful I am that you said yes to this adventure."

"Thank you for trusting me with something this important. I'll do everything I can to help make it as special as all your other productions."

"Oh, I have no doubt about that," Dorothy said, her voice rich with confidence. "I can already tell you're going to bring something wonderful to this year's play. The children are going to absolutely adore working with you. And Nathan, I appreciate you so much. Thank you for everything you've done. You're so good at bringing the right people together."

Nathan's cheeks colored slightly at the praise. "I think we all found each other at exactly the right time," he said simply.

"Sometimes," Dorothy said, "the universe just lines things up perfectly."

As they began gathering up the scripts and planning materials, Emma realized she was genuinely looking forward to tomorrow's first rehearsal. The creative energy that had felt so elusive lately was beginning to stir, sparked by Dorothy's passion and the prospect of helping children discover their own storytelling magic.

"I'll see you both tomorrow afternoon," Dorothy said as they reached the library door. "Two o'clock sharp for our first read-through. Come prepared for the kind of joy that happens when fourth-graders realize they get to become characters in a real story."

Emma fell into step beside Nathan as they walked through the school's quiet hallways toward the main entrance.

"That went really well," Nathan said as they pushed through the front doors into the crisp November afternoon. "Dorothy looked happier than I've seen her in weeks. I think you've put her mind completely at ease about all this."

"She's remarkable," Emma said, pulling her cardigan tighter against the cool air. "I can see why she's so beloved. There's real magic in the way she talks about helping children discover what they're capable of."

"Everything I know about seeing the best in people, I learned from Dorothy," Nathan agreed. "She has this gift for helping people become the person they didn't know they could be."

Emma paused on the front steps, looking back at the school building where, tomorrow, she would begin her first official collaboration with Dorothy and Nathan. The late afternoon light warmed the brick facade, and she could almost imagine the sounds of children's laughter.

"You know what?" she said, surprised by the certainty in her own voice. "I think saying yes to this play might be one of the best decisions I've made in a long time."

Nathan's smile was soft and genuine as he studied her face. "I'm really glad you feel that way. The children are lucky to have you working with them."

He paused, his expression growing more serious. "And so am I."

Emma's breath caught at the quiet intensity in Nathan's words. The way he looked at her suggested he was thinking about far more than Christmas play logistics, and she suddenly became aware of how close they were standing.

"I should probably let you get back to your afternoon. I'm sure you've got a million things waiting for you."

"I do," Nathan agreed, but he made no immediate move to step away. "Emma?"

"Yeah?"

"Thank you. For everything. For saying yes, for bringing your passion to this project, for making Dorothy light up like she did in there." His voice dropped slightly. "For making me remember why I love this work so much."

As Emma drove home through the quiet November afternoon, she found herself replaying not just the practical details of their planning session but the way Nathan had looked at her when he'd said the children were lucky to have her—and so was he. The warmth in his voice and the sincerity in his eyes suggested their partnership was becoming something deeper than professional collaboration, and Emma was eager to see where this might lead.

Chapter 10

Nathan leaned against the back wall of the multipurpose room as the fourth-graders filed in with barely contained excitement. They'd been talking about the Christmas play all day.

"Walking feet, everyone," he called out.

"Mr. Reid, is it true that Miss Emma wrote the books about Princess Buttercup?" Madison Torres asked as she bounced on her toes in front of him, her voice pitched with excitement.

"She did," Nathan confirmed, smiling at Madison's enthusiasm. "Along with a lot of other wonderful stories."

"That's so cool," Madison breathed, then hurried to claim a seat near where Emma was standing beside Mrs. Benson.

Nathan's attention was immediately drawn to Emma as she knelt down to Madison's level, her face lighting up with genuine interest. "You know about Princess Buttercup?"

"I love those books," Madison said, suddenly shy now that she was face-to-face with her favorite author. "I have all the books. Sometimes I read them to my little sister."

"That's wonderful," Emma said warmly. "Princess Buttercup stories are always better when they're shared. What's your sister's favorite part?"

Madison giggled, her shyness evaporating. "The dragon! She makes me do the voice all growly and funny like this—" She demonstrated a silly, rumbling dragon voice that made Emma burst into delighted laughter.

Nathan grinned as he took in the interaction, struck by how effortlessly Emma connected with children and how she made Madison feel heard and important rather than brushed off. This was exactly what he'd hoped for: not just someone to manage logistics, but someone who genuinely understood and enjoyed working with kids.

"All right, my incredible actors," Dorothy called from the front of the circle, her voice carrying that special mix of warmth and authority that could capture fourth-grade attention. "Let's gather 'round so we can begin this adventure."

The students settled into their chairs with unusual focus, and Nathan took a seat along the side wall where he could observe without getting in the way. Emma sat beside Dorothy, looking completely comfortable in the circle of eager faces.

"Now then," Dorothy began, holding up her script, "who can tell me what makes a story come alive?"

Hands shot up around the circle, and Nathan's gaze moved to Emma's face as the children offered their answers.

"Characters that feel like real people!" Jake Morrison called out. He was usually the quiet one, but theater had a way of bringing out unexpected sides of kids.

"And exciting stuff happening that makes you wanna know what's next," added Chloe Kincaid, bouncing in her seat.

"And feelings," said Zach Williams thoughtfully. "Like when you care about what happens to the people in the story."

"Those are all perfect answers," Dorothy said, beaming at them. "Emma, would you like to add anything?"

Emma looked around the circle of eager faces, her expression thoughtful. "I think stories come alive when the people telling them—or acting them out—really believe in the characters they're playing. When you become the character instead of just pretending to be them."

"Ooh, like method acting!" Sarah Tillman bounced excitedly. She'd been in community theater since kindergarten and loved showing off her vocabulary. "Where you really think like the person you're playing thinks!"

"Exactly like that," Emma said. "And the wonderful thing about 'The Christmas Light Keepers' is that every single character gets to be brave and kind, and all are important to the story."

Emma opened her script and began reading the opening scene aloud. Her voice shifted and changed for different characters—the worried Village Mayor, the wise Grandmother, and the eager children who discover the lights going out one by one. The fourth-graders were completely captivated, leaning forward in their chairs as they pictured themselves in the magical Christmas village.

When Emma finished the opening, the room stayed quiet for just a moment before hands started shooting up like popcorn.

"Miss Emma," Madison said, her voice smaller than before, "what if someone gets scared and can't talk loud enough for everyone to hear them?"

Emma's expression immediately softened with understanding. She scooted her chair closer to Madison's, her voice gentle but confident. "You know what I've learned about being brave, Madison? It's not about not being scared. It's about doing important things even when your heart's beating super fast and your stomach feels all fluttery."

Madison nodded slowly, and Nathan could see her shoulders relax a little.

"Plus," Emma continued, "when you're in a play, you're never alone up on the stage. You've got all your friends with you, and Mrs. Benson, Mr. Reid, and I will practice with you until you feel totally ready. And you know what else?"

"What?" Madison asked.

"Princess Buttercup gets scared sometimes too. But she always finds her courage when she remembers she's helping her friends."

Madison's whole face lit up. "Really? Princess Buttercup gets scared?"

"Absolutely. Being brave and being scared can happen at exactly the same time."

Nathan smiled. Emma's intuitive understanding of how to encourage without dismissing Madison's fears was undoubtedly the kind of gentle wisdom that helped children grow.

"Now then," Dorothy said, "let's talk about our rehearsal schedule. We'll meet every Tuesday and Thursday at two o'clock, right here in our magical multipurpose room. That gives us six weeks to learn our parts, practice our scenes, and create something absolutely wonderful together."

"Six whole weeks?" Ben Ingalls started counting on his fingers. "That's like... a million practices!"

"Twelve practices," Emma corrected with a grin. "Just enough to become the most amazing Christmas Light Keepers Mistletoe Falls has ever seen."

Nathan listened as Emma and Dorothy began explaining how practice would take place, how they'd read through scenes together, and how they'd help each other perfect their lines. The children listened quietly and absorbed every word.

"Mr. Reid," Emma called across the circle, "would you help us out? We need someone to read the Village Mayor parts so the children get a better idea of how different characters sound and work together."

"Sure thing," he said, moving to join the circle.

Emma handed him the script, and their fingers brushed briefly as she pointed out the Mayor's lines. The simple touch sent warmth up his arm.

As they read through the scene together—Dorothy playing the Wise Grandmother, Emma voicing several of the children's characters, and Nathan as the Village Mayor—he was struck by how their different styles complemented each other. Dorothy brought years of experience and understanding of what worked with children; Emma contributed genuine enthusiasm and creative insight, and Nathan provided practical grounding when the kids got too excited.

"That was perfect," Dorothy said as they finished the scene. "Children, can you see how each character has something special to contribute? Just like each of you has something special to bring to our play."

They all nodded in unison.

"Miss Emma," Jackson Ford raised his hand, "when you write your stories, do you act out all the parts to see how they sound?"

Emma's laugh was pure delight. "You know what, Jackson? I totally do. When I'm trying to figure out what a character would say, I'll walk around my apartment talking to myself in different voices. I probably look completely ridiculous, but it really helps the stories feel real and come alive."

The children giggled at this image, and Nathan found himself grinning at Emma's easy honesty. She had such a natural way of making herself approachable while keeping the respect the kids clearly had for her.

"All right, my wonderful actors," Dorothy said as the clock crept toward three, "let's wrap up for today. Before you go, I'd love to hear which character each of you is most excited about."

Nathan listened as several children shared their opinions, noting how many had been influenced by Emma's enthusiastic reading of the different parts.

"I like the narrator," said Zach Williams thoughtfully. "He gets to tell the story and help the audience understand what's happening."

"Narrators are so important—they're like the bridge between the story and the people watching," Emma said.

As the children gathered their backpacks and prepared for dismissal, Nathan noticed how many made a point to say goodbye to Emma specifically—thanking her for the rehearsal, asking questions about her books, or simply telling her how excited they were for Thursday.

"Miss Emma," Madison said shyly as she passed, "thank you for saying it's okay to be scared and brave at the same time."

Emma knelt down to Madison again, her voice gentle. "Madison, you're going to be wonderful in this play. I can tell already."

Nathan's throat tightened as he saw Madison beam with pride before skipping out of the multipurpose room, clearly feeling confident.

"Well," Dorothy said as the last student headed for the buses, "I'd call that a complete success. Emma dear, you have such a gift with children. They were hanging on your every word."

Emma's cheeks flushed pink. "They're such an amazing group. So thoughtful and enthusiastic about everything."

"They really are," Nathan agreed, starting to stack chairs while Dorothy gathered scripts. "And they responded to you incredibly well.

I could actually see them relaxing and getting more excited as the rehearsal went on."

"I forgot how much I love this age," Emma admitted, helping with the chairs. "They're old enough to really understand character development and story themes but young enough to still believe in magic completely."

Nathan paused in his chair-stacking, struck by Emma's observation. "That's exactly what makes fourth grade such a perfect fit for this kind of project. They can handle the responsibility of a real performance, but they still approach it with pure wonder instead of self-consciousness."

As they finished cleaning up, Nathan realized he was already anticipating Thursday's rehearsal with an excitement that had everything to do with watching Emma work with the children again. Her warmth, her intuitive understanding of how to encourage without pressuring, and her ability to make each child feel seen and valued—these weren't just helpful qualities for a Christmas play director. They were the kind of gifts that made someone truly special.

"Same time Thursday, or do you need me to come earlier?" Emma asked Dorothy.

"Two o'clock is perfect," Dorothy said. "Though feel free to come early if you'd like."

Nathan walked with Emma through the quiet hallways toward the main entrance, their footsteps echoing softly in the after-school stillness. The familiar sounds of buses rumbling to life and children's voices carried from the front parking lot.

"You were amazing in there," he said as they pushed through the front doors into the crisp November afternoon. "The way you connected with the kids, especially Madison—you said exactly what she needed to hear."

Emma smiled. "Thanks. There's something magical about being around kids who are genuinely excited about stories."

"They just..." Nathan paused, searching for the right words. "They lit up around you."

Emma glanced up at him, and Nathan felt a flutter in his chest.

"I think this is going to work out even better than I had hoped," he said quietly.

Emma's smile widened, and Nathan thought he caught something in her expression that matched what he was feeling. "I hope so. See you Thursday?"

"Thursday," Nathan confirmed, watching as she walked to her car.

Chapter 11

99 —and the dragon looked down at the tiniest mouse in the whole kingdom and said—" Emma's voice dropped to a theatrical rumble that made the fourth-graders lean forward in delighted anticipation, "You want to do WHAT?"

Nathan watched as Emma sat cross-legged on the polished floor, surrounded by a perfect circle of children who hung on her every word.

"Tell him, little mouse!" Madison Torres burst out, bouncing on her crossed legs. "Tell him you're gonna help!"

Emma's expression shifted to wide-eyed mouse innocence, her voice squeaking with determination. "I want to help you find your missing treasure, Mr. Dragon. 'Cause that's what friends do—they help each other, even when they're scared and their knees are all wobbly."

Nathan grinned as he stood nearby. This wasn't even part of today's Christmas play practice—Emma had simply noticed that the children seemed restless after running through their first full read-through, and she'd seamlessly transitioned into an impromptu storytelling session to help them refocus.

"What happened next?" Maya Patel whispered. She pressed closer to the circle, dark eyes bright with wonder.

Emma leaned forward conspiratorially, her voice dropping to a whisper that somehow reached every corner of the room. "Well, the dragon was so surprised that somebody actually wanted to help him that he forgot all about being scary. And the mouse? She was so busy thinking about helping her new friend that she forgot to be afraid."

From the costume table, Dorothy had stopped sorting angel wings entirely. When she caught Nathan's eye, her knowing smile held twenty-five years of watching children fall under storytelling spells.

"And that's when they discovered something amazing," Emma continued, building toward her climax with the practiced rhythm of someone who understood the hearts of children. "The real treasure wasn't gold or sparkly jewels at all. It was the friendship they'd made by being brave enough to care about each other."

The room erupted in spontaneous applause, small hands clapping with genuine delight. Emma's whole face transformed with joy—radiant and alive.

"Miss Emma!" Jackson Ford's hand shot up. "Did you just make that whole story up? Right now? Out of your head?"

"I did. Sometimes the best stories are the ones that show up exactly when you need them."

"Like how our Christmas play showed up when we needed to learn about working together?" Zach Williams asked.

"Exactly like that," Emma said, her smile warming.

Nathan pushed off from the doorframe, unable to resist joining them. "That was quite the performance. I don't think I've ever heard a more convincing dragon voice."

"Mr. Reid!" several children called out in greeting.

"Miss Emma," Chloe Kincaid practically vibrated in her seat, "will you tell us another story?"

Before Emma could answer, Dorothy's voice carried across the room with sudden inspiration. "Actually, Chloe, we're running out of time today, but you just gave me the most wonderful idea." She approached their circle, silver hair catching the overhead lights, eyes twinkling with the same mischief. "Emma, dear, how would you feel about reading to our kindergarten classes during Friday story time? We usually depend on parent volunteers, but having a real live children's book author..." She let the possibility hang in the air like Christmas magic waiting to be unwrapped.

Nathan watched Emma's face cycle through surprise, consideration, and then unmistakable excitement that made his pulse quicken for reasons he didn't want to examine too closely.

"The kindergartners?" Emma asked, her voice lifting. "When do they have story time?"

"Fridays at one o'clock," Dorothy explained. "It's become quite a beloved tradition. The little ones curl up in the library, and we read them stories before they head home for the weekend. They'd be absolutely over the moon to meet the author of the Princess Buttercup books."

"Would it be okay if I started this Friday? Tomorrow? I mean, if that's not too soon—"

"Of course!" Dorothy clapped her hands with delight that could've powered the school's Christmas lights. "Oh, they're going to be beside themselves with excitement. Should I tell them who their special reader will be, or would you prefer it to be a surprise?"

Emma's smile could've melted snow. "Let's surprise them."

Nathan studied Emma's expression as she and Dorothy worked out the details. There was an energy radiating from her that he hadn't seen before—not just enthusiasm, but a kind of hopeful anticipation that made her whole face more animated, more alive.

"Miss Emma," Tyler Rodriguez piped up, "are you gonna write a book about us? About our Christmas play and stuff?"

Emma turned back to the children, her expression growing thoughtful. "You know what, Tyler? I wasn't planning to, but now that you mention it..." She paused, looking around the circle of eager faces. "There might be a story hiding in here somewhere."

"That would be so cool!" Madison breathed. "We'd be like, famous and stuff!"

"You're already gonna be famous," Emma laughed, the sound bright and warm. "At least, you will be after our Christmas performance."

"All right, my wonderful actors," Dorothy announced as the wall clock crept toward three, "let's gather our scripts and backpacks. Remember, next week we'll be diving into actual scene work for the first time, so practice your lines as often as you can."

As the children collected their belongings and began their usual end-of-practice ritual of saying goodbye to Emma, Nathan began stacking chairs and cleaning up the room. But his attention kept drifting to Emma, who was kneeling beside Maya's chair, listening intently as the girl chattered excitedly about her character.

"She's spectacular... I think she'll be great with the kindergartners," Dorothy murmured, appearing at Nathan's side. "Look how wonderfully she connects with children."

Nathan followed Dorothy's gaze to where Emma was now helping Ben Ingalls figure out which scenes his character appeared in, her patience clear as she walked him through the script page by page.

"She's a natural," Nathan said. Emma wasn't just good with children—she was extraordinary. She had an intuitive understanding of how to meet each child exactly where they were, whether that meant encouraging Maya's newfound confidence or channeling Tyler's boundless energy into character development.

"You know," Dorothy continued, "it's rare to find someone who fits so naturally into our school community. Emma has such a gift for this work."

"She does," he said simply.

"And she seems quite happy here," Dorothy added, her eyes twinkling with satisfaction. "Happier than I've seen her in months, actually. The bookshop's wonderful, but I think Emma needed this play as much as we needed her."

Nathan nodded, remembering Emma's remarks about feeling stuck in her usual patterns, about needing new challenges to shake up her routine.

"Miss Emma," Sarah Tillman called as she headed toward the door, backpack bouncing, "you're gonna come to our Thanksgiving program next week, right?"

"Wouldn't miss it," Emma replied warmly. "I'll be in the audience cheering you on."

"You should totally sit with Mr. Reid," Madison suggested with the kind of innocent directness that made Nathan's cheeks warm and several other children perk up with interest. "He always sits in the back so he can see everything and make sure we're all doing good."

"Madison," Nathan said mildly, though he couldn't quite keep the smile out of his voice as multiple pairs of eyes ping-ponged between him and Emma with obvious speculation.

"What?" Madison asked with wide-eyed innocence that fooled absolutely no one. "You do sit in the back. And Miss Emma's super nice. And you both like kids and stories and stuff."

"Well, when you put it like that..." Emma said with a laugh, catching Nathan's eye across the room with a look that made his pulse stutter.

"I think what Madison's trying to say," Dorothy interjected with barely concealed delight, "is that she thinks you two make a good team."

Nathan watched Emma's cheeks turn pink as she gathered her things, but her smile suggested she wasn't bothered by the children's amateur matchmaking attempts.

"Well," Emma said a few moments later as the last student disappeared into the hallway, "I should probably get back to the bookshop. Cora and Molly are covering, but Thursday afternoons can get pretty busy at times."

"Of course, dear," Dorothy said. "And Emma? Thank you again for agreeing to story time tomorrow. You have no idea how happy this'll make Mrs. Druthers and Mrs. Hartman. They've been struggling to find readers who can really capture those little ones' attention."

"I'm so excited," Emma replied, her eyes bright with anticipation. "Five-year-olds and Princess Buttercup stories? That sounds like the perfect way to spend a Friday afternoon."

Nathan fell into step beside Emma as they headed toward the exit.

"You were incredible in there," he said as they pushed through the main doors into the crisp November afternoon. "The way you just seamlessly shifted from Christmas play practice to impromptu storytelling... that's not something everyone can do."

"It felt really good," Emma admitted, pulling her cardigan closer against the cool air. "And the idea of reading to the kindergartners tomorrow…" She trailed off, but Nathan could see the anticipation practically glowing in her expression.

"They're gonna love you," Nathan said, and realized he meant it with every fiber of his being. "Those teachers have been trying to find engaging readers all semester. You're gonna be exactly what they need."

Emma's smile was warm with gratitude. "I hope so. And Nathan? Thanks for… well, for making all this possible. If you hadn't walked into my bookshop that day looking all desperate and principal-y…"

"I'm the one who should be thanking you. You've brought something special to our school. To the children, to Dorothy, to…" He caught himself before he could finish the thought that was becoming increasingly dangerous to his peace of mind.

"To what?" Emma asked, tilting her head with the kind of gentle curiosity that made him want to tell her exactly what he'd been thinking.

"To all of us."

"I should get going," Emma said, glancing at her watch. "But I'll see you tomorrow? Maybe after story time?"

"Definitely," Nathan said, watching her walk to her car with that graceful confidence he was beginning to recognize as uniquely Emma.

He stood on the front steps until her taillights disappeared around the corner, then shook his head and headed back inside. One o'clock tomorrow. He was already wondering what legitimate excuse he could manufacture to be in the library during kindergarten story time.

Chapter 12

99 —and Princess Buttercup realized that the most powerful magic wasn't in her sparkly crown or her big castle." Emma's voice dropped to a whisper that somehow carried to every corner of Mrs. Hartman's kindergarten classroom, twenty-two little faces leaning forward like flowers turning toward the sun. "It was right here—" She pressed her hand to her heart, watching their eyes widen with wonder. "Cause when you love somebody enough to be brave for them, that's when the real magic happens."

A soft collective "Ohhh" rippled through the circle, and Emma felt that wonderful surge of joy watching children discover something beautiful.

The scent of crayons and apple juice mingled in the air, and in the corner of the room a hamster wheel squeaked softly in its cage. Emma breathed it all in—the pure magic of childhood curiosity suspended in a cozy classroom on a Friday afternoon in November.

She hadn't noticed Nathan appear in the doorway, but when she glanced up during Princess Buttercup's final scene, there he was.

Leaning against the doorframe with his arms crossed, watching her with such focused attention that her voice nearly stumbled on the next line. The look on his face wasn't principally interested—it was something deeper, warmer, that made her suddenly aware of how she must look crouched on a kindergarten carpet.

"And Princess Buttercup and the Dragon became the very best of friends," Emma concluded, closing the picture book with a satisfying snap. "Because sometimes the scariest things turn out to be the most wonderful adventures."

Enthusiastic applause erupted from tiny hands, and Emma laughed as several children reached out to touch the book's cover, desperate to see the illustrations one more time.

"Miss Emma! Miss Emma!" A girl with lopsided pigtails bounced on her knees. "Do you think Princess Buttercup was scared when she first met the dragon? Like, super scared?"

Emma considered the question with the seriousness it deserved. "You know what, Lucy? I think she was probably scared. But here's the thing about being brave—it doesn't mean you're not scared. It means you do the right thing even when your tummy feels all fluttery and your heart goes boom-boom-boom really fast."

"Like when I had to get a shot, and I cried, but I still did it?" A gap-toothed boy named Marcus grinned proudly.

"Just like that, Marcus. That was incredibly brave."

Nathan's soft chuckle from the doorway made her look up again. Their eyes met across the circle of children, and something passed between them—admiration, maybe, or recognition. The kind of look that made her pulse skip.

"Miss Emma," called a voice from the circle, "will you come back next week? Please, please, please?"

"I'd love to," Emma said, meaning it with every fiber of her being. Surrounded by eager faces and boundless imagination, she felt more like herself than she had in months. "Mrs. Hartman, would it be okay if I made this a regular thing?"

Mrs. Hartman looked up from her desk. "Emma, we'd be absolutely thrilled. These little ones have been buzzing with excitement since I told them earlier this afternoon that a real author was coming."

"Miss Emma!" The pigtailed girl tugged on Emma's cardigan. "Mrs. Hartman said you write lots and lots of books. Like, books that live in real stores where people buy them with money!"

Emma was charmed by the awe in her voice. "I do write books. I love creating stories for kids just like you. Do you have a favorite story?"

Lucy's face lit up like Christmas lights. "I love the one about the bunny who loses her red mitten in the snow! My daddy reads it to me every single night, and I do the voices."

"That sounds like a wonderful story," Emma said. "I love writing about brave little animals too."

As the children began their usual post-story shuffle, Emma collected her book and the canvas tote she'd brought.

Nathan approached as the last kindergartner joined the line for afternoon activities, his presence somehow making the spacious classroom feel smaller. "That was incredible, Emma. I've never seen them so completely absorbed. You had them eating out of your hand."

Heat crept up Emma's neck at his praise, especially with the way he was looking at her—like she'd just performed actual magic instead of simply reading a picture book to five-year-olds. "They're easy to please at this age. Give them voices and a little drama, and they're happy."

"No, it's more than that. You have a real gift."

They fell into step together as they headed toward the hallway, Emma acutely aware of Nathan beside her—the way he waved to students peeking out of doorways, how he remembered names and asked about weekend soccer games and art projects.

"Would you like me to walk you to your car?" Nathan asked as they reached the main entrance. The afternoon light streaming through the glass doors caught the warm brown of his eyes.

"That'd be nice," Emma said, pushing through the heavy doors into November air that smelled like fallen leaves and approaching snow.

They crossed the front courtyard, and Emma found herself sneaking glances at Nathan—the confident way he moved, the slight smile that seemed permanently carved around his eyes, and the way he made her feel like the most interesting person in his day instead of just another volunteer.

"Emma. I wondered—would you maybe like to have dinner tonight? If you don't have plans already," he asked as they stood next to her car.

The invitation surprised her, and Emma nearly dropped her car keys.

Her mind immediately started racing. She liked Nathan—really liked him, if she was being honest. But what if she was reading too much into his kindness? What if this was just friendly appreciation for helping with the Christmas play? What if it was more than friendly and she wasn't ready for more than friendly?

"That's... that's really sweet of you," she said. "But I should probably work tonight. I really need to buckle down and do some writing."

Nathan's face fell for just a moment before he recovered with an understanding nod. "Of course. Your writing's important. I shouldn't have assumed you'd be free on a Friday night."

"It's not that I don't want to—" Emma started. "I mean, it sounds lovely. I just... deadlines, you know?"

"Emma, you don't need to explain." Nathan's voice was gentle, though she caught the disappointment underneath. "I get it. Work comes first."

As Emma drove back toward town, Nathan's invitation played on repeat in her mind like a song she couldn't shake. The November afternoon was crisp and bright, houses already sporting early Christmas decorations, but all she could think about was the careful way he'd asked, the hope in his expression, and how quickly she'd shut him down.

"Dinner tonight," she said aloud to her empty car. "He asked me to dinner. Tonight."

The way he'd said it—casual but with an underlying current of something more—had definitely felt like a date. Not a business discussion or a friendly thank-you for volunteering, but an actual, honest-to-goodness dinner date. With a man who made her laugh and understood her passion for storytelling, who looked at her like she was fascinating instead of just helpful.

And she'd panicked and said no.

Emma pulled into the narrow alley behind Once Upon a Time and sat for a moment, the engine ticking as it cooled. Her hands still gripped the steering wheel like it might anchor her to something solid.

"Really, Emma?" she muttered. "He asks you to dinner, and you claim you need to work? On a Friday night?"

But even as she berated herself, Emma knew exactly why she'd hesitated. Nathan wasn't just another dinner date. He felt different—bigger somehow. Not just handsome or easy to be around, but the kind of man who could matter. And that was what scared her most.

She gathered her tote bag and headed for the bookshop's back entrance, already composing the text she might send Nathan later.

Something casual but apologetic, leaving the door open for future possibilities without seeming desperate or wishy-washy.

"How'd story time go?" Cora's voice carried from the front counter, warm with genuine interest.

"Awesome," Emma called back. "The kids seemed to enjoy it."

And Nathan was there, she added silently, watching me like I was performing magic instead of just reading a picture book. *And then he asked me to dinner like it was the most natural thing in the world, and I got scared and said no, and now I'm standing here wondering if I just let something wonderful slip right through my fingers.*

Emma leaned against the back door for a moment, closing her eyes.

"I should've said yes," she whispered. "I really, really should've said yes."

Chapter 13

The numbers on the budget reports blurred into meaningless columns as Nathan pushed back from his desk, the parking lot conversation playing on repeat in his head.

I should probably work tonight.

Emma's polite decline still echoed in his ears, each word settling deeper into his chest like stones in still water.

He'd been so sure she'd say yes. Instead, he got a gentle brush-off.

A sharp knock rattled his office door. "Come in," Nathan called, grateful for any distraction from replaying his spectacular misreading of the situation.

Aaron Morgan appeared in the doorway, his perpetually rumpled dark hair sticking up at odd angles. His friend clutched a travel mug, and his slightly shell-shocked expression suggested the afternoon choir rehearsal had involved more enthusiasm than actual harmony.

"You look like someone stole your lunch money," Aaron said, dropping into the chair across from Nathan's desk without invitation—a privilege earned through three years of friendship and countless sessions of mutual venting about the unique joys of elementary education. "Rough afternoon with the budget battle?"

"Just trying to figure out how to keep art and music programs alive when the district keeps demanding cuts," Nathan said, gesturing at the scattered paperwork. "You know how it is."

"I do. Care to hit the trails tomorrow morning? The weather's supposed to be perfect, and I thought we could check out that new trail system. Get some fresh mountain air, clear our heads."

The suggestion was appealing—Nathan had always found peace in the woods, and Aaron's company made any outdoor adventure better. But the idea of spending a Saturday morning hiking felt oddly empty when what he really wanted was to spend time with Emma.

"Yeah, maybe," Nathan said, then caught his own lackluster tone. "Sorry, yes. That sounds good. I could definitely use some fresh air."

Aaron's eyebrows rose as he studied Nathan's face. "Okay, what's going on? You've been different all week. Distracted. And now you're sitting here looking like you've lost your best friend."

Nathan couldn't help smiling despite his current mood. Aaron's directness was one of the things he valued most about their friendship—no games, no dancing around issues, just honest conversation between people who genuinely cared about each other.

"You know Emma Sullivan, right?" Nathan asked. "She owns the Once Upon a Time Bookshop on Mistletoe Lane."

"Emma? Of course I know Emma. I stop by her store at least once a week. Why—" He paused, his grin returning with renewed interest.

"She's been helping Mrs. Benson with the Christmas play, and we've been working together on all the preparations. She's just... she's incredible with the children."

"Go on." Aaron's tone was carefully neutral, but Nathan caught the amusement dancing in his eyes.

"Today she read to the kindergartners, and Aaron, you should've seen her. She brought this fairy tale to life in a way that had every single five-year-old completely captivated. She wasn't just reading to them—she was connecting with each kid individually while somehow keeping the whole group spellbound."

"She's got that rare thing," Nathan continued, his voice warming as he remembered the scene. "The way she talks to them, the way she understands exactly what they need to hear... it's like she has this intuitive gift for meeting children right where they are. No talking down, no talking over their heads. Just... perfect."

Aaron listened, occasionally nodding or making encouraging sounds. When Nathan finished describing the story time session, Aaron was quiet for a moment, swirling the dregs of his coffee.

"So," Aaron said finally, his grin widening, "you're completely gone on her."

Nathan nearly choked on air. "I'm not—we're just—it's not like that."

"Right." Aaron's smile was pure mischief now. "That's why you lit up like a Christmas tree the second you started talking about her. And why you've been checking your phone like you're waiting for the most important text of your life."

Nathan started to protest, then stopped. "She's different," Nathan admitted.

"Different how?"

Nathan considered the question, searching for words to capture something he didn't entirely understand himself. "She gets it, you know? The work, the kids, why it all matters so much. Most people think we're nuts for caring as deeply as we do."

Aaron nodded slowly.

"And when she talks about what I do, about my work with the kids…" Nathan ran a hand through his hair. "She seems genuinely impressed. She thinks it's actually a good thing that I'm so dedicated. Most people act like caring too much about your job is some kind of character defect."

The words came out more bitter than Nathan had intended, carrying three years' worth of his ex-wife's accusations that had shaped every relationship decision since. Aaron's expression softened with understanding—they'd had plenty of conversations about the damage the wrong person could do to your sense of self-worth.

"She appreciates who you are," Aaron observed.

"I think so. I hope so." Nathan felt his shoulders relax slightly. "When we talk about the Christmas play, about the kids, about what we're trying to create for them—she gets as excited as I do. She sees the bigger picture, how these experiences shape who children become."

"That's huge," Aaron said. "So how does she feel about you?"

Nathan's brief optimism deflated like a punctured balloon. "I asked her to dinner tonight. She said she needed to work."

Aaron studied Nathan's expression carefully. "Did she seem as if she wanted to say yes?"

The question caught Nathan off guard. He thought back to Emma's reaction in the parking lot—the way her keys had slipped in her grip, the flustered quality of her response, the almost-apologetic tone when she'd declined.

"Maybe," Nathan said slowly. "She seemed surprised, and she kind of stumbled over her words when she was explaining why she couldn't. But Aaron, if someone wants to have dinner with you, they make it work, right? They don't immediately jump to excuses."

"Or," Aaron said, leaning back in his chair, "they get scared about what dinner might mean and default to the safe choice."

Nathan frowned. "What?"

"Think about it from her perspective." Aaron set down his mug and leaned forward. "You're the principal; she's volunteering at the school. There's this whole professional dynamic to navigate. Plus, you're clearly interested in her—don't even try to deny it; it's written all over your face—but maybe she's worried about complicating things. Or maybe she's just as gun-shy about relationships as you usually are."

The suggestion made sense. Nathan had been so focused on his own disappointment that he hadn't considered what might be driving Emma's hesitation. If she was feeling the same connection he was, the same growing attraction, maybe her decline had more to do with caution than disinterest.

"Besides," Aaron continued, "she's helping with the Christmas play. That means you'll be working together for weeks. Plenty of opportunities to show her you're serious about getting to know her better."

"You think I should try again?"

"I think you should stop overthinking and trust your instincts." Aaron's tone turned earnest. "Nathan, in the past few years since your divorce, I've never heard you talk about a woman the way you just talked about Emma. You're always Mr. Caution when it comes to relationships. But with her, you just... come alive."

"She makes me want to take risks," Nathan admitted. "And that terrifies me."

Aaron nodded. "Because taking risks means you might get hurt again."

"Jennifer used to say I was married to my job, that I'd always care more about other people's children than I would my own family."

Nathan's voice dropped. "What if she were right? What if I'm just not capable of the kind of balance a real relationship needs?"

"That's complete garbage, and you know it." Aaron's voice turned fierce with loyalty. "Jennifer left because she wanted you to be someone you're not, not because you cared too much about your work."

"What if I mess this up with Emma?"

"What if you don't?" Aaron countered.

Nathan was quiet for a moment. "She really is different."

"How so?"

"She makes everything feel possible," Nathan said, the words coming out more honest than he'd intended. "Nothing else matters when I'm around her. I feel a connection between us."

Aaron grinned. "And that scares the living daylights out of you."

"Yeah," Nathan admitted. "It really does."

"So what're you gonna do about it?"

Nathan considered the question. "Keep working with her on the play, I guess. See what develops."

"That's not very decisive for someone who just admitted he's found a woman who makes everything feel possible."

"Aaron, she turned me down for dinner. I can't exactly chase after her like some lovesick teenager."

Aaron stood, draining the last of his coffee. "No, but you can stop acting like one dinner invitation was your only shot." He paused at the door, fixing Nathan with a serious look. "Maybe she said no because you caught her off guard. Maybe she really did have work to finish. Or maybe she's just as scared as you are about where this might lead. Either way, giving up after one try doesn't seem like the Nathan Reid I know."

After Aaron left, Nathan sat in his quiet office as the November afternoon light slanted through the windows. The budget reports still waited for his attention, but his mind was elsewhere—replaying Aaron's words, thinking about Emma's flustered reaction in the parking lot, wondering if he'd misread the whole situation.

Maybe Aaron was right. Maybe Emma's hesitation didn't mean lack of interest. Maybe it just meant she was being careful, the same way he'd been careful for the past three years.

Chapter 14

Emma nearly dropped the stack of new books she held when she spotted Nathan squinting at the back covers of two novels like they might reveal the secrets of the universe. His forest green sweater made his eyes look darker than usual, and without his principal's tie, he seemed more like a man trying to decide between pizza toppings than someone who managed four hundred kids and their teachers.

Saturday morning light streamed through the bookshop windows, warming the space with that particular early winter glow that made everything feel softer. The espresso machine hissed gently from the coffee corner, and somewhere in the mystery section, Mrs. Whitaker was muttering about "too many red herrings" while browsing through cozy mysteries.

Nathan shifted his weight, running a hand through his hair. The motion made her stomach do something fluttery.

Stop staring, she told herself. *He's just a customer who happens to have really nice shoulders and—*

"Finding everything okay?" The words slipped out before she could stop them.

Nathan's head snapped up, and when he spotted her approaching, his whole face transformed.

"Emma, hey." He set down both books he'd been looking at and seemed oddly relieved to see her.

"Hey yourself. Need some help finding something to read?"

"Yes, actually. I finished the last book I was reading, and I thought maybe I'd try something different." He gestured vaguely at the surrounding shelves.

"What do you usually read?"

"Mostly crime stuff. Michael Connelly, John Sandford, that kind of thing."

Emma stepped closer, close enough to catch his scent—something clean and woodsy that made her want to lean in. "What did you like about the last book you read?"

Nathan considered this seriously, his brow furrowing in concentration, which she found ridiculously attractive.

"The detective wasn't perfect," he said finally. "He made mistakes, questioned himself, but he kept trying to do the right thing, anyway. And the mystery wasn't just whodunit—it was about understanding why people make the choices they do, even when those choices hurt others."

Emma felt her pulse quicken. Not because of how close they were standing—though that wasn't helping—but because of what his answer revealed. This was a man who understood that the best stories weren't about perfect heroes but about flawed people finding their way toward something better.

"Follow me," she said, leading him deeper into the fiction section.

The back corner of the store had always been her favorite spot. She ran her finger along the spines until she found what she was looking for.

"This one." She pulled out a book and turned to hand it to him, only to realize they were standing close enough that she had to tip her head back to meet his eyes. Close enough to see the way his gaze dropped to her mouth for just a heartbeat before returning to her face.

"It's got all the mystery elements I imagine you love," she managed, trying to ignore the way her pulse had decided to throw a little party. "But the main character's a librarian who gets pulled into investigating a decades-old disappearance."

Their fingers brushed as Nathan accepted the book, sending warmth shooting up her arm. "A librarian detective? Mrs. Benson would probably solve the case in chapter three."

Emma laughed, grateful for the excuse to step back a little. "Are you kidding? She'd have it wrapped up by the dedication page."

Nathan's laugh was pure delight. He examined the book's cover, then looked back at her with something like wonder. "How do you do that?"

"Do what?"

"Know exactly what someone needs." His voice had gone softer, more personal. "We barely know each other, and you're picking books like you've been inside my head."

Heat crept up Emma's neck. "It's nothing, really. You just pay attention to what people say or how they react to certain situations. Besides..." She shrugged, aiming for casual and probably missing by miles. "You're not that complicated."

"Is that so?" Nathan's eyes sparkled with mischief. "Should I be insulted?"

"Depends. Are you going to trust my judgment, or are you going to stand there questioning my professional expertise?"

"Your professional expertise?" Nathan's grin turned teasing. "Is that what we're calling it?"

"Maybe I'm rethinking my assessment," Emma said, fighting back a smile. "You might be more complicated than I thought."

"Good complicated or bad complicated?"

Dangerously complicated, Emma thought, but said, "The jury's still out."

They were both laughing now, the kind of easy laughter that made Emma forget they hardly knew each other. Nathan had this way of making everything feel natural, unforced, like they'd been having conversations like this for years.

"Okay," he said, extending his hand. "I'll trust your recommendation. But if I hate it, you owe me a better suggestion."

"Deal." Emma shook his hand, noting how his fingers lingered against hers just a moment longer than necessary. "Though I should warn you—I'm pretty confident in my book-matching abilities."

"Is that a challenge?"

"Maybe. I like being right about these things."

They walked back toward the register together, and Emma was grateful for the movement, for something to do with her hands besides think about how nice his had felt in hers. The familiar sounds of her bookstore—soft country music playing overhead, the whisper of pages turning, and Cora's gentle laughter with a customer—helped steady her racing pulse.

"So what's your Saturday looking like?" Nathan asked as they reached the counter. "Besides helping hopeless customers navigate their literary crises?"

"You're not hopeless," Emma said, then immediately wondered if that sounded too flirtatious. "And honestly, not much planned. I was thinking about doing some writing later this afternoon, maybe catching up on my own reading."

"How's the writing going?"

"Better, actually." Emma said as she rang up his book purchase. "Working with the kids on the Christmas play has really helped me. I think shaking up my normal routine a bit has given me some inspiration again."

Nathan nodded, his expression thoughtful. "Kind of like reading outside your comfort zone?"

"Exactly like that."

Emma handed him the receipt, their fingers brushing again in the exchange. Such a simple touch, but it sent warmth spreading through her chest like hot chocolate on a cold day.

"Emma," Nathan said, his voice carrying a note like someone about to jump off a diving board. "Would you maybe want to have lunch with me? I mean, if you're free."

The invitation made her pause; she'd been hoping for this.

"I'd love to."

The expression of relief on Nathan's face was so obvious it made her smile.

"Give me two seconds." Emma practically floated toward the back room, catching her reflection in the small mirror by the employee bulletin board. Her cheeks were flushed, and her eyes were bright with anticipation. She looked like someone who was about to have lunch with a man she was increasingly, hopelessly attracted to.

And for once, that didn't scare her.

"Cora," she called as she emerged, pulling on her coat, "I'm heading out for lunch. Mind holding down the fort?"

Cora glanced up from helping a customer, spotted Nathan waiting by the counter, and her eyebrows rose with obvious delight. "Take all the time you need, honey."

Emma felt heat flood her cheeks at Cora's knowing tone but couldn't bring herself to care.

"Ready?" Nathan asked as she approached.

"Ready."

As they walked toward the door together, Emma caught Cora's eye. Her employee gave her the most unsubtle thumbs-up in the history of workplace encouragement, followed by a grin.

Outside, the sidewalks along Mistletoe Lane buzzed with Saturday morning energy—families window shopping, teenagers sharing coffee outside the bakery, and couples walking arm in arm past storefronts.

Nathan fell into step beside her, close enough that their shoulders occasionally bumped as they navigated around other pedestrians. Each tiny contact sent awareness skittering across Emma's skin.

"So," she said, tucking her hands into her coat pockets to keep from doing something ridiculous like reaching for his, "where are we going for lunch?"

"How does the Pickle Barrel Deli sound?" Nathan glanced at her sideways.

"I love that place." Emma grinned. "I go there sometimes when I need to get out of the bookstore but don't want to drive anywhere. Lisa's sandwiches are to die for."

They'd almost reached the deli when Nathan suddenly stopped, turning to face her with an expression caught somewhere between sheepish and amused.

"Speaking of Lisa," he said, running a hand through his hair, "I should probably warn you. She's been dropping hints about my love life... or lack thereof... for a while now, and if she sees us together... well, she's going to assume we're... you know... on a date."

Emma raised an eyebrow, fighting back a smile. "And that's a problem because?"

Nathan's cheeks flushed, but his grin was pure warmth. "Not a problem at all. I just wanted to prepare you for Lisa's interrogation."

"Nathan," Emma said softly, stepping closer, "is this a date?"

"Would you like to be?"

Emma's heart did something acrobatic in her chest. "Yes."

His smile could have powered the entire town's Christmas lights. "In that case," he said, offering her his arm, "let's go give Lisa something to talk about."

Chapter 15

The moment Nathan and Emma stepped into the warm embrace of the Pickle Barrel Deli, Lisa Davenport's head snapped up from behind the counter like a bloodhound catching a scent.

"Well, well, well." Lisa's weathered hands stilled on the sandwich she'd been wrapping, a grin spreading across her face. "Nathan Reid and Emma Sullivan. Together. On a Saturday..." She dragged out the pause like she was savoring fine wine. "Now this is interesting."

Nathan felt heat creep up his collar as the familiar scents of roast beef and fresh bread wrapped around them. The deli buzzed with Saturday afternoon energy, and Lisa's delighted attention made him feel like they'd walked into a spotlight.

"Hi, Lisa," he managed, shoving his hands into his jacket pockets.

"Don't you 'Hi Lisa' me, Nathan Reid." She bustled around the counter, mischief dancing in her eyes. "Emma, honey, I am absolutely loving this. You two make the cutest couple I've seen walk through that door all month."

Emma glanced at Nathan, her lips twitching with barely contained laughter. The way her eyes sparkled with amusement instead of embarrassment made something warm unfurl in his chest.

"This just makes my day," she said, leading them toward a corner table with the purposeful stride of a woman on a mission. "I've got the perfect spot for you two—nice and cozy."

The table sat next to the front window, where sunlight streamed across the red-checkered cloth. "Best view in the house," Lisa announced, hands on her hips as she surveyed her handiwork. "Now, what can I get you to drink? Coffee? Sweet tea? Water?"

"Just coffee for me," Nathan said, settling across from Emma and trying not to notice how the afternoon light caught the warm brown of her hair.

"Sweet tea, please." Emma said as she hung her purse on the back of the chair, her movements graceful despite the obvious amusement still tugging at her lips.

"Perfect choices. I'll give you a minute with the menu. The roast beef special is absolutely divine today. Very impressive choice for a lunch date."

"Lisa—" Nathan's protest came out strangled.

"What?" Her expression turned innocently wide-eyed. "I'm just saying the roast beef is exceptionally good today. Could make a girl swoon, that's all."

She bustled away with obvious satisfaction, leaving them in a cocoon of soft conversation and clinking silverware. Nathan looked across the table to find Emma pressing her lips together, shoulders shaking with suppressed laughter.

"I'm really sorry about that," he said, running a hand through his hair. "She means well, but subtle isn't exactly in her vocabulary."

"Are you kidding?" Emma's laughter bubbled over like champagne, warm and effervescent. "I love that someone cares about you enough to thoroughly embarrass you in public. How long has she been playing matchmaker?"

"Since about six months after my divorce papers were signed. She's introduced me to her neighbor's daughter, her hairdresser's sister, and—" He shook his head, grinning at the memory. "A woman who came in once asking for directions to the highway."

"Oh, no." Emma leaned forward, eyes bright with interest. "Please tell me these did not go as badly as I'm imagining."

"The neighbor's daughter talked exclusively about her ex-boyfriend. For two hours. The hairdresser's sister was perfectly nice, but we had less in common than strangers at a bus stop." Nathan paused for effect. "And the woman asking for directions was married."

Emma's delighted laughter drew glances from nearby tables, but Nathan found he didn't care. The sound was like music, bright and unguarded, making him want to keep talking just to hear it again.

"Lisa felt so guilty about that last one she bought my lunch for a month," he added.

"Well then," Emma said, settling back in her chair with a playful smile that made his pulse skip, "I guess I should feel honored that I passed the Lisa Davenport seal of approval."

"You definitely should. She's got excellent instincts about people."

Lisa returned with their drinks and an expectant expression. "Have we decided?"

Nathan ordered the roast beef special, Emma chose the turkey club, and Lisa left with promises that lunch would be ready soon.

"So," Emma said, "tell me something I don't know about Nathan Reid."

The question caught him off guard. Most first-date conversations he remembered had felt like job interviews—safe questions about work and weather and weekend plans. But Emma's curiosity felt different, genuine, like she actually wanted to understand him as a person rather than just fill conversational space.

"Like what?"

"Anything. Any hidden talents? Secret fears? What did you dream about being when you were little?" Her eyes danced with mischief. "Please tell me you wanted to be something wonderfully impractical like a dinosaur hunter or a professional treasure finder."

"Close. I wanted to be a park ranger. Thought it'd be amazing to live in the mountains, help lost hikers, and maybe rescue the occasional bear cub."

"That's not so different from what you do now," Emma observed, tilting her head with genuine interest. "Different kind of helping, same heart behind it."

The insight surprised him. "I never thought about it that way, but you might be right. What about you? Always known you wanted to write children's books?"

Emma shook her head, tucking a strand of hair behind her ear. "I wanted to be a veterinarian at one point until I realized I'd have to deal with sick animals, not just cuddle healthy puppies all day. Then I thought maybe a teacher, but when I started helping with story time in the elementary school library while I was in high school, I realized I loved the stories themselves more than the classroom management."

Lisa appeared with their sandwiches and an extra side of pickles that Nathan definitely hadn't ordered, setting them down with the flourish of someone presenting a feast.

"Extra pickles on the house," she announced with a wink. "Pickles are good luck on first dates. Old family tradition."

Nathan opened his mouth to protest, but Lisa had already vanished back into the lunch rush.

"She really doesn't give up, does she?" Emma said, biting into her turkey club with obvious pleasure.

"Never." Nathan tasted his roast beef, and it was incredible. "So tell me about your family. Do they live around here?"

Emma's expression grew softer, more thoughtful. "Just my Aunt Lily, and she lives a few miles outside town. My parents are both gone." She traced the condensation on her tea glass with one finger. "You already know my mom passed away earlier this year, and my dad... well, he decided being a father wasn't what he wanted after all. He walked away from Mom and me without looking back when I was in grade school."

"I'm sorry," Nathan said, meaning it. The matter-of-fact way she spoke about abandonment made his chest ache for the little girl who'd had to learn too young that love wasn't always permanent.

"It was hard, but I've come to accept it. His loss. He chose to walk away from us. But losing Mom, well... it still hurts," Emma continued, her voice steady but vulnerable. "She was my biggest cheerleader, my first reader, and my best friend. She always read my first drafts out loud to me so I could listen to the words and make sure everything sounded right. She was simply an amazing person. Without her... well, life is different, and my writing has become more challenging. I miss her voice cheering me on."

"I wish I could have met her."

Emma's smile was watery but genuine. "Me too. What about your family?"

"My parents are living their best retirement life in Florida. Dad spent his career with the State Department of Education—moving us around every few years as he took on new regional posts. Mom was the classic stay-at-home wife, always making sure the family adjusted. Now they're loving the beach life and constantly trying to guilt me into visiting more often." Nathan grinned. "According to my mother, I work too much and don't call enough."

"Do you? Work too much, I mean."

"Probably. But I love what I do, you know? Those kids, the teachers—it doesn't feel like work when you enjoy what you do. I really love my job."

"That's beautiful," Emma said softly. "Not many can say something like that."

"What about hobbies?" Nathan asked. "What does Emma Sullivan do when she's not writing or directing Christmas plays?"

"I read voraciously. Hike or go jogging when the weather's nice. And I'm absolutely terrible at cooking but keep trying new recipes anyway." Her grin turned mischievous. "Last week I attempted homemade bread and created something that could probably stop bullets."

Nathan burst out laughing. "I'm not much better. I've mastered exactly three dishes, and everything else is a disaster waiting to happen."

"What are your three specialties?"

"Spaghetti, grilled cheese and canned tomato soup, and scrambled eggs. That's literally my entire culinary repertoire."

"Hey, those are solid comfort foods," Emma said with mock seriousness. "And I bet you don't set off smoke alarms regularly like I do."

"How regular are we talking?"

"Let's just say my neighbors have stopped calling the fire department when they hear mine going off. They've learned to distinguish between 'Emma's cooking' and 'actual emergency.'"

Nathan watched her face as she talked—the way her eyes crinkled when she laughed, the graceful gestures she made with her hands, and the unconscious way she leaned forward when she was engaged in conversation. Everything about her drew him in and made him want to keep discovering new layers.

"Can I ask you something?" Emma said, and Nathan realized he'd been openly studying her face.

"Shoot."

"What made you decide to become a principal? Most people go into education for the classroom experience—working directly with kids. Administration is a whole different animal."

"I started as a third-grade teacher and loved it. But I kept seeing systemic problems that could be solved at the administrative level—budget issues affecting multiple classrooms, policies that didn't serve the kids well. I realized I could have a broader impact from the principal's office."

"Do you miss the classroom?"

Nathan considered this as he finished his sandwich. "Sometimes. But when I see teachers thriving because they have the support they need, or when I can solve a problem that helps multiple classrooms, it brings me joy." He paused, meeting her eyes. "Working on the Christmas play is reminding me how much I enjoy direct interaction with the kids, though."

"They adore you. You have a way of being authoritative without being intimidating. You're approachable. They respect you because they know you genuinely care about them."

"That means a lot, especially coming from you. You're pretty incredible with them yourself."

Pink bloomed across Emma's cheeks, and Nathan realized he liked being able to make her blush with honest compliments.

They'd both finished eating, and Nathan was surprised to realize they'd been talking for over an hour. The lunch rush had flowed around them like a river around stones—families claiming tables, orders being called out, the steady rhythm of a busy deli—but their conversation had created its own intimate bubble.

"I should probably head back," Emma said, glancing at her watch with obvious reluctance. "Cora and Molly can handle the shop, but Saturday afternoons can get pretty hectic."

Nathan nodded, though every instinct screamed against letting this end. He wanted to suggest coffee, or a walk, or dinner—anything to extend their time together. But something held him back. Maybe the newness of whatever this was becoming, or perhaps just not wanting to seem too eager and risk spoiling the easy connection they'd built.

"Of course," he said, signaling Lisa for the check.

Emma reached for her purse as Lisa approached with the check.

"I asked you to lunch," Nathan said firmly. "My treat."

"So," Lisa said, clasping her hands together, "will I be seeing you two lovely people together again soon?"

Nathan felt his face heat up again, but Emma's warm laughter made the embarrassment worthwhile.

"That depends," Emma said with sparkling eyes, "on whether Nathan can survive more of your professional matchmaking services."

"Honey, that wasn't professional matchmaking," she protested with a grin. "That was just friendly curiosity. You should see what I do when I'm really trying to meddle."

Nathan left a generous tip and stood quickly, eager to escape before Lisa could demonstrate her advanced meddling techniques.

Outside, the November air felt crisp after the deli's warmth. Nathan fell into step beside Emma as they walked back toward the bookshop.

"Thanks for lunch; I truly enjoyed spending time with you."

"Thank you for saying yes," Nathan replied. "And for not running away when Lisa started her matchmaking routine."

Emma's grin was pure mischief. "I thought it was sweet. She obviously adores you."

They'd reached the bookshop, and Nathan felt the afternoon slipping away like sand through his fingers. He wanted to ask when he could see her again outside of Christmas play practice. He wanted to suggest dinner or a movie or anything that would give him another excuse to watch her laugh and listen to her speak. But instead he simply asked, "I'll see you Tuesday?"

"Tuesday," Emma agreed, but she made no move toward the door. "Should be interesting now that the kids have their actual roles."

"Yeah, it'll be good to see them work with their individual characters."

They stood there for a moment, neither quite ready to break the spell of the afternoon. Nathan caught himself memorizing details—the way the wind ruffled her hair, the soft smile that lingered at the corners of her mouth, and the way she looked at him like he was someone worth her time and attention.

"Well," Emma said finally, "I should let you get on with your Saturday. Thanks again for lunch."

"Anytime," Nathan said, meaning it more than any casual phrase he'd ever spoken.

As Emma disappeared into her bookstore, Nathan stood on the sidewalk longer than was probably dignified, replaying their conversation and already counting the hours until Tuesday's practice. For the first time in years, his anticipation had nothing to do with lesson plans or school meetings. It had everything to do with the woman who'd just made him remember what it felt like to want something more than just getting through another day.

Chapter 16

"Miss Emma, Miss Emma!" Madison Torres bounced on her toes beside the doorway, clutching her script to her chest like precious treasure. "My mom said she's gonna help paint the backdrops on Saturday, and I get to come too! Can I help paint the stars?"

Emma knelt to Madison's level, catching the girl's infectious excitement. "Of course you can. We'll need all the star-painting experts we can get."

"I'm really good at stars," Madison announced with nine-year-old confidence.

The last group of fourth-graders finally disappeared down the hallway, their voices trailing like musical notes until the heavy doors muffled their chatter. In the sudden quiet, Emma could hear the distant hum of the heating system and catch the lingering sweetness of peppermint—Mrs. Benson's traditional end-of-practice candy canes.

"Well," Mrs. Benson said, settling into her chair with the careful movements that had become more pronounced this week. She flexed her fingers slowly before reaching for her legal pad. "That went remarkably well for our fourth practice. The children are really starting to get into the play."

Emma pulled her chair closer to the table where Mrs. Benson had arranged several manila folders like a general planning a battle strategy. Nathan dragged a third chair over, completing their cozy circle near the multipurpose room's windows. Outside, the November afternoon light filtered through the glass, casting everything in that soft, pre-winter glow that made ordinary moments feel touched with magic.

"Tommy's completely lost in his role as the Village Lamplighter," Emma said, unable to hide her smile. "Did you see his face when he was explaining to the other kids that the lights were going out? He looked genuinely worried about the whole village."

Mrs. Benson's eyes crinkled with fond pride. "Twenty-five years of Christmas plays, and I still get goosebumps when a child stops acting and starts being their character. Tommy's not reciting lines anymore—he's living the story."

Nathan leaned forward. "And Sara's finding her voice. Last week I could barely hear her when she read her lines, but today she projected all the way to the back wall. Clear as a bell."

Emma grinned at Nathan's observation. Sara Tillman's transformation from whisper-quiet to cautiously confident had become her personal mission. Knowing that Nathan had noticed—that he cared enough to watch for the girl's progress—felt wonderful.

"She just needed someone to believe she could do it," Emma said. "Kids surprise themselves when they discover adults actually have faith in them."

"Speaking of having faith," Mrs. Benson said, reaching for her legal pad with that mischievous twinkle Emma was learning to recognize, "we need to nail down Saturday's plans. I've got our volunteer list here, and honestly… I'm once again amazed by this community."

Emma accepted the paper Mrs. Benson slid across the table, scanning names that read like a who's who of Mistletoe Falls' most creative residents.

"This is incredible," she said, passing the list to Nathan. "Though I'll admit, I'm kinda nervous about managing all these helpers. I've never coordinated a construction project before."

Nathan glanced up from the list, and his smile was reassuring in a way that made her pulse skip. "That's what I'm here for. Three years of these Saturday construction marathons taught me a few things. The secret's having everything organized ahead of time and trusting that folks know their own skills better than we do and that they're genuinely interested in helping in any way they can."

Mrs. Benson nodded. "Nathan's absolutely right. The parents who volunteer for these projects? They're not doing it out of obligation. They want to create something special for the kids. Each of the people who volunteered has unique skills. I think Saturday will run smoothly, and we'll get a lot of work done."

"Okay," Emma said, pulling out her notebook and clicking her pen. "So what exactly are we building? I've been sketching ideas, but I wanna make sure we're not forgetting anything important."

"Let's start with the big pieces." Nathan said. "We'll need village buildings for the Light Keepers story, something that shows the community where the Christmas lights are failing. The main square's gotta be large enough for all the ensemble scenes but still portable enough to move around."

Emma started sketching rough rectangles on her notepad. "What if we built the village square in sections? Several building facades that connect with hinges, so they fold flat for storage but create this whole world when they're set up."

"That's brilliant," Nathan said, leaning over to see her sketch. His shoulder bumped hers gently, sending awareness skittering across her skin. "Way easier than wrestling with one huge piece. What about the lighting effects? We need to show the Christmas lights going out and the kids bringing them back to life."

Emma tapped her pen against her lip, thinking. "Could we use actual string lights? Battery-powered ones that we can control with a remote? Turn them off to show the lights failing, then have the kids 'fix' them during their scenes?"

"Perfect. And if we weave them through all the village buildings, around the whole stage area, it'll create this magical atmosphere that serves the story too."

Mrs. Benson watched their planning ping-pong with satisfaction, occasionally making comments but mostly content to let them work through the logistics together. Emma noticed how easily she and Nathan had fallen into sync—his practical problem-solving balancing her creative vision, ideas building on each other like a conversation that had been waiting to happen.

"What about the other scenes?" Emma asked, flipping through her script notes. "We've got the village square for the opening, but there's also that scene where the Wise Grandmother gathers everyone to solve the lighting problem."

"A town setting should be easy," Nathan said. "A few painted backdrop panels showing storefronts, maybe some potted plants to suggest a little marketplace. The hillside scene's trickier though."

"Risers," Emma said suddenly. "What if we covered portable risers with green fabric? Different heights to create rolling hills. Add some artificial trees to break up the straight lines."

Nathan's face lit up. "The school's got risers in storage—I'd completely forgotten about those. That'd work perfectly."

Emma felt that familiar flutter of creative excitement, the sensation she'd been missing for months that was slowly starting to come back to her. Ideas were flowing again, her mind painting pictures she could actually bring to life. Having Nathan there to solve the practical puzzles made it even better—like having a creative partner who spoke her language.

"Should we make a materials list?" she asked. "I'm guessing Thompson's Hardware can handle most of the lumber and basic supplies."

"Chuck's already said he'd donate the wood and hardware; just email him the list, and he'll make sure everything is delivered in time," Nathan said, consulting Mrs. Benson's volunteer list. "And Lynn Palmer mentioned she's got extra paint and brushes in the art room here at the school we can use for the backdrops."

Emma made a note to herself to email Chuck, then looked up to find Nathan watching her with an expression that made her suddenly conscious of how close they were sitting. Their knees were almost touching under the small table, and there was something in his gaze that made her pulse quicken.

"What?" she asked, tucking a strand of hair behind her ear—a nervous habit that seemed to activate whenever Nathan looked at her like that.

"Nothing," he said. "Just thinking about Saturday. It's gonna be great seeing all these plans come together."

Mrs. Benson cleared her throat gently, and Emma caught the older woman watching their interaction with barely concealed delight. "Before you two get completely carried away with Saturday logistics," she said, "we should probably inventory what props and set pieces we've already got in storage. There's no point building from scratch if we've already got what we need gathering dust back there."

"Good thinking," Nathan said, standing and stretching, and Emma tried not to notice the way his sweater pulled across his shoulders. "Dorothy, why don't you stay here and brainstorm some props we might need? Emma and I can handle the inventory expedition."

"That would be wonderful. These old bones are aching more than usual today."

Emma felt a flutter of anticipation at the prospect of exploring the storage closet with Nathan. Professional curiosity about theatrical treasures, she told herself. Nothing to do with spending time alone with the man who made her stomach do little flips when he smiled.

"Lead the way," she said, following Nathan toward the closet doors.

Nathan pulled open the double doors, revealing a space that looked like Santa's workshop had collided with a theater department. Metal shelving lined the walls, loaded with cardboard boxes, fabric-draped shapes, and props that were instantly recognizable as Christmas magic.

"This is incredible," Emma breathed, stepping into the closet and turning in a slow circle. "It's like stepping into Mrs. Benson's memory box."

"She never throws anything away if there's a chance it might be useful someday," Nathan said, reaching for a box labeled "VILLAGE CHARACTERS" in Mrs. Benson's precise handwriting.

Emma gravitated toward the painted backdrop panels leaning against the back wall. "These are gorgeous," she said, carefully pulling one forward to examine the details. "Look at this brushwork—someone really knew what they were doing."

"That'd be Mrs. Benson. She's quite the artist when she has time to paint."

Emma studied the backdrops, mentally cataloging possibilities. There was a perfect village scene with cozy cottages that would work beautifully for the Light Keepers' community and a starry winter night that could be magical for the moment when the lights come back to life. As she shifted panels to see the ones behind them, Nathan moved to help support their weight.

"Here, let me—" he said, reaching around her to steady a panel that was starting to tip.

The movement brought him close enough that Emma could feel warmth radiating from his body. When she turned to thank him, she found herself looking directly into his eyes from maybe six inches away. For a heartbeat, neither of them moved, and Emma was acutely aware of the way Nathan's gaze dropped to her lips before returning to her eyes.

"We should probably—" she started to say, but her words disappeared when Nathan shifted and their hands brushed as they both reached for the same backdrop.

The contact was brief—just the warm pressure of his fingers against hers—but it sent electricity shooting up Emma's arm.

Instead of pulling away, Nathan let his fingers linger against hers. Then, slowly and deliberately, he turned his hand to capture hers in a gentle clasp. His thumb brushed once across her knuckles, a touch so tender and intentional that Emma felt her breath catch.

"Emma," he said, and there was something in his voice that made her name sound like the beginning of a question and a promise.

"Yeah?" she managed, though the word came out softer than she'd intended.

"Have dinner with me tomorrow? Not to talk about the play. Not because we need to plan anything. Just because I'd really like to spend an evening with you."

Emma felt her heart thump with excitement and nervousness. "I'd love to," she said, watching Nathan's expression transform into relief and pleasure that made her understand why people wrote songs about moments like this.

"Really?" he asked, as if he'd been prepared for her to need time to think about it.

"Really," Emma confirmed. "When?"

"Six o'clock?"

"Perfect." Emma's smile felt like sunshine. "We could go to the Fireside Diner."

"That sounds great," Nathan said, his own smile widening.

Emma looked up at him. "We should probably get back to work," she said softly, though she made no move to step away.

Nathan seemed to have the same thought. He slowly released her hand, though he squeezed her fingers once before stepping back.

Emma grabbed the nearest box without really reading the label. "We should bring some of this stuff out so Mrs. Benson can see what we found."

Nathan cleared his throat and reached for another box, his movements suddenly more careful. "Good idea."

They emerged from the storage closet with their arms full of props and costume boxes, both trying to look like they'd been efficiently working the entire time rather than having had a moment that felt like the beginning of everything.

Chapter 17

The Fireside Diner hummed with Friday evening energy—silverware clinking against ceramic plates, bursts of laughter from nearby tables, the rich scent of homemade bread and Pete's famous pot roast drifting from the kitchen—but in their corner booth, Emma felt wrapped in a cocoon of privacy. The vintage fixtures cast everything in a honey-warm glow, and she found herself thinking that this—this easy conversation, this comfortable teasing, the way Nathan leaned forward as if every word she spoke mattered—felt more natural than any date she'd experienced in years.

"Okay, I have to ask," Emma said, twirling her fork through the creamy mashed potatoes beside her pot roast, "what's your favorite Christmas movie? And please don't tell me you're about to say Die Hard."

Nathan nearly choked on his bite of meatloaf. "Why would you automatically assume I'd pick an action movie for my favorite Christmas film?"

"Because you read crime novels and have this whole steady, protective thing going on." Emma grinned, savoring the way his eyebrows rose in mock offense. "I can absolutely picture you arguing that Die Hard counts as holiday viewing because it happens at a Christmas party."

Nathan set down his fork with exaggerated dignity. "For your information, Ms. Sullivan, my favorite Christmas movie is It's a Wonderful Life. Very traditional, very wholesome, completely free of explosions."

"Really?" Emma's face brightened, and she leaned forward, elbows on the red-checkered tablecloth. "That's so perfect for you. The whole community coming together, everyone's life mattering..."

"Right? Though I'll confess, watching it as an adult, I couldn't stop wondering what kind of principal Mr. Gower would've been. He probably had excellent classroom management skills."

Emma's laughter bubbled up, bright and unguarded, making Nathan realize he was already cataloging that sound, wanting to bottle it up and keep it forever. "Only you would analyze the educational leadership implications of It's a Wonderful Life."

"What about you?" Nathan asked.

"Little Women. The 1994 version with Winona Ryder. I watch it every Christmas Eve while I wrap presents. Jo's determination to write despite everyone telling her to be practical, the way the family supports each other through everything..." She paused, reaching for her sweet tea. The glass was slick with condensation, cold against her palm in the diner's cozy warmth. "Plus, it makes me cry in all the right places."

"Jo March. A writer who refuses to give up on her stories, no matter what. The movie suits you."

"Your turn for twenty questions," Emma said. "If you could travel anywhere in the world, where would you go?"

Nathan was quiet for a moment, his brow furrowing in that thoughtful way that made Emma want to reach across and smooth the lines with her fingertips.

"Alaska," Nathan said suddenly, and Emma heard longing thread through his voice like silver. "I've always wanted to see the northern lights. Maybe stay in one of those glass dome cabins where you can watch the aurora from bed. There's something about that kind of wonder..." He trailed off, meeting her eyes with an expression that made her stomach flutter.

Emma pictured Nathan beneath a star-filled sky, watching the shimmering lights, his expression filled with awe. Something warm and dangerous unfurled in her chest as she imagined herself beside him, sharing that moment of wonder.

"That sounds magical," she said softly.

"Maybe someday." Nathan's shrug seemed casual. "It's just a dream vacation I've thought about."

"You should go. Dreams like that—they matter. They keep us believing in possibilities."

Nathan studied her face, and Emma felt heat creep up her neck under his attention. "When did you become so wise about dreams?"

"When I realized ignoring them doesn't make them go away."

Rita, their waitress, appeared beside their table, coffee pot steaming. "Y'all need any refills? Pie? The apple's fresh out of the oven."

"Just coffee, thanks," Nathan said.

"Same for me," Emma added, watching Rita top off their cups with practiced efficiency.

"Take your time and enjoy your evening," Rita said with a knowing smile. "Friday nights were made for good conversation."

When Rita bustled away, Nathan leaned forward, cradling his coffee mug between his hands. "Speaking of dreams—what's next for you? With your writing?"

Emma felt a familiar flutter of nervous excitement at the question. "I'd love to write longer books someday. Middle-grade novels, maybe. And I've been thinking about teaching writing workshops for kids, helping them find their voices." She paused, studying Nathan's face for any sign of polite dismissal. "You probably think that sounds impractical."

"Emma." Nathan's voice was firm, immediate. "That would be incredible. You'd be wonderful at it."

"You really think so?"

"I know so." His enthusiasm made her sit straighter, hope blooming in her chest. "I can picture it—kids discovering they have stories worth telling and building confidence in writing."

Emma smiled, charmed by how easily he could envision her dreams becoming reality. "What about you? What other dreams are you hiding behind all that principal responsibility?"

Nathan's fingers stilled on his coffee mug, and Emma caught the vulnerability that flickered across his features.

"I've always wanted to create outdoor educational programs," he said finally. "Take kids into the mountains; let them learn science and history through hiking and camping. Most children spend so much time indoors they never discover how capable they can be in nature."

"Nathan, I love that!" Emma's mind sparked with possibilities, imagining children learning about ecosystems while standing in actual forests and studying history where it happened. "Kids would learn so much more that way."

"It's probably too ambitious," Nathan said with a self-deprecating smile. "Budget constraints, liability issues..."

"It's not too ambitious. It's exactly the kind of vision that makes you exceptional at what you do. You see what children actually need, not just what's convenient to provide."

Nathan's expression shifted, vulnerability, and old hurt shadowing his features. "My ex-wife used to say my ideas about education were unrealistic. That I cared more about changing the world than building a practical life."

Heat flared in Emma's chest—protective indignation that surprised her with its intensity. How could anyone not see the beauty in Nathan's dreams? "That's awful. Passion for meaningful work isn't a character flaw—it's attractive."

The words came out more forcefully than she'd intended, and Nathan's eyebrows rose, surprise and something that might have been hope flickering in his eyes.

"You think a passion for work is attractive?"

"I think," Emma said, holding his gaze steadily, "that a man who cares about making children's lives better—that's not competition for love. That's the kind of man you'd want to build a life with."

Nathan went very still, his dark eyes searching hers with an intensity that made her breath catch. The sounds of the diner—conversations, clinking dishes, Rita's laughter at another table—faded to background noise.

"Emma." His voice was quiet, careful. "I need you to know something." He paused, as if weighing his words. "I'm falling for you."

The simple honesty hit her like a physical force. Emma's heart stuttered, then began racing as the truth of what he'd said—and how deeply she felt it too—washed through her.

"Nathan," she said, reaching across the table.

The moment her fingers touched his hand, Nathan turned his palm up, and their fingers intertwined with startling naturalness. The contact sent electricity racing up Emma's arm—his hand was warm and slightly rough from his woodworking, calloused but gentle, and the way he held hers made her feel simultaneously treasured and safe.

"I want you to know," she managed, her voice barely above a whisper, "I feel it too."

Nathan's smile was soft, relieved, and utterly beautiful. His thumb traced gentle patterns across her knuckles, and Emma realized this moment—sitting in a small-town restaurant with her hand held by a man who saw her as worthy of someone to spend his time with—was exactly the kind of life she'd envisioned for herself but never quite believed could happen to her.

They sat like that for a long moment, hands linked across the red-checkered tablecloth, not saying a word. Emma could feel her pulse in her fingertips where they touched Nathan's skin and could see her own wonder reflected in his eyes.

"Can I ask you something personal?" Nathan said, still tracing those gentle patterns on her hand.

Emma nodded, nerves and anticipation fluttering in her stomach.

"Where do you see yourself five years from now?"

"Five years from now... that's difficult to think about. Since Mom passed, I've felt lost, like part of me is missing. I've had a hard time moving forward in life. I hope that in five years the feeling of being lost without her eases some. I hope I'm writing freely again without feeling like I'm constantly reaching for words I can't find." She paused, meeting his eyes. "I'd love to settle down with someone who was meant just for me. Maybe even have a family someday." Her cheeks warmed. "What about you? Do you think about getting married again? Maybe a few children running around?"

Nathan's expression grew thoughtful. "I do. I've always imagined being a dad. Jennifer, my ex... she wanted kids too, but only after I cut back my hours at school. She saw my dedication as competition for the attention our children would need."

Emma's protective indignation returned, sharper this time. "That's awful. I think your devotion to your work would only make you an even better father. Your future kids could learn so much from seeing that dedication."

"I hope so," Nathan said, and she caught the longing in his voice. "I've always believed parenting, teaching, even my job—they all come from the same place. Wanting to help kids become their best selves."

"Exactly. And the right person won't see that passion as competition." Emma's voice was firm, wanting him to understand just how wrong his ex-wife had been.

They smiled at each other across the table, both recognizing they'd just shared something weighty—not plans or promises, but compatible dreams that could one day weave together into something beautiful.

"Emma," Nathan said, glancing at their joined hands before looking back up at her. "I should probably tell you... I'm not good at dating or keeping things light."

Her pulse quickened, but something in his expression made her lean closer instead of pulling away.

"After my divorce, I swore off anything that didn't feel..." He paused, searching. "I'm not looking just to have fun or see where things go. If I'm here with you like this, it's because I think your someone really special, and I can see a future with you."

Emma's breath caught. "Nathan—"

"I know that probably sounds intense," he said quickly, "but I wanted you to know where my head's at."

"You don't sound intense to me—you sound honest." Her thumb brushed across his knuckles. "And for what it's worth, I've never been good at casual either. When I care about someone..." She drew a steadying breath. "When I care, I really care."

Nathan's smile was relief and something deeper. "So we're both the all-in type."

"Looks like it." Emma's own smile felt tremulous, hopeful.

Nathan lifted her hand and pressed a gentle kiss to her knuckles, his eyes never leaving hers. The gesture was tender and old-fashioned, yet charged with promise that made Emma's heart race.

In the warm glow of the Fireside Diner, with the quiet clatter of dishes and the murmur of conversations drifting through the air, Emma realized how right this felt—holding hands with a man who wasn't afraid to show her his heart, who saw her dreams as beautiful, and who made her feel cherished.

Chapter 18

Emma wrestled a large insulated coffee dispenser through the front doors of Mistletoe Falls Elementary, the weight tugging at her arm as she nudged the door open with her shoulder. She could already hear the buzz of conversation and the whir of a drill coming from the multipurpose room, along with laughter echoing off the walls.

When she stepped inside, Nathan looked up from where he was kneeling beside a sheet of plywood, a pencil tucked behind his ear and a measuring tape in his hand. The sight of him in dark jeans and a forest green flannel shirt, his hair slightly mussed from working, made her pulse skip.

"I brought reinforcements," Emma announced, hoisting the dispenser a little higher.

"You're an absolute angel," Margaret Foster said, glancing up from the backdrop panel she'd been painting near the windows. Drops of forest green dotted her apron, and her gray hair had escaped its neat bun in artistic wisps.

Emma set the dispenser on a folding table and began pouring steaming cups for volunteers scattered around the room. Nathan's entire face lit up when she handed him his—black coffee, no sugar, exactly how he liked it. The simple fact that she'd remembered seemed to mean something to him.

"Thank you," he said, his voice low. "Ready to create some Christmas magic this morning?"

She smiled and glanced around the multipurpose room, breathing in the mingled scents of paint and fresh lumber. Sheets of plywood in various sizes were stacked against one wall, with lumber that would clearly need cutting outside. Paint cans sat neatly on a tarp in the center of the room, surrounded by brushes, rollers, and enough drop cloths to protect every surface in the building.

"What can I help with?"

"How about the village storefronts? Three connected panels that fold flat for storage but create a realistic street scene when they're set up. Think Christmas-card perfect."

"Christmas-card perfect is right up my alley. What do you need me to do?"

"Well, I was thinking you could help me paint the panels after we get everything cut to the right size."

Emma watched as Nathan selected pieces of wood, automatically checking each board for straightness. There was something grounding, even comforting, about the way he moved—focused, capable, steady.

"I like watching you work," she said before she could stop herself.

Nathan paused mid-measurement and looked up. "I like having you watch," he said with a grin. "Though you might get bored once I start the actual cutting. I get pretty obsessive about making sure everything lines up right."

"Obsession has its charms," she teased.

"Good to know." His smile widened in a way that made her stomach flutter pleasantly.

Twenty minutes later, Emma stood in the parking lot watching Nathan set up the power tools he'd need. The crisp air carried the scent of fresh-cut pine, mingling with the faint aroma of coffee drifting from the multipurpose room.

"Here," Nathan said, handing her safety glasses from his well-organized toolbox. "I know they're not exactly fashionable, but I've seen too many people get hurt by flying wood chips."

Emma slipped on the oversized glasses, acutely aware of how ridiculous they probably looked on her. "How do I look?"

Nathan's gaze lingered on her face, his expression softening. "Like someone smart enough to protect her beautiful eyes."

Heat crept into her cheeks, and she glanced quickly toward the saw as if it could distract her from the way his words had landed.

The cutting process took about an hour, and Emma found herself genuinely fascinated. Nathan worked with smooth efficiency, adjusting blade heights, securing boards with clamps, transforming raw lumber into neatly measured panels for their village storefronts. The steady whir of the saw, the sharp scent of sawdust, and the focused ease of his movements created a rhythm that was almost meditative—like watching an artist at work.

"You're really good at this," she said as he finished the last cut.

"I like working with my hands." Nathan began stacking the pieces with care, lining them as precisely as if they were puzzle parts. "There's something satisfying about starting with raw materials and ending up with something useful and beautiful."

"Like teaching," Emma said, meeting his eyes as she bent to lift a board.

Nathan paused, surprise flickering across his features. "Yeah. Exactly like teaching. I never thought about it that way, but you're right."

Back inside the multipurpose room, they spread Mrs. Benson's sketches across a folding table. The paper crackled softly beneath their hands, covered in careful pencil strokes that revealed a charming main street scene: three distinct storefronts—a bakery, a bookshop, and a toy store—that would serve as a backdrop for several Christmas play scenes.

After Nathan had assembled the panels, they focused on artistic details.

"Can you hand me that detail brush?" Nathan asked, leaning close to examine the bakery window she'd been painting. "I want to add some trim work around the window frame."

Emma passed him the brush, their fingers touching briefly. A small spark of awareness shot up her arm. "You're really good at fine detail work."

"I'm good at following your vision," Nathan corrected, carefully painting a thin line of white trim. "You're the one making this look like a real place instead of just painted plywood."

The easy rhythm they'd found surprised her—Emma sketching flourishes, Nathan refining edges, both stepping back periodically to admire their progress. The bakery storefront was coming to life with warm yellow walls, red-checkered curtains in the windows, and a hand-painted sign reading Sugarplum Bakery in cheerful script.

"This is gonna be gorgeous when we're finished," Emma said.

Nathan's mouth curved into a smile as he looked at her. "It already is." Reaching over, he gently wiped away a streak of yellow paint on her cheek, his thumb brushing across her cheekbone with careful tenderness.

The touch was practical, but his hand lingered just long enough to send warmth racing through Emma's body. His gaze followed the spot he'd wiped before lifting to meet hers, and for a suspended heartbeat, the air between them shimmered with possibility.

"Better," he said.

"Thanks," Emma managed, her voice barely above a whisper.

They settled back into their work, the comfortable quiet broken only by the sound of brushes on wood and the murmur of other volunteers. Emma bent close to add delicate details to the bakery window, pretending not to notice Nathan watching her.

"What're your plans for Thanksgiving?" Nathan asked.

"My Aunt Lily and I will spend the day together. What about you?"

"It'll be pretty low-key for me this year. I'll probably work on projects around the house and maybe catch up on reading."

Emma looked up from her painting. "Wait... are you saying you'll be alone on Thanksgiving?"

Nathan nodded. "Mom, Dad, and my brother are on a cruise, and my sister in California is spending the holiday with her husband's family."

Emma set down her brush. "Nathan, why don't you join Aunt Lily and me? I know she'd love to meet you. And honestly, I'd love to have you there."

He hesitated. "I wouldn't want to intrude."

"You wouldn't be intruding," Emma said firmly. "Aunt Lily always cooks enough for an army, and she loves having company."

A smile tugged at his mouth. "If you're sure..."

"I'm sure."

"Then I'd love to join you."

"Perfect. Aunt Lily'll be thrilled." Emma grinned. "Fair warning though—she'll talk your ear off and probably send you home with enough leftovers to last a week."

"I wouldn't complain about leftovers," Nathan said, his smile widening. "Especially when they come from a meal shared with good company."

Emma felt her cheeks warm. "Well, you'll definitely get both."

"I'm looking forward to it," Nathan said, his voice carrying a note of something more than simple anticipation.

Emma pulled out her phone. "You'll need Aunt Lily's address. And we usually eat around one, if that works." She typed quickly and hit send. "There—you're all set."

Nathan's phone buzzed. "Got it. Is there anything I can bring?"

"Just yourself."

Nathan met her gaze, his smile gentle but sure. "I can definitely do that."

Something in his tone made Emma's heart skip as she picked up her brush again.

As they continued working side by side, their conversation drifted from holiday logistics into favorite Thanksgiving traditions and childhood Christmas memories. Nathan told her about the year he'd unwrapped his first real set of tools, his father spending hours in the garage teaching him to measure twice and cut once. His voice carried a fondness that made Emma picture a younger Nathan, eyes bright with pride as he tried to copy his dad's careful movements.

Emma, smiling at the image, then shared how one Christmas she'd stayed up until midnight trying to finish personalized storybooks for every member of her family—handwritten, hand-illustrated, and bound with nothing more than staples and ribbon. "The drawings were terrible," she admitted with a laugh, "but I thought if I gave them a story, it would mean something."

"What was the story about?"

"A little girl who wanted to give everyone in her family the perfect Christmas gift but didn't have any money," Emma said, smiling at the memory. "So she decided to give them stories instead—personalized fairy tales where each family member was the hero of their own adventure."

"That's beautiful," Nathan said softly. "Did they like them?"

"They loved them. My mom cried when she read hers. She kept it in her jewelry box." Emma's voice grew quiet. "I think that was another one of those moments in my life when I knew I wanted to be a writer. Not because I was particularly good at it, but because I'd made someone I loved feel special through words."

For a long moment, Nathan was silent, studying her face with something that looked like admiration. "You still do that," he said at last. "Make people feel special through words."

Something tight in Emma's chest loosened, like a knot she hadn't realized she'd been carrying finally coming undone. His quiet certainty meant more than any professional review ever could. "Thank you for saying that. I've been so afraid lately that I'd lost that."

"Never," Nathan said, his gaze steady. "A gift like yours doesn't disappear. Maybe it goes quiet for a while... but only so it can find the right moment to speak again."

By late afternoon, they'd completed all three storefront panels, and Emma had to admit they looked better than anything she'd imagined. The village scene was charming and detailed. She could already imagine the children's delight when they saw it.

"Mrs. Benson's gonna be over the moon," Nathan said as they stood back to admire their work. "This looks professional. Like something you'd see in a real theater production."

"We make a good team. Our skills complement each other well."

Nathan glanced at her, his expression unreadable but his tone carrying layers that reached far beyond plywood and paint. "We do make a good team," he agreed softly. "In more ways than one."

Emma's breath caught, her pulse quickening at the quiet weight of his words.

They began cleaning up their supplies in comfortable silence, working together to fold drop cloths with the kind of natural coordination that came from people who understood each other's rhythms. Emma found herself stealing glances at Nathan, noting the careful way he rinsed each brush and the methodical precision with which he packed away his tools.

"Want to come over to my place tomorrow... for dinner and maybe watch a movie or something?"

"I'd love to," she said without hesitation. "What time?"

"How about four?"

"Perfect." Emma shouldered her purse, already looking forward to tomorrow. "Should I bring anything?"

"Just yourself." Nathan pulled out his phone. "You'll need my address though—I'm up on Whisper Ridge." He typed quickly and sent her a text.

Emma's phone buzzed, and she smiled as she read the message. "Got it. See you tomorrow at four."

Tomorrow couldn't come fast enough.

Chapter 19

Emma's breath caught as she rounded the final curve on Whisper Ridge Road. Through the swirling snowflakes dancing across her windshield, Nathan's house emerged like something from a winter dream—cedar and stone rising from the mountain ridge as if it had always belonged there. Her Honda's tires crunched softly on the gravel drive, and she couldn't help but smile. This was so perfectly Nathan: thoughtful, strong, and built to last.

The front door opened before she'd even turned off the engine, and there he was—charcoal-colored sweater, dark jeans, hair slightly mussed in a way that made her stomach flutter. His smile was different here, she realized. Softer. Unguarded in a way she'd never seen at school.

"You made it," he said, jogging down the porch steps despite the falling snow. "I was starting to worry."

"GPS is my friend," Emma said as she stepped out into the crisp mountain air, breathing in the scent of pine and wood smoke. "Nathan... wow. This place is incredible."

"Thanks. Come on, let's get inside before you freeze."

The warmth hit her the moment she crossed the threshold—not just from the heating, but from the space itself. Rich wood floors gleamed under soft lighting, and a stone fireplace dominated the far wall, flames crackling behind the screen. Through the massive windows, the snow-dusted mountains stretched endlessly, like nature's own masterpiece hung on the wall.

"Nathan, this is... absolutely gorgeous," Emma breathed, turning in a slow circle.

"I had a lot of help with the design," he said, taking her coat. "But I knew what I wanted—something that felt like part of the surrounding area, not just a home sitting on top of a mountain. A home, not a showplace."

"You succeeded." She moved deeper into the room, taking in every detail. Built-in bookcases flanked the fireplace, filled with an intriguing mix of leadership texts and well-worn novels.

"You built these bookshelves yourself, didn't you?" She asked, running her hand over the smooth wood.

"Guilty." He shoved his hands in his pockets, rocking slightly on his heels.

"They're beautiful. Really beautiful." She moved toward the fireplace, drawn to the framed photos on the mantel—smiling faces that radiated warmth and happiness. "Your siblings and parents?"

"Yeah. Brother and sister, plus their families. That one was from Mom and Dad's anniversary party last summer."

"You have a lovely family."

"I do," Nathan said with a smile. "Come on, let me show you around."

He led her down a hallway lined with windows that showcased the snowy evening, past a guest bedroom that looked like it rarely saw guests, to his home office. The space was organized to the point of being austere—the desk was clear except for a laptop and a single, neat stack of papers. Behind his desk, a large corkboard told a different story entirely, covered with children's artwork, handwritten thank-you notes, and school photos spanning years. A private shrine to the hearts he'd touched and the reason he did what he did.

Nathan followed her gaze to the corkboard, his expression growing tender. "They keep me grounded. Remind me why the budget battles and district politics matter."

From there, he showed her his bedroom—glimpsed only briefly through an open doorway, but she caught sight of a king-sized bed with a simple wooden frame that he'd crafted himself and more windows framing the mountain view. Everything was neat, masculine, and comfortable without being fussy.

"The workshop's through here," he said, leading her back through the living area to a door off the kitchen.

The moment he flipped the lights on, Emma understood why he disappeared here on weekends. The attached garage had been transformed into a craftsman's paradise that smelled richly of sawdust and wood stain. Tools hung in precise rows on pegboard walls, each in its designated place. Lumber was sorted by type and size along one wall, and the central workbench held a half-finished birdhouse, its tiny windows already cut with perfect precision.

"This is where you hide out on weekends," Emma said, immediately drawn to a shelf displaying finished projects—a pair of bookends carved from deep red wood and polished to silk, a small jewelry box with intricate inlay work, and a set of cutting boards that looked too beautiful to actually use.

"Something like that." Nathan moved beside her. "When my head gets too full of budgets and district politics, working with my hands helps quiet everything down. You start with rough wood, and if you're patient enough..." He picked up one of the bookends, turning it in his hands like he was remembering the hours it had taken to shape. "You end up with something that'll last."

Emma watched his fingers trace the wood's grain. "You build everything to last," she said softly.

"I try to," he said, his voice carrying layers of meaning.

When they returned to the kitchen, Emma noticed the careful preparations Nathan had made for their evening. The granite counters gleamed under warm pendant lighting, and ingredients were spread across the surface with the precise organization of someone determined to make a good impression. San Marzano tomatoes, fresh garlic and basil, and a block of Parmesan cheese waited next to a bottle of olive oil.

"Fair warning," he said, washing his hands at the sink. "This is one of only three dishes in my culinary arsenal. I'm hoping quality ingredients make up for the basic dish we'll have for dinner."

Emma laughed, tying on the apron he'd pulled from a drawer. "I'm the last person to judge anyone's cooking. My smoke alarm and I are on a first-name basis. What can I do?"

"You're in charge of garlic and basil." He handed her a knife and cutting board. "I tend to get heavy-handed with the garlic."

"Heavy-handed garlic sounds perfect to me."

They fell into an easy rhythm—Emma chopping while Nathan browned ground beef, their conversation flowing naturally. He told her about a kindergartner who'd tried to pay for lunch with a shiny rock he'd found at recess. She shared the story of Mrs. Harvey, who was convinced she'd encountered Mark Twain's ghost browsing the history section in her store.

"Did you check the security cameras?" Nathan asked, stirring the sauce.

"No," she said with a chuckle.

The snow was falling harder now, tapping against the windows like nature's percussion section. The kitchen felt like a warm cocoon, separate from the rest of the world—just the two of them, enjoying comfortable conversation punctuated by easy laughter.

Nathan put a large pot of water on to boil for the noodles, then returned to stir the simmering sauce. But the heat was apparently higher than he'd realized—the sauce gave an enthusiastic bubble and pop, sending a splatter of red across his dark sweater and a small splash onto his cheek.

Nathan froze, looking down at the mess with such comical dismay. "Well," he said gravely, "that wasn't in the recipe."

"Are you okay?" Emma asked. "That's hot—did it burn you?"

"I'm fine," Nathan assured her, touching his cheek gingerly. "More wounded pride than anything else."

"Here, let me." Emma grabbed a damp cloth, reaching up to gently wipe the sauce from his cheek. Her fingers brushed his skin. He went very still, dark eyes fixed on hers, and the air between them shifted into something electric.

For a heartbeat, neither moved. Emma was acutely aware of everything—his warmth, the way his gaze dropped to her lips, and the flutter of her pulse where her fingers touched his face.

"You, uh... got it," Nathan said, his voice rougher than before.

Emma pulled her hand back, cheeks burning. "Right. So... uh... what next?"

***

The meal was perfectly imperfect when they finally sat down at Nathan's dining table. The spaghetti was slightly past al dente, the sauce thinner than intended, but neither of them cared—it was delicious in the way that mattered most.

"How's the book coming along?" Nathan asked, his attention focused entirely on her in a way that made her feel like the most important person in his world.

Emma twirled pasta around her fork, considering how honest to be. "Better. I'm actually making progress toward my deadline." She hesitated, then decided on truth. "But something's still missing. It feels like I'm writing from my head instead of my heart. The story has all the right pieces, but no soul."

"Maybe the soul of a story isn't something you can force," he said finally. "Maybe it shows up when you're not looking for it."

"Like inspiration?"

"Like happiness."

The simple insight hit her with unexpected force. She set down her fork, really looking at him across the table. She'd been treating her writing like a problem to solve, a deadline to meet.

"When I first moved to Mistletoe Falls after my divorce," Nathan continued, his voice dropping slightly, "this house was just a blueprint and empty land. I'd come up here every day after work and just... sit. For months, it felt impossibly lonely. Empty property for an empty life."

Emma's chest tightened at this glimpse into his pain, the wound he rarely showed.

"But then I started focusing on one small thing at a time. Clearing brush for the driveway. Hiring someone to pour the foundation. Picking out colors. Things like that. I stopped thinking about the empty space I had to fill and just focused on the next step." He paused, swirling pasta on his plate. "Eventually, a home started taking shape."

"You built a new life here," Emma said softly. "Not just a home."

"I'm trying." His eyes met hers across the table. "And lately, it's been feeling a lot less empty."

The words hung between them, weighted with meaning that made Emma's heart skip. Without thinking, she reached across the table, covering his hand with hers. He turned his hand immediately to intertwine with hers. They sat like that for a long moment—connected, understanding passing between them without need for words.

"Thank you," Emma said finally, "for sharing that with me."

Nathan's thumb traced gentle circles across her knuckles. "I appreciate you listening so openly. It's not always easy to speak about tough times in our past, but with you... I'm completely comfortable."

They finished their meal in comfortable quiet, hands still linked across the table, occasionally sharing smiles or remarks about the snow that continued to fall outside. When Emma finally released his hand to take their plates to the kitchen, she felt the loss of contact like a small ache.

"Let me help," Nathan said, standing as she gathered their dishes.

"You did most of the cooking; I'll clean," Emma protested.

"My kitchen, my rules," he said with a grin that made her stomach flutter. "Besides, we both cooked.. we're a team, remember?"

They moved around each other in the warm kitchen with surprising ease, falling into a natural rhythm of washing dishes together. Emma stood at the sink, sleeves rolled up as she scrubbed plates and glasses in the soapy water, while Nathan rinsed and dried, their conversation flowing as naturally as it had all evening.

When the last dish was clean and the kitchen restored to order, Nathan dimmed the lights and led her back to the living room. The fire had died down to embers, and he knelt to add another log, muscles moving beneath his sweater as he worked. Bright sparks danced up the chimney before the flames caught and settled into a steady warmth that painted everything in golden light.

"Movie?" he asked, settling onto the large sofa and reaching for the remote.

"Sounds good," Emma said, curling her feet under her as she settled beside him.

He found an old black-and-white movie—something familiar and soothing that required no real attention. As the opening credits rolled, Emma leaned back against the plush cushions. The heat from the fire, Nathan's solid presence beside her—it all combined into a cozy comfort she hadn't felt in months. Without conscious thought, she shifted closer to him.

Nathan responded by draping his arm along the sofa behind her, creating a circle of warmth and protection that felt like coming home. They sat like that as the movie played—her head eventually finding its way to his shoulder, his fingers occasionally brushing through her hair.

This was intimacy, Emma realized. Not just physical closeness, but this quiet sharing of space and time, this comfortable silence that said more than words ever could.

When the credits rolled, she was surprised to see it was past nine.

"I don't want to, but I need to go," she said. "Morning comes early, and I have to open the shop in the morning."

"I understand." His reluctance matched her own.

Nathan retrieved her coat from the closet, holding it open for her. Emma slipped her arms through the sleeves, acutely aware of his hands settling the fabric across her shoulders.

They stepped out onto the porch together, and Emma's breath caught at the transformation. The world had become a winter wonderland—snow blanketing the deck railing, the trees, and even her little Honda.

"Oh my," Emma breathed, turning in a slow circle. "It's beautiful."

"Yeah," Nathan said, but when she looked at him, his gaze was fixed on her face, not the snow. "Beautiful."

Heat bloomed in her cheeks despite the cold air. Snow caught in her hair, dotted her eyelashes, and she laughed softly as flakes melted on her face.

"Thank you," she said, looking up at him. "For tonight, for dinner, for sharing your home with me. I had a wonderful time."

"I'm glad you came. I haven't had an evening like this in… well, in a very long time."

Nathan reached out slowly, brushing a snowflake from her hair. His fingers traced down to cup her cheek, his thumb gently sweeping across her skin. Emma's breath caught as she felt the pull between them, a silent question hanging in the snowy air.

For a heartbeat, time seemed suspended. Then Nathan leaned down and pressed a soft, tender kiss to her other cheek—sweet and old-fashioned and full of promise. His lips lingered for just a moment before he pulled back, his warm breath creating small clouds in the cold air.

"Drive safe," he said, his hand still cradling her face.

Emma's heart fluttered like snowflakes in the wind. "I will."

She made her way carefully down the snowy steps to her car, turning back once to see Nathan watching from the porch, hands in his jean pockets, snowflakes catching in his dark hair. He raised one hand in a small wave, and she waved back before getting into her car.

As Emma navigated the winding mountain road back to town, her cheek still tingling where his lips had touched, her heart felt full to overflowing. The gentle kiss had been perfect—romantic without being rushed and tender. It spoke of patience and respect and promises yet to come.

Some stories, she thought as her windshield wipers swept away the steadily falling snow, *were worth waiting for.*

Chapter 20

The rich, savory scent of roasting turkey and thyme wrapped around Emma like her favorite quilt, a fragrance so deeply tied to Thanksgiving it felt like a memory in itself. She hummed a tuneless melody as she basted the golden-brown skin of the bird, the heat from the open oven door warming her cheeks. In the cozy, sunlit kitchen of her Aunt Lily's house, everything felt perfect.

"If you baste that turkey one more time, it's gonna float right out of the pan," Aunt Lily said, her voice laced with the gentle teasing that had been the soundtrack to Emma's life. She stood at the wide farmhouse sink, her hands moving with practiced efficiency as she peeled the last of the potatoes, the brown skins falling away in long, elegant spirals.

Emma closed the oven and grinned, wiping her hands on the green-and-white striped apron tied around her waist. "I'm just trying to make sure everything is perfect for dinner."

Lily paused, a potato in one hand and her peeler in the other, and looked at Emma with eyes that held a lifetime of affection and a spark of knowing humor. "I know. Nathan's really important to you, I can tell. You talk about him like he hung the moon, you know."

A warm blush crept up Emma's neck. "I do not."

"Honey, you light up like a Christmas tree when you mention his name," Lily chuckled. "I'm happy for you. It's been a long time since I've heard this much joy in your voice."

Emma leaned against the counter, the worn butcher block cool against her elbows. "I really like him, Aunt Lily. He's such a good person. And he looks at me like…" She trailed off, unsure how to put the feeling into words.

"Like you're the only person in the room?" Lily supplied.

Emma nodded. "Something like that."

"That's how your Uncle Ben used to look at me," Lily said, her gaze distant for a moment. "Like I was a puzzle he was delighted to be solving for the rest of his life. That's a good look on a man." She turned back to the sink, her smile returning. "I can't wait to meet this principal of yours. Any man who can make my niece blush just by being mentioned is someone I need to properly inspect."

Just then, a flurry of excited yaps erupted from the living room, followed by the scrabble of tiny paws on the hardwood floor. Trixie, Aunt Lily's fluffy white terrier mix with the personality of a dog ten times her size, was announcing an arrival.

"Well, speak of the devil," Lily said, drying her hands on a towel. "He's early. That's another point in his favor."

Emma untied her apron and smoothed the front of her burgundy sweater, catching her reflection in the glass of the kitchen window. Her eyes were bright, her cheeks flushed with a combination of oven heat and anticipation.

She walked into the living room just as Aunt Lily opened the front door. Nathan stood on the porch, holding a vase—not just a bouquet, but a heavy glass vase filled with a stunning arrangement of flowers: deep orange lilies, golden sunflowers, creamy white roses, and sprigs of fragrant eucalyptus. His smile was warm and a little shy as he looked past Lily to find Emma.

"Nathan, welcome," Lily said, her voice full of genuine warmth as she took the vase from him. "Oh, my goodness, these are beautiful! You didn't have to do that."

"It was my pleasure," Nathan said, his gaze still on Emma. He was dressed in dark, well-fitting jeans and a soft, cream-colored cashmere sweater that made his shoulders look even broader. He looked relaxed, happy, and so handsome it made Emma's heart pound. "I hope I'm not too early."

"Not at all," Lily declared, already moving to place the vase in the center of the mantelpiece. "Come in, come in! Don't mind Trixie; her bark is much bigger than her bite."

Trixie, who had been circling Nathan's feet with suspicious sniffs, seemed to decide he was acceptable and promptly sat on his shoe, looking up at him expectantly. Nathan chuckled and bent down to scratch her behind the ears.

"Hello there," he said softly. "You must be the lady of the house." Trixie's tail began to wag furiously, her entire body wiggling with delight.

Emma watched the scene, a warmth spreading through her chest that had nothing to do with the crackling fire in the hearth. He'd brought flowers for her aunt and won over the dog in less than a minute.

"I see you've passed the Trixie test," Emma said, walking toward him.

Nathan stood, his smile widening as she drew near. "Rigorous examination, but I think I managed a passing grade." His voice dropped so that only she could hear. "You look beautiful."

"Thank you," she replied, her cheeks warming at the sincere compliment.

"What can I do to help?" Nathan asked, turning to Lily.

"A man who volunteers for kitchen duty?" Lily pressed a hand to her heart in mock astonishment. "Emma, you've found yourself a keeper. Now, Nathan... let's see... the turkey's handled and the potatoes are about ready to go on the stove, but I do believe we can find something for you to do."

"Lead the way," Nathan said, pushing up his sweater sleeves to reveal strong forearms.

For the next half hour, the kitchen was filled with the comfortable sounds of shared work and easy conversation. Nathan stood beside Emma at the island, helping Lily with each task she assigned them. He listened with genuine interest as Lily recounted the story of her first disastrous Thanksgiving as a newlywed, which involved an undercooked turkey.

"I was so mortified," Lily said, laughing at the memory. "Ben, bless his heart, just pulled a pizza out of the freezer and told me he'd always preferred pepperoni to poultry, anyway."

"Smart man," Nathan commented, eyes crinkling with amusement. "He knew the secret to a happy marriage is knowing when disasters become adventures."

Emma found herself stealing glances at him as they worked side by side, mesmerized by how naturally he fit into her aunt's kitchen. He wasn't playing the part of a polite guest—he was simply himself, teasing Lily about her quilting obsession, asking thoughtful questions about Uncle Ben, and even sneaking Trixie tiny snacks when he thought no one was looking.

This was how it would feel, she realized with a start. Having him as part of her life permanently. The thought settled warm and comfortable in her bones.

Later, as they sat around the dining room table, with the low afternoon sun slanting through the windows illuminating the steam rising from the platters of food, Emma felt a profound sense of peace.

"Nathan, will you do the honors?" Lily asked, gesturing toward the turkey with the carving knife.

"I'd be happy to," he said, proceeding to carve with a confident skill that impressed both women, arranging perfect slices on the serving platter.

The conversation flowed as easily as the gravy. They discussed the Christmas play, and Lily listened with rapt attention as Nathan described how Emma had coaxed a beautiful performance out of the shyest little girl in the fourth grade.

"She has a gift for that," Lily said, looking at Emma with pride. "Always has. She can see the story inside a person, even when they can't see it themselves."

Emma felt her cheeks warm at the praise, but it was the look on Nathan's face that made her heart swell—a look of such profound agreement and admiration that it felt like a caress.

After the main course, while Lily insisted on whipping fresh cream for the pumpkin pie, Nathan stood and began clearing plates without being asked.

"You don't have to do that," Emma protested, starting to rise.

"I want to," he said firmly, gathering dishes with practiced efficiency.

Emma followed him into the kitchen, washing the dishes while he dried.

"Your aunt's incredible," he said quietly, his voice full of sincerity.

"She's everything to me. After Mom passed… she's been my anchor, my safe harbor."

"I'm glad you have such a wonderful person in your life." He paused, then added, "Thanks for including me today, Emma. This is the best Thanksgiving I've had in longer than I can remember."

She turned to look at him, soap bubbles clinging to her fingers. The gratitude in his eyes was so open, so vulnerable, it made her chest ache. She saw past the confident principal to the man who'd spent too many holidays alone, who poured everything into his work because he didn't have anyone to come home to.

In that moment, watching him in her aunt's kitchen with his sweater sleeves pushed up and genuine joy lighting his face, she knew she loved him. Wholeheartedly loved him, no questions asked.

It wasn't a possibility anymore—it was a fact. Watching him laugh with her aunt, seeing him win over Trixie, listening to him talk about his dreams for the children of Mistletoe Falls—every small moment had been a brushstroke, painting a portrait of the man she'd fallen for. And now, seeing him here in the heart of her aunt's home, the picture was complete.

The realization didn't scare her. It felt like coming home.

"I'm so glad you're part of my life," she said, the simple words carrying everything she was feeling.

Nathan's expression softened. He reached out slowly, his fingers gently brushing a stray strand of hair from her cheek, the touch lingering. "Me too."

***

Later, Lily produced an old photo album, and soon the three of them huddled together on the overstuffed sofa, Trixie snoring softly at their feet. Lily pointed out gap-toothed Emma on her first day of school, teenage Emma at graduation, and laughing photos of Emma and her mother in this very room.

Nathan didn't just politely look—he engaged completely, asking questions about the stories behind the pictures, laughing at Lily's tales, his arm resting comfortably along the back of the sofa behind Emma. When his fingers occasionally brushed her shoulder, she leaned into his warmth, feeling utterly content.

Hours melted away like snow in sunshine. As twilight painted the sky in soft purples and roses, Nathan stood to leave. Emma felt a sharp pang of disappointment that their perfect day was ending.

"Miss Lily, thank you for your incredible hospitality and a wonderful meal," Nathan said, giving her a warm hug at the door.

"The pleasure was all mine, sweetheart," Lily said, patting his arm affectionately. "You come back anytime, you hear? Your family now."

Emma walked him out onto the porch, the air crisp and cold after the warmth of the house. As Nathan turned to face her, a single perfect snowflake drifted down and landed on his shoulder. Then another, and another.

"It's snowing again," Emma whispered, watching the flakes dance in the porch light like tiny ballerinas.

Nathan looked at Emma, his face illuminated by the golden glow of the porch light, the snowflakes catching in his dark hair. He stepped closer, his hands finding hers. "Emma, I almost forgot to ask. The town's tree-lighting ceremony is tomorrow night. Would you go with me?"

"Absolutely," she said, her heart soaring.

He squeezed her hands gently. "Good. I'll see you tomorrow then."

He leaned closer and pressed his lips to her forehead in a gesture so tender it made her knees weak.

"Sweet dreams, Emma."

"Goodnight, Nathan."

Chapter 21

Emma's gloved hand was tucked into the crook of Nathan's arm, a small point of warmth that seemed to anchor him in the swirling energy of the evening. The sound of the town square grew with every step they took, a symphony of cheerful voices, the distant jingle of bells, and the underlying hum of a community gathered in happy expectation of the tree-lighting ceremony.

"I think half the town is already here," Emma said, her voice a soft cloud in the frosty air. She squeezed his arm gently, and Nathan felt the simple gesture resonate all the way to his core.

"I agree," he replied, his gaze sweeping over the crowd. "Mistletoe Falls sure doesn't take the Tree Lighting Ceremony lightly."

He'd attended this event for the past two years, always as Principal Reid—a respected, if somewhat solitary, figure. He'd shaken hands with parents, accepted compliments on the school's performance, and watched families create memories, all while feeling a professional satisfaction that was neatly walled off from anything personal.

Tonight was different. Tonight, with Emma beside him, he felt like he belonged at the celebration, not just an observer. When a second-grader named Leo spotted him and waved frantically, his face smeared with chocolate, Nathan didn't just offer a polite nod. He grinned, waving back with a warmth that felt new and unguarded.

The square was a masterpiece of festive charm. The Victorian gazebo at its center was draped in evergreen garlands and white lights, looking like a giant, glowing snow globe. All around the perimeter, local businesses had set up small booths.

They made their way to one of Claire's booths, where the Sugarplum Bakery owner was serving steaming cups of hot chocolate and coffee. The air around the booth was sweet with the scent of melted chocolate, cinnamon, and vanilla; fairy lights strung between the tent poles cast everything in soft, welcoming light.

"Claire has outdone herself," Emma murmured, her gaze taking in the tiered platters of gingerbread men and sparkling sugar cookies. Steam rose from giant silver urns of coffee and hot cocoa.

"Nathan! Emma! So good to see you two out and about. Isn't this wonderful? Best turnout we've had in years." Claire Whitfield, her cheeks rosy from the cold, beamed at them from behind the counter. "What can I get for you, lovebirds?"

Nathan felt a pleasant warmth spread through his chest at the casual endearment. He glanced at Emma, who was smiling. "Two hot cocoas, please, Claire. With everything."

"You got it." Claire worked with practiced efficiency, topping the steaming mugs with whipped cream and a generous shower of peppermint shavings. As she handed them over, her gaze was full of friendly, unconcealed approval. "You two make the cutest couple."

"Thanks, Claire," Emma said, a blush appearing as she accepted her cup.

They found a spot near the edge of the crowd where they could see both the tree and the children's choir. Nathan positioned himself slightly behind Emma, close enough to feel her warmth. Around them, conversations hummed with excitement as families gathered for one of Mistletoe Falls' most beloved traditions.

The enormous evergreen stood in the center of the square, easily twenty feet tall and full enough that its branches created perfect symmetry. Thousands of lights were wound through its needles, dark now but ready to transform the entire square into something magical. At its base, a nativity scene had been arranged with figures carved by local artisans, surrounded by poinsettias in deep green ceramic pots.

"I always forget how big it is," Emma said, tilting her head back to see the star that would crown the tree once the lights came on.

"I heard it took the tree-lighting committee a few hours to get the tree in place," Nathan said.

Aaron stepped up to the small microphone that had been set up near the gazebo. "Ladies and gentlemen, if I could have your attention, please. Our third-grade choir would like to start tonight's celebration with a few of your favorite songs."

The children arranged themselves in their practiced formation, some standing tall with confidence while others fidgeted nervously. Nathan automatically scanned their faces, noting which students seemed comfortable and which ones needed encouraging smiles. Sonia Gallagher caught his eye from the front row and waved shyly. He waved back, pleased to see her smiling and not looking a bit shy.

Aaron raised his hands, and twenty-four young voices began the opening notes of "Silent Night." The familiar melody drifted across the square, sweet and slightly imperfect in the way that made it utterly authentic. Parents pulled out phones to record while grandparents dabbed at their eyes, and Nathan felt that familiar swell of pride that came from watching children he knew and cared about share their gifts with the community.

Emma leaned back slightly, her shoulders settling against his chest. The contact was casual, natural, but it sent awareness racing through Nathan's entire body. He could smell her perfume—something light and floral that seemed to capture her personality perfectly. When she shifted to get a better view of the choir, her hair brushed against his chin, soft and carrying a hint of vanilla from her shampoo.

"They sound wonderful," she murmured, her voice barely audible above the singing.

"Aaron's done amazing work with them this year."

The choir moved through three songs, their voices growing stronger with each verse as they forgot their nerves and lost themselves in the familiar melodies. By the time they finished "Jingle Bells," half the crowd was singing along, creating a chorus that filled the entire square with joy.

Mayor Williams stepped up to the microphone as the applause died down. "Thank you, Aaron, and thank you to our incredible third-grade choir. Now, ladies and gentlemen, it's time for the moment we've all been waiting for."

The crowd pressed closer to the tree, children pushing forward for the best view while parents called gentle warnings about staying together. Nathan instinctively moved closer to Emma, his hands settling lightly on her shoulders as the crowd shifted around them.

"This is my favorite part," Emma said, her voice full of anticipation.

"The tree lighting?"

"The moment right before. When everyone's holding their breath, waiting."

Nathan looked around at the upturned faces surrounding them—children wide-eyed with wonder, teenagers trying to act too cool but clearly caught up in the excitement, and adults whose expressions had softened with memory and hope. Emma was right. There was something special about this suspended moment when an entire community shared the same anticipation.

"Let's count down together," Mayor Williams called. "Ten!"

"Nine!" the crowd responded, their voices creating a unified sound that echoed off the surrounding buildings.

"Eight!"

Emma's hands came up to cover Nathan's where they rested on her shoulders. Her fingers were cold from the evening air, but her touch sent warmth shooting up his arms.

"Seven!"

She was trembling slightly—whether from cold or excitement, Nathan couldn't tell. Without thinking, he shifted closer, his arms coming around her waist in a protective embrace that felt as natural as breathing.

"Six!"

Emma melted back against him, her head finding the perfect spot against his shoulder. They fit together like puzzle pieces that had been searching for their match.

"Five!"

Nathan's world narrowed to this moment, this woman in his arms, the shared anticipation thrumming between them.

"Four!"

He'd attended this ceremony every year since moving to Mistletoe Falls, but he'd never felt part of it the way he did right now. Emma's presence had transformed him from observer to participant, from principal fulfilling a community obligation to a man celebrating with the woman who was quickly becoming central to his world.

"Three!"

Emma's grip tightened on his hands, and Nathan realized his pulse was racing with anticipation that had nothing to do with Christmas lights.

"Two!"

This was what true joy felt like, he realized with startling clarity. Not the satisfaction of a job well done or the quiet contentment of a peaceful evening. This was joy, pure and bright and shared with someone who made everything better just by being there.

"One!"

The tree blazed to life.

Thousands of lights burst into brilliance simultaneously, transforming the evergreen into something that belonged in dreams. White lights outlined every branch, while colored bulbs nestled deeper in the needles, creating layers of red, gold, and green that seemed to pulse with their own magic. The star at the top blazed like a beacon, visible from anywhere in the square.

But Nathan barely saw the tree.

Emma had tipped her head back against his shoulder, her face turned up toward the lights with an expression of pure wonder. The colored bulbs painted her skin in shifting hues—rose and amber and the soft blue-white of the star—and her eyes reflected the brilliance like captured starlight. Her lips were slightly parted in amazement, and the smile that curved across her face was luminous.

She was the most beautiful thing he'd ever seen.

The surrounding crowd erupted in cheers and applause, children shrieked with delight, and someone started singing "O Christmas Tree." But Nathan heard it all as if from a great distance. His entire focus had narrowed to Emma's face, to the joy radiating from her like warmth from a fireplace.

She turned in his arms, her hands coming up to rest against his chest, and looked up at him with eyes that held all the wonder of the lit tree behind them.

"Nathan," she said softly, his name barely a whisper in the celebration surrounding them.

He saw the moment she registered the intensity in his expression, the way her own breathing quickened in response. The noise of the crowd faded until it was just the two of them in a bubble of awareness and possibility.

Her gaze dropped to his lips, then returned to his eyes with unmistakable invitation. Time seemed to slow as Nathan cupped her face in his hands, his thumbs brushing across her cheekbones with infinite tenderness. She was precious and perfect and looking at him like he was the answer to every question she'd ever asked.

When he lowered his head, she rose on her toes to meet him halfway.

Their lips met in a kiss that was everything their first should be—soft and sweet and full of promise. Emma's hands fisted in his coat, pulling him closer, and Nathan felt something fundamental shift in his chest. This wasn't just attraction or affection. This was love. Complete, overwhelming, life-changing love.

The kiss lasted only seconds, but it rewrote Nathan's understanding of everything. When they broke apart, Emma's eyes were bright with happiness, and her smile was radiant enough to compete with the Christmas tree.

"Perfect," Nathan said, his forehead resting against hers.

"Perfect."

Around them, the celebration continued. Families posed for pictures in front of the tree, children ran between the adults with the boundless energy that came from too much sugar and excitement, and the choir had launched into an impromptu version of "Deck the Halls" with half the crowd joining in.

But Nathan felt separated from all of it, existing in a private world that contained only Emma and the certainty that everything in his life had just changed for the better. The fear that had kept him cautiously distant for three years was gone, replaced by a certainty so complete it was staggering. He wasn't afraid of failing at love anymore. He wasn't afraid of his past repeating itself. He looked at Emma, this brilliant, kind, creative woman who made stories come alive, and he knew, with every fiber of his being, that this was different. This was real.

They stayed like that for another minute, wrapped in the glow of the tree and their own private magic, before the cold finally seeped back in as the crowd of people surrounding them began to spread out.

They began walking slowly toward Emma's apartment, stopping to speak with friends and mutual acquaintances. Nathan introduced Emma to parents of some fourth-grade students she hadn't met yet, his hand never leaving the small of her back, and watched with growing pride as she charmed everyone with her genuine interest in their families and her obvious love for their community.

They continued to make their way slowly through the thinning crowd, saying goodnight to neighbors and friends.

Emma stopped walking, turning to face him under one of the old-fashioned streetlamps that lined the square. The warm light caught the gold threads in her hair and made her eyes seem luminous.

"Nathan Reid," she said, her voice firm with conviction, "you are the best thing that's happened to me in a very long time. You make me laugh, you make me think, and you make me want to be brave enough to take risks again." She stepped closer, her free hand coming up to rest against his chest. "You're good for me in every way that matters."

The simple honesty of her words hit him like a physical force. His ex-wife had made him believe he was too much, too dedicated to his work, and too focused on everyone else's needs to be a good partner. But Emma looked at the same qualities and saw them as strengths rather than flaws.

"Emma," he said, his voice rough with emotion.

Her smile was radiant.

When they reached her apartment above the bookshop, Nathan walked her to the door, neither of them ready to say goodnight.

"Thank you," Emma said, turning to face him on the small landing. "For tonight, for the tree lighting, for… just being you." She gestured helplessly, as if encompassing everything that had passed between them.

He cupped her face in his hands and kissed her again, soft and sweet and full of promise. When they broke apart, Emma's eyes were bright with happiness.

"I had a wonderful night, Nathan," she said, her eyes shining up at him.

"Me too." He couldn't stop himself from reaching out to brush a snowflake from her eyelashes. His fingers lingered on her cheek. "Emma, there's something I've been meaning to ask you. The Mistletoe Ball is in a few weeks." He took a breath. "I was wondering if you'd go with me."

Her smile was immediate and radiant. "I would love to, Nathan. I'd love that more than anything."

Nathan kissed her forehead gently, breathing in her scent and committing this moment to memory. Then he stepped back, knowing that if he didn't leave soon, he'd find excuses to stay on her doorstep all night.

"Goodnight, Emma, and sweet dreams."

"Goodnight, Nathan."

He watched until she was safely inside; the door clicking softly shut behind her. As he walked back to his truck, the cold air felt invigorating, the snowflakes a benediction. He started the engine; the heater blasting warm air into the cab, but the warmth he felt came from within.

As he drove home through the quiet streets, Nathan found himself thinking about his marriage to Jennifer. They'd been compatible on paper—both ambitious and both committed to building respectable careers. But there had never been this sense of rightness, this feeling that they brought out the best in each other.

With Jennifer, love had been work—constant negotiation, compromise that felt like sacrifice, and the exhausting effort of trying to be someone other than who he was. But with Emma, love felt like coming home. She didn't want him to change; she wanted him to be more of himself.

The difference was staggering.

Nathan pulled into his driveway and sat for a moment, looking up at the star-filled sky visible above the mountain ridge. This time last year, he'd been convinced that his dedication to his work made him unsuitable for lasting love. Tonight, he'd kissed a woman who saw that same dedication as one of his most attractive qualities.

Nathan was struck by the sheer magnitude of what had been happening in his life. He had fallen in love. Fast, hard, and completely. His first marriage hadn't been love; it had been a partnership of convenience and shared ambition that had buckled under the first real pressure. This feeling for Emma was something else entirely—a deep, soul-level recognition. It wasn't just that he wanted her in his life; it was that he couldn't imagine his life without her in it anymore. The empty spaces in his home, in his future, suddenly had a shape, and it was hers.

Life, he reflected as he finally headed inside, was full of the most wonderful surprises.

Chapter 22

Emma stared at the last paragraph she'd just typed, her fingers hovering over the keyboard as satisfaction settled warm in her chest. The story was flowing again. Princess Buttercup's latest adventure was practically writing itself, the words coming as naturally as conversation with an old friend.

She saved the document and stretched her arms above her head. The soft sounds of the bookstore drifted from beyond her office door—Molly's cheerful voice helping a customer, the gentle chime of the register, the whisper of pages turning in the reading nooks.

A sudden thought struck her with the force of a cold mountain wind.

The Mistletoe Ball was next week. And she had absolutely nothing to wear.

The ball wasn't just any party; it was the kind of event where women wore gowns and men donned their finest suits, where couples danced to live music under twinkling lights.

Panic fluttered in her throat like a trapped bird. She grabbed her phone and quickly typed a message to Cora.

Emergency shopping mission needed. Care to hit the Velvet Boutique with me? I need a dress for the Mistletoe Ball!

The response came back almost instantly.

Give me five minutes to make sure Molly and Anna have everything covered. Crisis shopping is my specialty.

Emma smiled. If anyone could help her navigate the treacherous waters of formal dress shopping, it was Cora—practical, honest, and blessed with an eye for style that Emma had always envied.

Ten minutes later, Cora appeared in the office doorway, pulling on her wool coat. Her ash-blonde hair was twisted into its usual sleek ponytail, and her gray-blue eyes held the determined glint of a woman preparing for battle.

"Okay, formal dress," Cora said, settling into the chair across from Emma's desk. "Cocktail dress or full-length gown?"

"I honestly don't know." Emma saved her work and closed her laptop.

"Full-length," Cora said decisively. "It's the town's biggest fundraiser, and everyone goes all out. Plus, Nathan's going to be in a tux, so you want something that'll make you feel like you belong on his arm."

Emma's cheeks warmed at the mental image of Nathan in formal wear. "I haven't shopped for anything like this in years. What if I look ridiculous? What if—"

"Emma." Cora's voice was firm but kind. "Stop spiraling. We're going to find you something gorgeous that makes you feel like the amazing woman you are. That's what friends are for."

They bundled into their coats and stepped out onto Mistletoe Lane. The December afternoon was crisp but not bitter, with the kind of clear sky that made the mountains look close enough to touch. Holiday decorations twinkled in every shop window, and the scent of fresh bread from the bakery mingled with the clean mountain air.

The Velvet Boutique sat like a jewel box on Jingle Bell Lane, its sage green storefront framed by evergreen wreaths and white lights. Through the large windows, Emma could see elegant displays of evening wear that looked both inviting and intimidating.

A small bell chimed as they entered. The interior was a study in refined elegance—soft lighting, plush velvet seating, and gowns displayed like pieces of art rather than mere clothing. The air held a faint scent of lavender and something expensive that spoke of quality and care.

"Good afternoon, ladies!" A woman with silver hair styled in a perfect bob approached them with a warm smile. Her name tag read "Patricia," and she had the confident bearing of someone who understood both fashion and the women who wore it. "How can I help you today?"

"We need a miracle," Emma said, then immediately felt her cheeks burn. "I mean, I need a dress for the Mistletoe Ball, and I'm not sure what would be appropriate."

Patricia's eyes lit up with the enthusiasm of a professional presented with an interesting challenge. "The Ball is such a wonderful event. What's your style preference? Classic, modern, or something with a bit of sparkle?"

"I honestly don't know," Emma admitted. "It's been so long since I've dressed up for anything formal."

"That's perfectly fine. Sometimes the best approach is to try a variety and see what speaks to you." Patricia's gaze moved over Emma with the practiced assessment of someone who fit women for a living. "You have a lovely figure—we have several styles that would be absolutely stunning. Let me pull a few options."

While Patricia disappeared into the depths of the boutique, Cora settled into one of the velvet chairs arranged near the fitting area. "This is going to be fun," she said, pulling out her phone. "I'll text Molly and Anna to let them know we might be awhile."

Patricia returned with an armful of gowns in various colors and styles. Emma's breath caught as she saw them—each dress was more beautiful than the last, with the kind of craftsmanship and attention to detail that transformed fabric into dreams.

"Let's start with this one," Patricia said, holding up a midnight blue dress with delicate beading across the bodice. "The color would be stunning with your complexion."

The first dress was beautiful but felt wrong somehow—too formal, too much like she was playing dress-up rather than being herself. The second, a soft pink number with flowing layers, was pretty but made her feel like she was trying too hard to look younger.

But the third dress...

Emma stepped out of the fitting room and heard Cora's sharp intake of breath.

"Oh my," Patricia murmured.

The dress was deep burgundy, the color of winter roses or expensive wine. The neckline was elegant without being revealing, the fitted bodice flowing into a classic A-line skirt that moved like water when she walked. The fabric had a subtle shimmer that caught the light without being flashy, and the length was perfect—formal enough for the ball but still comfortable for dancing.

"That's the one," Cora said, her voice certain. "Emma, you look absolutely radiant."

Emma turned to face the three-way mirror and felt her breath catch. The woman looking back at her was confident, elegant, and beautiful in a way that had nothing to do with perfect features and everything to do with inner glow. The dress didn't make her look like someone else—it made her look like the best version of herself.

"How does it feel?" Patricia asked.

"Like me," Emma said softly. "But... more."

"That's undoubtedly what the right dress should do." Patricia adjusted the shoulder seams slightly. "And the fit is nearly perfect. Just a small alteration to the length, and you'll be all set."

As Patricia pinned the hem, Emma found herself imagining next Friday night—walking into the ball on Nathan's arm, dancing with him while wearing this dress that made her feel beautiful and confident and completely herself.

"I think," she said, meeting Cora's eyes in the mirror, "this is the first time I've been truly excited about dressing up since Mom died."

Cora's expression softened. "She would have loved seeing you like this. Happy and in love and glowing."

"Do I really look like I'm glowing?"

"Honey, you've been glowing since the day you met Nathan."

After scheduling the alterations for tomorrow afternoon, they stepped back out onto Jingle Bell Lane. The afternoon had grown cooler, and the streetlights were beginning to twinkle on, casting pools of warm light on the brick sidewalks.

"Thank you," she said. "For coming with me and for being such a good friend."

"Anytime," Cora replied. "It's been wonderful watching you bloom these past few weeks."

They walked back toward the bookshop through the twinkling downtown streets, their breath creating small clouds in the cold air. Emma's phone buzzed with a text from Nathan.

Hope you had a good day. Can't wait to see you tomorrow at practice.

Emma smiled as she typed back.

Day was perfect. Can't wait to see you too.

"Let me guess," Cora said with a knowing smile. "Nathan?"

"Yes, he's just... wonderful. These little texts throughout the day, asking about my writing or telling me something funny that happened at school. It's like having someone who genuinely cares about the small details of my life."

"That's what a good relationship looks like," Cora said. "When someone chooses to be interested in your ordinary moments, not just the big ones."

They reached the bookshop, where warm light spilled from the windows onto the sidewalk. Through the glass, Emma could see Molly helping a customer while Anna restocked the featured books display. Her life was full—work she loved, friends who cared about her, a community where she belonged, and now Nathan, who made all of it feel even more meaningful.

For the first time in months, the future felt full of possibility rather than uncertainty.

Chapter 23

Emma pushed back from her desk and rolled her shoulders, stretching muscles that had been hunched over her laptop for the past two hours. The latest Princess Buttercup chapter was flowing beautifully—her protagonist was finally finding her courage to face the Shadow Dragon—but Emma's eyes needed a break from the screen. Through her office window, she could see fresh snow dusting everything in sight.

Her phone buzzed against the desk, and Nathan's name lit up the screen. Emma's pulse quickened the way it always did when she saw his contact photo—the candid shot she'd taken of him at Thanksgiving, laughing at something Aunt Lily had said while Trixie sat hopefully at his feet.

Perfect day for a winter hike. Want to explore Cascade Trail with me?

Emma glanced through her office doorway toward the main shop floor, where Saturday afternoon business hummed along at its usual comfortable pace. Cora stood behind the register helping Mrs.

Williams find a cookbook for her daughter-in-law, while Molly re-arranged the holiday display near the front window. Anna was re-stocking the children's section.

The shop was in excellent hands, Emma realized. And when was the last time she'd done something purely for fun on a Saturday after-noon?

She typed back quickly: *Sounds perfect. Give me thirty minutes, and I'll be ready.*

Nathan's response was immediate: Sounds good, see you in a few.

Emma smiled as she saved her work and closed her laptop.

"Cora," she called, stepping out of her office. "Would you mind if I snuck out for a few hours? Nathan's invited me on a hike, and you three seem to have everything well in hand."

Molly looked up from the holiday display with barely contained delight. "Ohhhh... a romantic winter adventure?"

"It's just a hike," Emma protested, though her cheeks warmed.

"Go," Cora said firmly. "Bundle up warm, and don't worry about anything here. We've got it all covered."

Emma hurried upstairs and pulled on her warmest hiking clothes—thermal leggings under sturdy jeans, a wool sweater, and the down jacket she'd bought last winter but rarely had occasion to wear. She was tugging on her hiking boots when she heard the familiar rumble of Nathan's truck pulling up outside.

Through her bedroom window, she watched him hop out of the cab, moving with the easy confidence of someone completely com-fortable in the world. He wore dark jeans and a forest-green fleece jacket.

Emma grabbed her knit hat and gloves and opened the door as Nathan was climbing the stairs with a smile that made her forget about the cold mountain air.

"Ready for an adventure?" he asked, his breath creating small clouds in the crisp afternoon air.

"More than ready."

The drive to Cascade Trail wound through snow-dusted mountains that looked like they belonged on Christmas cards.

"Tell me about this trail," she said, watching snow-heavy pine boughs flash past her window. "Is it one of your regular haunts?"

"I discovered it about six months after moving here. It's not too strenuous, but it leads to this incredible overlook where you can see three different mountain ranges." Nathan slowed to navigate a particularly sharp curve, his hands steady on the steering wheel. "I've hiked it in every season, but winter might be my favorite. Everything is so quiet and peaceful."

Emma studied his face, noting the way his expression relaxed when he talked about the mountains. "You really love the outdoors, don't you?"

"I do," Nathan said simply. "Spending time in the mountains reminds me what actually matters in life."

"Which is what?"

Nathan was quiet for a moment, considering. "Beauty. Peace. The reminder that most of our daily worries are pretty small in the grand scheme of things." He glanced over at her with a smile that made her pulse skip.

The trailhead parking area was nearly empty, just Nathan's truck and one other vehicle whose owners were probably already deep into their own winter adventure. Nathan shouldered his pack and offered Emma his arm as they made their way across the snow-dusted gravel toward the trail entrance.

"Careful here," he said, steadying her as they navigated a particularly uneven patch near the wooden trail marker. "The first hundred yards can be tricky."

The trail was well-maintained but not overly developed, winding through stands of evergreen trees whose branches hung heavy with fresh snow. Their footsteps created a rhythmic crunch-crunch-crunch that was oddly soothing, and the cold air felt clean and sharp in Emma's lungs.

"This is gorgeous," Emma said, pausing to examine a cluster of icicles hanging from a rock outcropping like nature's chandelier. "I can't believe I've lived in Mistletoe Falls my entire life and never explored this trail."

"To be fair, you've been a little busy building a career and running a business," Nathan pointed out, adjusting his pace to match hers as they began a gentle uphill climb. "But I'm glad you're exploring it with me now."

They fell into an easy hiking rhythm, conversation flowing as naturally as their synchronized footsteps. Nathan pointed out different types of trees, shared stories about wildlife he'd encountered on previous hikes, and listened with genuine interest as Emma described how the winter landscape reminded her of scenes from her favorite children's books.

"You see stories everywhere, don't you?" Nathan observed as Emma described how a snow-covered boulder looked exactly like a sleeping bear from one of her Princess Buttercup adventures.

"I do. Mom always said I had an overactive imagination, but she meant it as a compliment." Emma ducked under a low-hanging branch heavy with snow. "She used to tell me that people who see stories in ordinary things are lucky because they're never really bored."

"Your mom sounds like she was incredibly wise."

Emma felt the familiar tightness in her chest that came with missing her mother, but it was gentler now, more like wistful gratitude than sharp grief. "She was. She loved these mountains. And she would have loved watching you geek out about tree species and elevation changes."

Nathan chuckled. "Am I geeking out?"

"Completely. It's adorable."

They'd been hiking for about thirty minutes when Emma bent to scoop up a handful of snow, packed it into a loose ball, and lobbed it gently at Nathan, who was ahead of her.

The snowball exploded against his fleece jacket in a shower of white crystals. Nathan stopped walking and turned to face her with an expression of mock outrage that made Emma burst into helpless laughter.

"You didn't?"

"I did." Emma said, already backing away from him with her hands up in surrender.

"Oh, you're in trouble now," Nathan said, but his eyes were dancing with mischief. He bent to scoop up his own handful of snow, and Emma shrieked with laughter as she scrambled behind a tree.

What followed was less a snowball fight than a playful chase through the snowy woods, both of them laughing too hard to aim properly. Emma managed to land one good hit on Nathan's back as he tried to take cover behind a boulder, and he retaliated by scooping up enough snow to threaten a direct assault on her knit hat.

"Truce!" Emma called, holding up both hands as Nathan advanced with a snowball the size of a softball. "Truce, I surrender!"

"What are the terms of your surrender?" Nathan asked, though he was grinning too widely to look particularly threatening.

"I'll share my emergency chocolate stash," Emma offered, pulling a small wrapped candy bar from her jacket pocket. "Peace offering?"

Nathan dropped his snowball and stepped closer, brushing snow from her jacket with gentle hands. "Deal. But next time you start a snowball fight, you better be prepared for serious retaliation."

"Noted," Emma said, slightly breathless from the cold air and laughter and Nathan's proximity.

They continued up the trail, both still grinning from their impromptu battle. Emma felt lighter than she had in months—playful and carefree in a way she'd almost forgotten was possible. When was the last time she'd engaged in something so purely fun? When was the last time someone had made her feel safe enough to be silly?

The honest answer, she realized, was before her father left. Before she'd learned that the people you loved most could disappear without warning, leaving you to wonder what you'd done wrong. But here with Nathan, tossing snowballs like children and laughing until her cheeks hurt, she felt like that little girl again—the one who believed in adventures and happy endings.

After another twenty minutes of steady climbing, the trees began to thin, and Emma caught glimpses of expansive views through the branches. When they finally reached the overlook Nathan had mentioned, her breath caught in genuine amazement.

The view stretched for miles in every direction—rolling mountains covered in snow-dusted trees, distant peaks that seemed to touch the pale winter sky, and valleys that looked like they'd been sketched by an artist with an eye for perfect composition. The silence was profound, broken only by the whisper of wind through the evergreens and their own slightly labored breathing from the climb.

"Nathan," Emma breathed, turning in a slow circle to take in the full panorama. "This is incredible."

"I know. It was pure luck when I first found it," Nathan said, settling his backpack on a large, flat rock that provided natural seating.

"I was exploring different trails my first winter here, trying to learn the area. This one looked promising, and when I reached this spot..." He gestured toward the view with something approaching reverence. "It felt like discovering buried treasure."

Emma settled beside him on the rock, close enough that she could feel warmth radiating from his body despite the cold air. Nathan pulled a thermos of hot chocolate from his pack, along with two insulated mugs.

"You thought of everything," Emma said, accepting the steaming cup he offered.

"I tried."

They sat in comfortable quiet for a few minutes, sipping hot chocolate and absorbing the majesty spread out before them. Emma found herself thinking about perspective—how the daily concerns that felt so enormous in town seemed smaller from up here, set against the backdrop of ancient mountains and endless sky.

"Nathan," she said finally, "may I ask you something personal?"

"Of course." His attention focused on her completely, the way it always did when she spoke. Like she was the most important person in his world.

"I'm honestly curious, and if this is too personal... you don't have to answer, but it's been on my mind for some time now from a comment you made before. When your marriage ended, did you honestly think you weren't cut out for... this?" Emma gestured vaguely between them. "For building something lasting with someone?"

Nathan was quiet for so long that Emma began to worry she'd overstepped. But when he spoke, his voice was thoughtful rather than defensive.

"Every day," he said finally. "Jennifer used to say that I cared more about other people's children than I'd ever care about her or my own future children. That my dedication to work was really just selfishness dressed up as service."

Emma felt indignation flare in her chest. "That's terrible. And entirely wrong."

"Is it though?" Nathan turned to face her more fully, and Emma saw the vulnerability he was trying to hide. "I did work late most nights. I did bring school problems home. When budget cuts threatened to eliminate the music program, I spent an entire weekend researching grants instead of... I don't know, planning romantic dates or whatever husbands are supposed to do."

"Nathan." Emma set down her mug and turned to face him completely. "You fought to save the music program because you care about children's well-being and development. That's not selfishness—that's undoubtedly the kind of man anyone would want as a partner and father."

"You really believe that?"

"I know it." Emma's voice was firm with conviction. "The woman who couldn't see that your passion for helping children was one of your most attractive qualities? She was the wrong person for you. It doesn't mean there's anything wrong with who you are."

Nathan studied her face for a long moment, and Emma watched as something shifted in his expression—relief, maybe, or the beginning of real healing from old wounds.

"You make me feel good about myself. I never feel I have to be anyone other than who I am when I'm with you," he said quietly.

Emma felt her throat tighten with emotion. "You make me feel brave enough to hope for things I thought I'd lost forever."

"Like what?"

Emma was quiet for a moment, gathering courage for the kind of honesty that felt both terrifying and necessary. "Like family. Like partnership. Like waking up every day with someone who chooses to love me not despite my flaws, but including them."

Nathan reached for her gloved hand, intertwining their fingers with the gentle certainty that had become so familiar and precious to her.

"Emma," he said, "I need you to know something. These past few weeks with you... they've been the happiest I've been in years. Maybe ever."

Emma's pulse quickened at the seriousness in his tone.

His thumb traced patterns across her knuckles through the wool of her gloves. "I know we haven't been together very long, but I also know that what I feel for you isn't going to change or fade or turn out to be something I imagined. This is real. You're real. And if you'll let me, I want to build something lasting with you."

Emma felt tears prick at the corners of her eyes—not from sadness, but from the overwhelming relief of being seen and wanted and chosen by someone who understood her completely.

"I want that too," she whispered. "More than I've ever wanted anything."

Nathan's smile was radiant as he lifted her gloved hand to his lips, pressing a soft kiss to her knuckles.

"So what does that look like?" Emma asked. "Building something lasting?"

"I don't know exactly," Nathan admitted. "But I know I want to find out with you. I want to wake up on Saturday mornings and plan adventures like this. I want to support your writing and celebrate your successes. I want to introduce you to my parents and watch you charm them the way you've charmed me."

Emma's breath caught. "You want me to meet your parents?"

"They're coming for a visit after Christmas. I'm sure they'd love to meet the woman who's made me happier than I've been in years. If you're ready for that."

"I'm ready," Emma said without hesitation. "I'm ready for all of it."

They sat in the mountain quiet, hands linked, both absorbing the magnitude of what they'd found in each other.

"Are you getting cold?" Nathan asked eventually, noticing that Emma had begun to shiver slightly despite her warm layers.

"A little," she admitted.

Nathan released her hand and pulled off his gloves, then reached for hers. "Here, let me warm these up."

He tugged off her gloves and captured her cold hands between his warm palms, rubbing gently to restore circulation. The simple act of care made Emma's chest tighten with affection for this man, who noticed when she was uncomfortable and immediately moved to fix it.

"Better?" he asked, his voice soft with concern.

"Much better," Emma said, meaning it in more ways than he probably realized. Everything was better with Nathan—her writing, her confidence, her willingness to believe in happy endings. He hadn't just warmed her hands; he'd warmed her entire world.

"We should probably head back soon," Nathan said regretfully, glancing at the sky where the late afternoon sun was beginning to sink toward the mountain peaks. "I don't want you getting too cold, and some of those trail sections can be tricky in low light."

Emma nodded, though part of her wanted to stay in this perfect bubble forever—just the two of them and the mountains and the quiet certainty of love acknowledged and returned.

They packed up their supplies and began the descent, moving more carefully now as the afternoon shadows lengthened across the trail. But Emma found she wasn't sad about leaving their mountain sanctuary. She was carrying its peace with her, along with the promise they'd made to build something beautiful together.

"Thank you," she said as they reached the trailhead parking area. "For this, for the hike, for… everything you said up there."

Nathan stopped beside his truck and turned to face her, his expression serious but soft. "Thank you for trusting me with your heart."

He cupped her face in his hands and kissed her gently, a promise sealed under the winter sky. When they broke apart, Emma felt like the heroine of her own love story—brave enough to believe in happy endings because she was living one.

"Come on," Nathan said, opening the passenger-side door with old-fashioned gallantry. "Let's get you home where it's warm."

Chapter 24

Emma was pulling her seatbelt across her chest when Nathan's phone buzzed from the cup holder. He glanced at the screen as he started the truck, his face breaking into a grin.

"Aaron," he said, tapping the message open. "His girlfriend Tracey drove down from Gatlinburg for the weekend, and they want to know if we'd like to meet them for dinner at the Fireside Lodge."

"Aaron's girlfriend? I'd love to meet her. What's she like?"

Nathan backed out of the trailhead parking area, his expression thoughtful as he considered the question. "I've only met her twice, but she seems perfect for Aaron. Creative, funny, and doesn't take his dramatic musician tendencies too seriously." He glanced over at her with that smile that always made her stomach do pleasant flips. "So, a double date this evening?"

"Absolutely. I haven't been to the Fireside Grill in a while... am I underdressed?"

Nathan's laughter filled the truck cab. "It's still the same laid-back bar and grill. Thermal layers are probably overdressed, if anything."

Emma typed back a quick response on Nathan's phone while he navigated the winding mountain road. The idea of meeting Aaron's girlfriend felt significant in ways she couldn't quite articulate—another step into Nathan's world, another piece of the life they were building together.

The Fireside Lodge sat nestled among tall pines, its rustic exterior lit by string lights that created pools of warmth against the gathering twilight. Through the large windows, Emma could see the cozy interior—knotty pine walls, wooden tables and chairs, and the kind of comfortable atmosphere that invited lingering conversations over comfort food.

Nathan's hand settled naturally on the small of her back as they walked toward the entrance, a gesture so automatic it spoke of how quickly they'd become a unit. Emma found herself standing straighter, feeling cherished in a quiet way that still surprised her with its intensity.

"There they are," Nathan said, nodding toward a corner table where Aaron sat next to a woman with shoulder-length auburn hair and an infectious smile.

Aaron stood as they approached, his grin widening as he took in their flushed cheeks and hiking attire. "Look what the mountains dragged in. How was Cascade Trail?"

"Incredible," Emma said, accepting Aaron's warm hug. "Nathan promised spectacular views, and he definitely delivered."

The woman rose gracefully, extending her hand with genuine warmth. "You must be Emma. I'm Tracey Walsh, and I've been dying to meet the woman who's made Aaron's stories about Nathan so much more interesting lately."

"All good stories, I hope."

"The best kind," Tracey assured her, gesturing for them to sit. "Tales of romantic dinner dates, tree lighting ceremonies, and a certain principal who apparently smiled more in the past month than he has in quite some time."

Nathan shook his head with good-natured exasperation as he helped Emma out of her jacket. "Aaron, remind me why we're friends again?"

"Because I'm the only person willing to listen to you analyze school budget proposals for entertainment," Aaron shot back, then turned to Emma with theatrical concern. "Has he subjected you to his filing system yet? It's color-coded by urgency level."

Emma laughed, settling into the chair beside Nathan. "Actually, I find his organizational skills oddly attractive. There's something appealing about a man who knows where everything is and can stay organized."

Tracey raised her water glass in mock salute. "A woman after my own heart. Organization is severely underrated as a romantic quality."

The conversation flowed as naturally as the creek outside the lodge's windows. Emma learned that Tracey ran a freelance graphic design business from her apartment in Gatlinburg, specializing in branding for small businesses and nonprofits. Her enthusiasm for her work reminded Emma of her own passion for storytelling—the way creative people lit up when discussing projects they cared about.

"Children's books must be such a rewarding field," Tracey said after Emma had described her latest Princess Buttercup adventure. "Do you do your own illustrations or work with someone else?"

"I work with an illustrator in Nashville who's absolutely brilliant. Nicole Braxton. She has an astonishing ability to capture the emotion behind the story." Emma paused as the server appeared with menus, then continued. "Though I'll admit, the business side of writing sometimes feels overwhelming. Marketing, social media, keeping my website current—it's not exactly where my strengths lie."

Tracey's eyes lit up with professional interest. "What does your website look like currently? If you don't mind my asking."

Emma pulled out her phone, navigating to her author site with a slight grimace. "It's functional, but definitely not inspiring anyone to buy my books or get excited about story time events at the bookstore."

Tracey studied the screen, her expression thoughtful. "The content is great, but the design feels a bit... static. Like it's not reflecting the magic of your actual stories." She looked up with growing excitement. "Would you be interested in some design help? I'd love to create something that captures the whimsy and warmth of your writing."

"Really?" Emma felt a flutter of hope. "I'd love that, but I should probably mention upfront that my budget for website redesign is approximately zero dollars."

"How about we trade services?" Tracey suggested. "I'll design you a website that makes parents and librarians immediately want to book story time sessions or buy your books, and you can do a reading and signing at the community center in Gatlinburg for our literacy fundraiser next spring."

Emma glanced at Nathan, who was watching the exchange with obvious pleasure. "That sounds perfect. Are you sure?"

"Positive. It'll be fun working on something creative and meaningful." Tracey pulled out her own phone. "Let me get your contact information, and we can set up a time to talk through ideas."

Aaron leaned back in his chair, grinning at Nathan. "Look at that—fifteen minutes and they're already planning projects together. This is what happens when you introduce two creative powerhouses."

Emma found herself relaxing completely into the evening's rhythm and conversation. Nathan's knee pressed gently against hers under the table, a constant reminder of his presence that felt both exciting and comfortingly familiar.

"So, Emma," Aaron said, cutting into his barbecue sandwich the server had just delivered, "has Nathan told you about his legendary dating disasters from his first year in Mistletoe Falls?"

"Aaron," Nathan warned, though his tone held more amusement than genuine annoyance.

"Oh, this should be good," Emma said, settling back with obvious anticipation.

Tracey leaned forward conspiratorially. "I've already heard the highlights, and they're spectacular."

Aaron launched into a tale about Nathan being set up by well-meaning colleagues with a series of women who were completely wrong for him. "There was the kindergarten teacher who spent the entire dinner critiquing his classroom management philosophy. The bank teller who wanted to know his five-year financial plan before they ordered appetizers. And my personal favorite—"

"Please don't," Nathan interrupted, but he was smiling despite himself.

"The librarian from the county system who brought her own checklist of relationship compatibility questions." Aaron turned to Emma with gleeful satisfaction. "Actual printed checklist. She made him fill it out between the salad and main course."

Emma burst into laughter, imagining Nathan's polite bewilderment at such systematic romance. "Did you complete the checklist?"

"I felt rude not finishing it," Nathan admitted, his cheeks reddening slightly. "Though I may have answered a few questions less than honestly to speed the process along."

"That was when I knew my friend had officially given up on dating," Aaron said, his expression growing fond. "He came back from that disaster and announced he was focusing exclusively on work and bachelorhood."

Tracey reached across the table to squeeze Emma's hand. "Thank goodness you came along to rescue him from a life of building bird-houses in solitude."

Emma felt warmth spread through her chest as Nathan's arm settled across the back of her chair, his fingers brushing her shoulder in a gesture that felt both possessive and protective. "I think we rescued each other," she said, meeting Nathan's gaze across the table.

As the evening wound down, they lingered over coffee and the lodge's wonderful apple pie, conversation meandering through topics ranging from Christmas traditions to favorite books to Aaron's latest musical compositions for the play. Emma found herself thinking how natural this felt—not just being with Nathan, but being part of a foursome, contributing to the easy back-and-forth that spoke of genuine friendship.

"We should definitely do this again," Tracey said as they finally gathered their coats. "Maybe after the holidays, when things settle down a bit."

"Absolutely," Emma agreed, meaning it completely. "And thank you again for the website offer. I'm so excited to work with you."

They said their goodbyes outside the restaurant, Aaron clapping Nathan on the shoulder. "Have a good evening, my friend," he said.

Nathan's hand found hers as they walked to his truck. The night air was crisp and clean, carrying the distinct scent of nature wrapped in winter.

"That was wonderful," Emma said as Nathan started the engine. "I can see why Aaron's your closest friend. And Tracey is delightful—I feel like we've known each other for years."

Nathan backed out of their parking space, his free hand reaching across to grasp hers. "She loved you," he said simply. "Just like I do."

"Nathan," she began, then stopped, overwhelmed.

He glanced over at her, his expression tender in the dashboard's soft glow. "Too much? Too soon?"

"Not too much," Emma said quickly, turning to face him fully. "Not too soon. Just... perfect. Because I love you too, Nathan Reid. Completely and absolutely."

Nathan's smile was radiant as he pulled into her apartment building's parking area a few moments later. He cut the engine and turned to cup her face in his hands. "Tell me again."

"I love you," Emma repeated, the words feeling more natural each time she spoke them. "I love your dedication to your students and your thoughtfulness about everything from hiking supplies to restaurant reservations. I love you."

Nathan's answering smile was everything she'd ever dreamed of finding in another person—love and acceptance and the promise of countless evenings just like this one, filled with friends and laughter and the quiet certainty that they were precisely where they belonged.

Chapter 25

Emma wiped down the last of the elementary school cafeteria tables. Pizza boxes stood empty, evidence of what Mrs. Benson had declared "the best post-rehearsal celebration ever."

"Miss Emma! Miss Emma!" Tommy Martinez bounced up to her, his face still glowing with the excitement that had radiated from him during their final run-through of "The Christmas Light Keepers." "My mom says she's gonna cry tomorrow night when I do my big speech about keeping the lights burning in our hearts."

Emma knelt to Tommy's eye level, her own chest warm with pride for the boy who'd transformed from a shy mumbler into a confident young actor over the past month and a half. "You know what, Tommy? I think a lot of people are going to shed happy tears tomorrow night. You've all worked so hard, and it shows."

"Are you gonna cry too?"

"Probably," Emma admitted, ruffling his dark hair. "But they'll be the good kind of tears."

Tommy's mother appeared beside him, car keys jingling in her hand and with a slightly frazzled expression parents wore after long workdays. "Come on, mijo. We need to get home for dinner. Thank you again, Emma, for everything you've done with all these kids and especially for helping my son."

"It's been my pleasure," Emma said, standing and accepting the woman's grateful hug. "Tommy's been a joy to work with."

As the Martinez family headed toward the cafeteria's double doors, Emma turned back to survey the cleanup progress. Nathan was placing the empty pizza boxes into a large trash bag. Mrs. Benson sat at one of the round tables, slowly sorting through costume pieces that had migrated from the multipurpose room during the children's post-rehearsal excitement.

"I think that went about as well as we could have hoped," Nathan said.

"Better than we could have hoped," Mrs. Benson corrected, holding up a pair of angel wings that had somehow lost half their feathers during the evening's festivities. "Did you see Sara Tillman during the lighting ceremony scene? That little girl projected all the way to the back of the room without a microphone. A month ago, she could barely speak loud enough for the front row to hear."

Emma felt a familiar flutter of satisfaction that came from watching children discover their own capabilities. "She found her voice. Sometimes that's all they need—someone to believe they have something worth saying."

"Which is exactly why you're so good at this," Nathan said as he walked toward their table. "You see potential where other people just see problems."

"I'm going to miss this. The regular practices, working with the kids, having a reason to be at the school so often," Emma said.

"You'll have to find excuses to visit more," Mrs. Benson said with a twinkle in her eyes. "I'm sure Nathan wouldn't mind the company."

Nathan chuckled, settling into the chair beside Emma. "Subtle as always, Mrs. B."

"Subtlety is overrated at my age," Mrs. Benson replied cheerfully. "Life's too short not to say what you mean."

Emma smiled at the easy banter between Nathan and his mentor. Their relationship reminded her of the one she'd shared with her mother—built on mutual respect, gentle teasing, and the kind of affection that came from years of shared experiences.

"Are you two excited about the Mistletoe Ball tomorrow?" Mrs. Benson continued, carefully folding a costume. "It's going to be quite a day for you, Emma—your theatrical debut in the afternoon followed by a lovely evening of dancing."

Emma's cheeks warmed, but the nervousness she might have felt a month ago had transformed into anticipation. "I'm looking forward to both. Though I have to confess, I'm a little worried about dancing in a long dress. It's been a while since I've worn anything that requires that much coordination."

"What color did you end up choosing?" Mrs. Benson asked with genuine interest.

"Deep burgundy," Emma said, unable to suppress the smile that came with thinking about the dress hanging in her bedroom closet. "It's so elegant and beautiful. Cora helped me pick it out, and the seamstress at the Velvet Boutique worked miracles with the alterations."

Nathan's expression grew unexpectedly tender. "Burgundy is a good color on you. Though you'd look beautiful in anything."

The simple compliment, delivered without fanfare or dramatic flourish, made Emma's chest tighten with affection. Nathan had a gift for saying exactly the right thing at exactly the right moment, never too much or too little.

"Well," Mrs. Benson said with obvious satisfaction, "I can't wait to see you two together tomorrow night. You're going to be the most elegant couple at the ball."

Emma was about to respond when Mrs. Benson's phone buzzed against the table. The older woman glanced at it, her eyebrows rising slightly as she read whatever message had appeared on her screen.

"How interesting," she murmured, then looked up at Nathan with an expression Emma couldn't quite interpret. "Nathan, did you know that Superintendent Morrison announced his retirement today?"

Nathan paused in the middle of folding a tablecloth, his attention focusing sharply on Mrs. Benson. "Really? I hadn't heard. That's sudden—I thought he was planning to stay through the district's reorganization project."

"Apparently, his wife accepted a new job that requires a move to California," Mrs. Benson said, still studying her phone. "The district's already starting the search process for his replacement, and chatter has started among the faculty."

Emma watched Nathan's face, noting the shift in his expression from casual interest to something more focused. "That's going to be a big change for the district. Morrison's been superintendent for what, eight years?"

"Nine," Nathan corrected. "He's done good work, especially with the rural school consolidation issues."

Mrs. Benson set down her phone and looked directly at Nathan. "You know, Nathan, your name has come up in some interesting conversations lately."

"What kind of conversations?"

"The kind where school board members and community leaders discuss leadership potential," Mrs. Benson said carefully. "You know, Nathan, your reputation extends well beyond Mistletoe Falls Elementary. Your work with budget management, community partnerships, and educational innovation—people notice these things."

Nathan laughed, but Emma caught a flicker of something in his expression that suggested Mrs. Benson's words weren't entirely unwelcome. "Mrs. B, I think you're giving me more credit than I deserve. I'm good at running an elementary school, but that's very different from overseeing an entire district."

"Is it though?" Mrs. Benson leaned forward, her voice taking on the tone she used when she was building toward an important point. "The best superintendents are the ones who remember what it's like to be in the classroom, who understand that every policy decision affects real children and real families. You have that perspective."

Emma studied Nathan's face, noting the way he was carefully not looking at her as Mrs. Benson spoke.

"Have you ever considered it?" Emma asked. "Moving into district-level administration?"

Nathan was quiet for a long moment, his hands stilling on the tablecloth he'd been folding. When he spoke, his voice carried the careful consideration that Emma had learned meant he was working through complicated thoughts.

"Sometimes," he admitted. "Not the politics or the bureaucracy, but the possibility of affecting educational policy on a larger scale. There are things I'd love to change—funding formulas that hurt rural schools, standardized testing requirements that ignore what children actually need, and programs that could serve more kids if they were implemented district-wide instead of school by school."

Emma listened to the passion building in Nathan's voice. This wasn't idle speculation—this was a man talking about dreams he'd held but never fully articulated.

"That outdoor education program you mentioned before," she said. "You could implement something like that across multiple schools as superintendent."

"Possibly," Nathan said, his eyes lighting up in a way that made Emma's heart skip and sink simultaneously.

Mrs. Benson nodded approvingly. "Leadership isn't about moving away from the work you love, Nathan. It's about finding new ways to serve the same mission."

Emma forced herself to smile, though something cold was settling in her stomach. "This sounds like it could be a wonderful opportunity for you."

Nathan seemed to register the shift in her tone, his attention focusing on her face with concern. "Emma, it's just speculation. Nothing's even been officially announced from the board yet."

"But if it were offered?" Mrs. Benson pressed gently. "Would you consider it?"

Nathan glanced between Mrs. Benson and Emma. "I... honestly don't know. It would depend on numerous factors."

Emma's mind was racing despite her efforts to appear calm. The superintendent position would mean increased responsibilities, longer hours, and travel to other schools in the district. It would mean Nathan's focus shifting from the intimate, hands-on work he loved to the broader but more abstract challenges of district management. It would mean less time for quiet evening dinners and weekend hikes.

It would mean everything changing just as they'd found their rhythm together.

"Well," she said, proud of how normal her voice sounded, "you'd certainly have my support whatever you decided."

The words were true, even as they made her chest ache. She loved Nathan, which meant supporting his dreams even when they scared her. But the fear was real and sharp—that success might pull him away from her, from them, just like her father's restlessness had pulled him away from their family all those years ago.

"The important thing," Mrs. Benson said, beginning to gather her costume pieces, "is that you have options, Nathan. And you have people who believe in your ability to make a difference on whatever scale feels right."

But even as she smiled and listened as Nathan and Mrs. Benson continued to talk, part of her mind remained fixed on Nathan's words, on the excitement she'd heard in his voice when he'd talked about district-wide policy change. She'd fallen in love with his dedication to education, but what if that same dedication required him to move beyond the small-town life he had here with her?

"Emma?" Nathan appeared beside her. "You okay? You're quiet... deep in thought?"

Emma looked up at him, taking in his familiar face—the concerned crease between his eyebrows, the gentle way he waited for her answer without pressing for reassurance she wasn't ready to give. She loved this man, loved his integrity and his dreams and his commitment to making children's lives better. Which meant she needed to be honest about her fears rather than pretending they didn't exist.

"I'm proud of you," she said finally. "And excited about the possibilities Mrs. Benson mentioned. It's just... the timing feels complicated."

Nathan stepped closer, his voice dropping to the intimate tone he used when they needed to have important conversations. "Complicated how?"

"We've just found each other," Emma said softly. "Just figured out how we fit together, how to balance your work and my work and this thing we're building. The idea of everything changing again so soon... forget I just said that. I'm being selfish..." She trailed off, not sure how to articulate fears that felt both rational and selfish.

Nathan's hand found hers, his thumb tracing gentle patterns across her knuckles. "Emma, look at me."

She met his gaze, finding the steady certainty that had drawn her to him from the beginning.

"Nothing that matters between us would change," he said quietly. "My feelings for you, my commitment to you—those aren't dependent on job titles or administrative responsibilities. If I ever decided to pursue something like this, it would be with the understanding that we're partners. That we make decisions together."

Emma felt some of the tension in her chest ease, though the worry didn't disappear entirely. "I want to support your dreams. I do. It's just..."

"It's just that change is scary, especially when you've been through loss before," Nathan finished gently. "I understand that, Emma. And I need you to know that any major career decision would be something we'd discuss together. You're not just along for the ride in my life—you're my partner."

Mrs. Benson appeared beside them, her purse slung over her shoulder and her coat buttoned against the December evening. "I hope I didn't stir up unnecessary worry with my speculation," she said, looking between them with concern. "The last thing I want is to create anxiety about possibilities that may never materialize."

"It's fine," Emma assured her, meaning it. Mrs. Benson had simply voiced what was probably already being discussed in administrative circles. Better to know than to be surprised later. "I'm glad you mentioned it. It's good to think about these things."

"Let's just forget I even brought all this up," Mrs. Benson said, adjusting her scarf. "Think instead about the play tomorrow. We have a day of celebration ahead of us. You've accomplished something wonderful with the children, and you deserve to enjoy the recognition. Whatever the future holds can be sorted out later."

Emma smiled, feeling genuine affection for this wise woman who'd brought them together and continued to offer guidance at exactly the right moments. "You're right. Tomorrow is about the play and celebrating all the good we've accomplished."

"And it's going to be magical," Nathan added, his arm settling around Emma's waist in a gesture that felt both protective and partnering. "The children will be incredible, and you will shine in that burgundy dress tomorrow night."

As they walked toward the cafeteria exit, Emma found herself thinking about the day ahead—the final preparations for tomorrow's performance, the anticipation of wearing her beautiful dress to the Mistletoe Ball, and the prospect of dancing the evening away with Nathan.

But underneath the excitement, a small voice whispered questions about the future. If Nathan were offered the superintendent position, would he take it? Would their quiet dinners and weekend adventures become casualties of increased responsibility and travel schedules? Would she find herself competing with an entire school district for his attention and emotional energy?

She pushed the thoughts aside as they stepped into the December evening, breathing in the crisp air. Tomorrow would be perfect—she was determined to make sure of that. Whatever challenges the future might hold could wait until after they'd celebrated the magic they'd created together with the children.

Nathan's hand found hers as they walked toward their vehicles, his fingers intertwining with hers in the gesture that had become familiar. "Penny for your thoughts?"

Emma squeezed his hand, choosing hope over fear and presence over worry. "Just thinking about tomorrow. About how proud I am of what we've accomplished with the kids and how excited I am to dance with you."

Nathan's smile was radiant in the glow of the school's security lights. "I can't wait to see you in your dress. And I can't wait to show off the most beautiful and talented woman in Mistletoe Falls."

Chapter 26

Nathan felt his throat tighten with pride as he watched the fourth-graders on the stage of the multipurpose room. Tommy Martinez stepped forward for his final line, his voice clear and confident as it carried to the very back of the packed room.

"And so the lights of Christmas burn bright in every heart that chooses to share its warmth with others."

The applause erupted immediately—parents leaping to their feet, grandparents dabbing at their eyes with tissues, and younger siblings clapping with the unrestrained enthusiasm that only children could muster. Nathan scanned the audience from his position in the wings, watching as they celebrated not just their children's performance but the magic that happened when a community came together for something beautiful.

"They were absolutely incredible," Emma whispered beside him, her voice thick with emotion. She stood close enough that he could see the tears of joy sparkling in her eyes as she watched the children soak up their well-deserved recognition. "Look at Sara—she's beaming."

Nathan followed her gaze to Sara Tillman, the shy girl who'd barely spoken above a whisper at their first rehearsal and was now curtsying with theatrical flair, her angel wings catching the stage lights as she smiled at her parents in the third row. The transformation had been gradual but remarkable, and Nathan knew it was Emma's gentle encouragement that had coaxed the confidence from hiding.

Mrs. Benson adjusted her navy cardigan as she prepared to join the children on stage. At sixty-seven, she moved more carefully than she once had, but her eyes held the same bright satisfaction Nathan remembered from his first year at the school. "Time for the directors to take their bows," she said.

Nathan's pulse quickened as Emma smoothed her ivory-colored sweater and checked that her hair was still neatly tucked behind her ears.

"Ready?" she asked, glancing up at him with that smile that never failed to make his chest feel too small for his heart.

"With you? Always."

They stepped onto the stage together, flanking Mrs. Benson as the applause shifted and intensified. Nathan had participated in dozens of school events through the years as principal, but this felt different. This felt like standing before his community not just as an administrator doing his job, but as part of something larger—a creative partnership that had produced something real and meaningful.

Emma held his hand as they took their bow, and the contact sent warmth up his arm that had nothing to do with stage lights. When they straightened, he caught sight of Aaron in the second row, grinning widely as he applauded. Beside Aaron sat Aunt Lily, who'd driven down from her mountain home specifically for today's performance, her expression radiant with pride as she watched.

Mrs. Benson stepped forward to the small microphone they'd positioned center stage, raising her hand for quiet. "Ladies and gentlemen, thank you so much for your support of our Christmas play tradition. These children have worked incredibly hard for the past month and a half, and I hope you're as proud of them as we are."

Another burst of applause, accompanied by whistles from proud parents. Mrs. Benson waited for the noise to die down before continuing.

"I'd like to thank our wonderful co-directors, Ms. Emma Sullivan and Principal Reid, for bringing fresh energy and creativity to this year's production. Emma's storytelling gifts and Nathan's organizational skills proved to be the perfect combination for bringing out the best in our young performers."

Nathan felt heat creep up his neck as the applause focused on him and Emma. Public recognition had always made him slightly uncomfortable, but standing here beside Emma, seeing how naturally she smiled at the crowd and how genuinely the audience responded to her presence, he felt only gratitude. Gratitude for Mrs. Benson's faith in him, for Emma's willingness to take on the project, and for the children who'd trusted them enough to be vulnerable and brave on stage.

"Before we all head to the cafeteria for refreshments," Nathan said, stepping closer to the microphone, "I want to say something about what we've witnessed tonight."

The room settled into expectant quiet, and Nathan looked out over the sea of familiar faces—teachers who worked alongside him every day, parents who trusted him with their most precious gifts, and community members who'd supported the school through budget cuts and difficult decisions.

"Theatre has a way of revealing truth," he began, his voice carrying easily to the back of the room. "Not just in the stories we tell, but in the courage it takes to tell them. Today, these children didn't just recite lines or hit their marks. They became light keepers—young people who chose to share their gifts with all of us, who reminded us that the best way to keep Christmas alive is to give pieces of our hearts to each other."

He paused, glancing at Emma, who was watching him with an expression of such warmth and pride that it made his words come easier.

"Mrs. Benson has been the heart of this tradition for twenty-five years, nurturing creativity and confidence in hundreds of children. Emma brought magic to this story, helping these kids discover that their voices matter. And these remarkable fourth-graders proved that when children are given the tools and encouragement to shine, they don't just meet expectations—they exceed them in ways that take your breath away."

The applause was immediate and sustained, but Nathan barely heard it. His attention was fixed on Emma's face, on the way her eyes had brightened with unshed tears, and on the smile that seemed to transform her entire expression from merely beautiful to luminous.

"Now," he said, raising his voice slightly to carry over the continuing applause, "please join us in the cafeteria for refreshments and more time to celebrate these remarkable young performers. The children are eager to hear how much you enjoyed their hard work."

The audience began to disperse, parents moving toward the stage to collect their costumed children while others headed directly toward the cafeteria, where the PTA had arranged a reception. The multipurpose room filled with the cheerful chaos of families regrouping, costumes being carefully removed, and the general bustle that followed any successful community event.

Nathan watched it all with the satisfaction that came from weeks of careful planning executed flawlessly. The play had succeeded beyond his most optimistic hopes; the children had risen to the occasion beautifully, and the community had responded with the kind of enthusiasm that would carry Mrs. Benson into a well-deserved retirement on a high note.

But more than professional satisfaction, he felt something deeper settling in his chest. Standing here beside Emma, watching her accept congratulations from parents and hearing her praise each child individually as they passed by, Nathan realized something that stopped his breath entirely.

He didn't want this to end.

Not just the play, not just this project—he didn't want this closeness with Emma to be limited to a single Christmas production. He wanted to work beside her on school fundraisers and community events and quiet Tuesday afternoon planning sessions. He wanted to see her animated face across committee meeting tables and hear her creative solutions to administrative challenges. He wanted their collaboration to extend far beyond the multipurpose room stage into every aspect of his life.

He wanted everything with her.

"Nathan?" Emma appeared beside him, her hand touching his arm gently. "Are you all right? You look like you've seen a ghost."

He turned to face her fully, taking in her flushed cheeks and bright eyes, the way her hair had come slightly loose from its careful arrangement, and the small smile that curved her lips as she waited for his response.

"Not a ghost," he said quietly, glancing around at the thinning crowd. "More like the future."

"The future?"

Nathan caught her hand in his. "Emma, can I steal you away for a minute? Before we join the reception?"

Her eyebrows rose slightly, but her smile widened. "Of course. Where are we going?"

"Backstage," Nathan said, leading her toward the area behind the stage where they'd stored props and costume changes during the performance. "I want to say something to you, and I'd rather not have an audience."

Emma's laughter bubbled up, light and musical in the way that always made him want to find excuses to hear it again. "This sounds mysterious."

They slipped behind the heavy curtain that separated the performance area from the storage space, and suddenly the sounds of the reception became muffled and distant. Back here, surrounded by carefully organized costume racks and prop boxes, the magic of the evening felt condensed into something intimate and private.

Nathan turned to face Emma, still holding her hand, and found himself momentarily speechless. She stood close enough that he could see the tiny flecks of gold in her blue eyes, could count the light freckles across her nose, and could watch the way her lips parted slightly as she waited for whatever he wanted to tell her.

"Emma," he began, then stopped, overwhelmed by the magnitude of what he was feeling.

But before he could find the right words, Emma stepped closer, her free hand coming up to rest against his chest. Her expression had shifted from curious to understanding, as if she could read the emotions he was struggling to articulate.

"Nathan," she said softly, "whatever you're trying to say—it's okay. No words needed."

Emma rose up on her toes, her hands framing his face with infinite tenderness, and kissed him.

This wasn't like their previous kisses—sweet and careful and testing new ground. This was Emma letting her happiness overflow, sharing the pure joy that radiated from her like warmth from a fireplace. Her lips were soft and sure against his, and when she pulled back just far enough to speak, her words came in a rush of breathless elation.

"Nathan Reid, you make me so incredibly happy," she said, her thumbs brushing across his cheekbones as she held his face between her palms. "I've never felt anything like this before in my life."

Nathan's hands settled at her waist, anchoring her close to him as he absorbed the radiance in her expression. "Emma—"

"Let me finish," she said, her smile so brilliant it competed with the stage lights still glowing beyond the curtain. "I'd been stuck for months. Grieving, blocked creatively, going through the motions of a life that felt half-empty. And then you walked into my bookshop, and I said yes without even thinking about it. Best decision I've ever made in my entire life."

Nathan felt his own smile building, fed by the joy radiating from the woman in his arms.

"And it's all because of you," Emma said. "You make me feel like the best version of myself every single day."

He couldn't speak for a moment, overwhelmed by the gift of her words and the certainty in her voice.

"I love you," he said, the words coming out rough with emotion. "Emma, I am completely, absolutely, head-over-heels in love with you."

Her answering smile was radiant. "I love you too. So much it scares me sometimes, but in the best possible way."

Nathan cupped her face in his hands, marveling at the woman who'd transformed his carefully organized life into something vibrant and unpredictable and more fulfilling than he'd ever imagined possible. "What we have—I want it in everything. Not just school projects or community events. I want to build a life with you, Emma. I want to wake up every morning knowing we're facing whatever comes next together."

"Is this a proposal?" Emma asked, her eyes dancing with mischief and hope in equal measure.

Nathan's laugh was slightly shaky with the intensity of his feelings. "Not yet. But it's a promise that there will be one... when the time is right."

Emma's kiss was her answer—soft and sure and full of the same certainty that had made her volunteer for the Christmas play without hesitation. When they broke apart, the sounds of the reception in the cafeteria seemed to call them back to the celebration.

"Let's go join the celebration," Emma said as she straightened his tie with gentle fingers. "How do I look? Do I look like a woman who is on top of the world?"

Nathan studied her face, taking in the bright eyes and flushed cheeks, the smile that seemed to start from somewhere deep inside and work its way outward. "You look like the woman I'm going to love for the rest of my life."

"Good," Emma said, rising up to press one more quick kiss to his lips. "Because that's exactly what I am."

Hand in hand, they pushed through the curtain back into the multipurpose room, where the last few stragglers were making their way toward the cafeteria. Nathan felt like he was floating as they walked toward the cafeteria.

"Nathan," Emma said as they approached the cafeteria doors, beyond which they could hear the cheerful noise of their reception. "Thank you."

"For what?"

"For seeing something in me that I couldn't see in myself. For trusting me with something that mattered to you. For showing me what partnership really looks like." She squeezed his hand, her expression serious despite the joy still sparkling in her eyes. "For loving me exactly as I am."

Nathan stopped walking, pulling Emma close for one more kiss in the empty hallway outside the cafeteria.

Chapter 27

Emma felt like a character from one of her own storybooks as Nathan's truck rounded the final curve toward the Mistletoe Lodge, the grand building emerging like something conjured from wishes and Christmas magic. Through the passenger window, she could see couples in formal attire making their way up the wide stone steps, their laughter carrying across the crisp mountain air as golden light spilled from every window of the century-old resort.

"You ready for this?" Nathan asked, his voice carrying a mix of excitement and nerves that made her stomach flutter with anticipation.

Emma smoothed the burgundy silk of her gown, the fabric whispering against her palms as she turned to study Nathan's profile in the dashboard's soft glow. He wore a classic black tuxedo that transformed him from the familiar principal she'd fallen for into something that belonged in old Hollywood films—elegant, confident, and devastatingly handsome in a way that made her forget how to breathe properly.

"With you? Always."

Nathan's smile was warm as he pulled into the circular drive where uniformed valets waited to assist arriving guests. Through the lodge's massive windows on the right side of the building, Emma caught glimpses of the ballroom—crystal chandeliers casting prisms of light across couples already lost in the rhythm of dance and the enormous Christmas tree decorated with what looked like thousands of ornaments that caught the light like captured stars.

The valet who approached Nathan's truck was young, probably a college student earning winter break money. "Good evening, folks. Beautiful night for the ball."

Nathan rounded the truck and extended his hand to help Emma step down onto the flagstone drive. The burgundy dress moved like liquid around her legs, the hemline Patricia had altered to perfection brushing just above her ankles. Emma had worried about navigating in heels and a long dress, but the moment Nathan's fingers closed around hers, steadying her as she emerged from the truck, she felt like she could dance on air.

"You look absolutely stunning," Nathan murmured, close enough that she caught the clean scent of his cologne—something subtle and woodsy.

"You clean up pretty well yourself, Principal Reid," Emma said, reaching up to adjust his bow tie with gentle fingers.

The lodge's entrance hall buzzed with elegant energy as they stepped through the heavy oak doors. Emma's heels clicked against the polished marble floors that reflected the soft glow of vintage sconces, and everywhere she looked, Mistletoe Falls' residents had transformed into their most glamorous selves. Women glided past in gowns that ranged from classic black to jewel tones that rivaled Emma's burgundy, while men in tuxedos and dark suits created a sea of sophisticated elegance.

"Nathan! Emma!" Aaron's familiar voice cut through the gentle din of conversation and distant music. He appeared through the crowd with Tracey on his arm, both of them beaming with the kind of happiness that radiated outward and made everyone around them smile in response.

Aaron looked distinguished in a charcoal gray tuxedo, his usually casual musician's aesthetic transformed into something that belonged at the Lincoln Center. Tracey was radiant in a deep emerald dress that complemented her auburn hair perfectly, her smile genuine as she reached for Emma's hands.

"Emma, you look absolutely gorgeous," Tracey said, stepping back to admire the burgundy gown. "That color is perfect on you—you're the most beautiful woman here tonight."

"Have you seen yourself in that dress?" Emma laughed, gesturing toward Tracey's elegant ensemble. "You look as if you stepped off the pages of a magazine."

"The ballroom's incredible," Aaron said, nodding toward the arched doorway where music drifted out along with the soft glow of chandelier light. "They've outdone themselves with the decorations this year. The Christmas tree has to be fifteen feet tall, and there's enough mistletoe hanging around to make even the most confirmed bachelors nervous."

"Speaking from experience?" Nathan asked with a grin.

"Absolutely," Aaron replied, slipping his arm around Tracey's waist. "I may have strategically positioned myself under a sprig or two earlier this evening."

Tracey's blush was charming as she swatted Aaron's arm playfully. "He's terrible. But the decorations really are spectacular—wait until you see them."

They moved as a group toward the ballroom entrance, Emma's hand resting naturally around Nathan's offered arm. The gesture felt both old-fashioned and exactly right, as if they'd been attending formal events together for years rather than experiencing their first together.

The ballroom took Emma's breath away completely.

The space was vast and elegant, with soaring ceilings supported by massive wooden beams draped in evergreen garland and twinkling lights. Crystal chandeliers cast warm, dancing light across couples already moving to the music of a seven-piece orchestra positioned on a small stage at the far end of the room. But it was the Christmas tree Aaron had mentioned that made Emma actually gasp aloud.

The enormous evergreen dominated one corner of the ballroom, its branches heavy with what had to be thousands of ornaments—some clearly antique, others obviously handmade by local children, all creating a tapestry of community history and shared tradition. Wrapped presents in elegant gold and silver paper were arranged beneath its sweeping boughs, and the whole display was illuminated by tiny white lights that seemed to pulse with their own magic.

"Oh my goodness," Emma breathed, her grip tightening on Nathan's arm. "It's like something from a fairy tale."

"Better than a fairy tale," Nathan said softly, his voice close to her ear as they paused just inside the ballroom entrance. "Because it's real, and we're here together."

The dance floor was already populated with couples moving to a waltz that the orchestra played with professional skill, and Emma recognized faces throughout the crowd—parents from the Christmas play, teachers from Nathan's school, business owners from Mistletoe Lane, and longtime residents whose families had been part of Mistletoe Falls for generations. Everyone looked elegant and happy, caught up in the magic of the evening and the celebration of another successful year in their beloved mountain community.

"Shall we find our table?" Aaron suggested, consulting a small card he'd pulled from his jacket pocket. "I think we're all seated together."

They wove through the ballroom, Emma marveling at the attention to detail that had transformed the space into something worthy of the grandest celebrations. Each round table was draped in pristine white linens and centered with arrangements of white roses, winter greenery, and candles that cast everything in a flattering, romantic light. Place cards were written in elegant calligraphy, and Emma felt a flutter of excitement when she spotted her name beside Nathan's at a table near the dance floor.

"Perfect placement," Tracey observed as they settled into their chairs. "We'll have an excellent view of all the dancing, and the orchestra sounds even better from here."

Nathan held Emma's chair as she sat, his hands lingering briefly on her shoulders in a gesture that felt both protective and possessive in the most wonderful way. When he took his own seat beside her, Emma felt completely happy in the moment.

"Wine?" Nathan asked, reaching for the bottle of white wine that had been placed at their table. "Or would you prefer champagne? I think I saw servers with champagne flutes circulating."

"Wine sounds perfect," Emma said, watching as he poured.

The evening unfolded like the best kind of dream. They talked with Aaron and Tracey about everything from holiday traditions to Tracey's latest graphic design projects to Aaron's spring concert plans. Emma found herself relaxing completely into the rhythm of the evening. Her earlier nerves about navigating formal social situations dissolved as Nathan's presence beside her created a pocket of comfort and confidence.

When the orchestra launched into another slow dance set, Nathan stood immediately and extended his hand with old-fashioned gallantry. "Ms. Sullivan, would you do me the honor?"

Emma's pulse quickened as she placed her hand in his, allowing him to guide her toward the dance floor where other couples were already swaying to the music. She'd worried about dancing in a long dress, about remembering steps she hadn't practiced in years, and about looking graceful enough to match Nathan's natural confidence. But the moment his arm settled around her waist and her hand found its place on his shoulder, everything else faded away.

Nathan was an excellent dancer—not showy or complicated, but smooth and sure in a way that made following his lead feel effortless. He guided her through the steps with gentle pressure at her waist, his right hand holding hers at exactly the right angle, his attention focused completely on her as if the rest of the ballroom had disappeared.

"You're a wonderful dancer," Emma said, looking up at him as they moved together to the orchestra's rendition of "The Way You Look Tonight." "Where did you learn?"

"My mother insisted on lessons when I was sixteen," Nathan admitted, his smile slightly embarrassed. "I complained about it for months, but she said any gentleman should know how to make a woman feel elegant on a dance floor."

"Your mother was very wise."

"She was. Though I have to admit, I never imagined those lessons would matter this much." Nathan's expression grew more serious as he looked down at her, his dark eyes reflecting the ballroom's twinkling lights. "Dancing with you feels like everything I learned these moves for."

Emma's chest tightened with emotion at the simple honesty in his voice. Nathan had a gift for saying exactly what she needed to hear without making it feel rehearsed or calculated. When he spoke, she believed him completely—not just because his words were beautiful, but because everything about him, from the way he held her to the attention he gave her responses, supported what he said.

They danced through three songs, conversation flowing as easily as their movements. Nathan told her about the first Mistletoe Ball he'd attended as a newcomer to town and how nervous he'd been about fitting into community traditions. Emma described watching the ball from outside as a teenager, pressing her face to the lodge windows with her friends and imagining what it would be like to wear a beautiful gown and dance with someone special.

"And now here you are," Nathan said. "In the most beautiful gown in the room, dancing with someone who thinks he's the luckiest man in Mistletoe Falls."

She looked up at Nathan's face, taking in the way the chandelier light played across his features, the warmth in his eyes as he looked down at her, and the slight smile that suggested he was exactly where he wanted to be. Surrounded by the music and the elegant crowd and the Christmas magic of the decorated ballroom, Emma felt like a princess in one of her stories.

"Nathan," she said, her voice barely audible above the music.

"Mmm?" He leaned closer to hear her, and Emma caught that familiar scent that had become home to her—clean cologne and something essentially him that made her feel safe and cherished and completely present.

"I want every dance for the rest of my life to be with you," she said, the words coming out in a rush of honesty that surprised her with its intensity. "Every dance, every celebration, every moment when music plays and people are happy—I want to be in your arms."

Nathan stopped moving entirely for a heartbeat, his eyes searching hers with an expression of such wonder it made her pulse race. Then his smile spread slowly across his face, transforming his already handsome features into something that made her understand why people wrote songs about moments like this.

"Emma Sullivan," he said, beginning to move again. "Do you have any idea what you do to me when you say things like that?"

"What do I do to you?"

Instead of answering with words, Nathan spun her in a graceful turn that made her burgundy dress flare around her legs like liquid silk, then pulled her back into his arms with smooth confidence. The movement was romantic and showy enough that several nearby couples smiled approvingly, but Emma barely noticed the audience. Her attention was completely captured by the look in Nathan's eyes—pride and love and possessiveness that made her feel like the heroine of every romantic story she'd ever read.

"You make me believe in forever," Nathan said when she was back in his arms, his voice quiet and serious. "You make me want to be the kind of man who deserves to hear you say things like that."

"You already are that man," Emma said firmly, her free hand moving from his shoulder to rest against his chest, where she could feel the strong, steady rhythm of his heartbeat through the fine fabric of his tuxedo. "You've been that man since the day you walked into my bookshop asking for help with the Christmas play."

Nathan spun Emma out once more, this time in a wider turn that showcased the elegant lines of her gown and the grace they'd found together on the dance floor. When he drew her back, instead of resuming their previous position, Nathan surprised her by dipping her low, supporting her weight with strong arms while her burgundy dress pooled around her like spilled wine.

Emma's breath caught as she looked up at Nathan's face from this new angle, seeing him framed against the ballroom's chandelier light, his expression tender and fierce and completely focused on her. Time seemed suspended as he held her there, both of them breathing slightly hard from the exertion of dancing, the music swelling around them like a soundtrack designed specifically for this moment.

"I love you," Nathan said, his voice carrying clearly despite the orchestra and the conversations of other couples nearby. "Emma, I love you more than I thought it was possible to love another person."

The simple declaration, delivered while he held her in this romantic pose with the entire Mistletoe Falls community dancing around them, undid every remaining barrier around Emma's heart. She felt tears prick at the corners of her eyes from the overwhelming rightness of this moment, this man, and this life.

Nathan brought her smoothly back to standing, his hands steadying her as she found her balance, but Emma couldn't seem to find words adequate to respond to what he'd just given her. Instead, emotion taking control of her actions, she reached up and framed his face with both hands, feeling the slight roughness of his evening stubble against her palms, the warmth of his skin, and the way his breathing quickened as she looked directly into his eyes.

And then she kissed him.

Nathan's arms came around her immediately, holding her close as he kissed her back. Around them, the music played and other couples danced, and the Mistletoe Ball continued its elegant celebration, but Emma felt wrapped in a cocoon of perfect happiness that existed separately from everything else.

Emma rested her forehead against Nathan's chest and listened to the strong, rapid rhythm of his heartbeat through his tuxedo shirt. His arms remained around her, one hand stroking gently through her carefully arranged hair, and she felt safer and more cherished than she'd ever experienced before.

"I love you too," she whispered against the fine fabric of his shirt. "So much it scares me sometimes, but in the most wonderful way possible."

Nathan's arms tightened around her as they continued to sway together, no longer really dancing but simply holding each other while the music played around them. Emma closed her eyes and breathed in the scent that had become home to her, committing this moment to memory.

This was what happiness felt like, she realized. Not the dramatic highs and lows of storybook romance, but this quiet certainty that she was exactly where she belonged, with exactly the right person. The Christmas lights twinkled overhead, the orchestra played songs about love and longing, and in Nathan's arms, surrounded by their community's celebration, Emma felt like the luckiest woman in the world.

Chapter 28

The budget spreadsheet on Nathan's computer screen blurred as he rubbed his eyes, the columns of numbers refusing to add up to anything that made sense for next year's textbook allocations. Winter break had settled over Mistletoe Falls Elementary like a soft blanket, leaving the hallways quiet.

His coffee had grown cold in the mug Emma had given him—white ceramic printed with "World's Most Patient Principal" in cheerful blue letters—and he was debating whether to brew a fresh pot when his office phone rang.

Nathan glanced at the caller ID: Dr. Margaret Hendricks, County School Board. Probably something routine about winter maintenance schedules or a question about enrollment projections. The board office typically used the break to catch up on administrative details that got pushed aside during the busy semester.

"Nathan Reid," he answered, leaning back in his chair and reaching for a pen in case he needed to jot down notes.

"Nathan, hello. I hope I'm not disturbing you." Dr. Hendricks' voice carried its usual professional warmth, but something in her tone made Nathan sit straighter. "Do you have a few minutes to talk?"

"Of course. What can I help you with?"

"Well, as you know, Superintendent Morrison officially announced his retirement last week, effective at the end of this school year." Dr. Hendricks paused, and Nathan could hear papers rustling in the background. "The board has been discussing possible candidates for his replacement, and your name has come up repeatedly in our conversations."

Nathan's pen stilled against his notepad. "My name?"

"We've been impressed with your work at Mistletoe Falls Elementary over the past three years. Your budget management, the way you've strengthened community partnerships, your innovative approaches to educational challenges—board members have taken notice. We'd like you to seriously consider applying for the superintendent position."

The words seemed to echo in the quiet of Nathan's office, bouncing off the walls lined with children's artwork and commendation letters from grateful parents. Superintendent. Him. Nathan was momentarily speechless, staring at the framed photo on his desk—himself with a fifth-grade class from last spring, all of them grinning at the camera after their science fair success.

"Nathan? Are you still there?"

"Yes, sorry. I'm just... surprised." Nathan set down his pen, running his free hand through his hair. "I didn't expect this."

"Which is part of what makes you an attractive candidate," Dr. Hendricks said with a slight chuckle. "You're focused on doing excellent work rather than positioning yourself politically. The board respects that integrity."

Nathan's mind was spinning, trying to process the magnitude of what he was hearing. Superintendent Morrison oversaw twelve schools across the county, managed a multi-million-dollar budget, and answered directly to the state education department. It was the kind of position that could define an entire career, the pinnacle of educational leadership that most principals only dreamed about.

"What would the timeline look like?" he heard himself asking, though part of his brain was still catching up to the reality of this conversation.

"We'd want to interview candidates in early January and make a decision by February so there's time for a smooth transition. Would you mind coming in next week to speak with us? Say Wednesday morning at ten? Nothing formal yet, just a chance to discuss the position and see if you're genuinely interested."

Nathan glanced at his desk calendar, though he already knew it was mostly empty during winter break. "Wednesday works."

"Excellent. I'll have my assistant send you an email with the details and some preliminary information about the position requirements. Nathan, I want you to know that you'd be entering the conversation as a serious candidate, not just as a courtesy interview. The board believes you have exactly the kind of vision and integrity we need for the district's future."

After the call ended, Nathan sat in his office chair staring at the phone as if it might ring again and reveal that the entire conversation had been some kind of mistake. Superintendent. The word seemed too big for the quiet elementary school office, too grand for someone who spent his days helping children tie their shoes and mediating playground disputes.

His computer chimed with an incoming email notification, and Nathan clicked over to see a message from the board office. The subject line read, "Confidential—Superintendent Position Discussion—Wednesday 12/29." Opening it, he found formal meeting details, and an attached document titled "Position Overview—County Superintendent."

Nathan downloaded the file, his pulse quickening as he scanned the responsibilities and requirements. Strategic planning for twelve schools. Budget oversight for the entire district. Policy development and implementation. Community leadership and public relations. The scope was staggering compared to his current role, yet as he read through the educational vision statements and goals, Nathan felt a stirring of excitement.

This was the kind of position where he could work on improving not just one school, but several schools across the entire county. Where he could advocate for the funding rural schools desperately needed. Where he could influence policy decisions that affected hundreds of teachers and thousands of students.

But even as professional ambition began to unfurl in his chest, another thought struck him with the force of cold mountain air: What would this mean for his private life?

Nathan pushed back from his desk, walking to the window that overlooked the empty playground. Snow had begun to fall while he'd been working, light flakes that danced past the glass and gathered in the corners of the swing set. In a few hours, he'd planned to leave work and drive to Emma's bookshop, maybe suggest they grab dinner at the Fireside Diner, and spend the evening planning what they might do with the rest of winter break together.

Now everything felt different, complicated by possibilities he hadn't completely imagined coming his way.

The superintendent position would require longer hours, more travel, and evening meetings with school board members and community leaders. There would be district events, conferences, and the kind of professional obligations that had strained his first marriage to the breaking point. Jennifer's accusations echoed in his memory: *You care more about other people's children than you'll ever care about building a real life with me.*

But this wasn't about caring more about work than relationships, Nathan told himself. This was about the opportunity to serve children on a larger scale. Emma understood his dedication to education—she'd said it was one of the things she loved about him. Surely she'd support a chance to expand that impact?

Yet doubt crept in as he considered the practical implications. The county school board offices were in Gatlinburg, an hour's drive from Mistletoe Falls on winding mountain roads. The position would almost certainly require relocating, or at minimum a long daily commute that would eat into the time he and Emma had been treasuring together.

Nathan's phone buzzed with a text message, and he glanced down to see Emma's name on the screen.

How's the budget wrestling match going?

The message made him smile despite his churning thoughts.

He needed to talk to her about this. Not just because the decision would affect both of them, but because Emma's perspective had become essential to how he processed important choices. She saw angles he missed, asked questions that clarified his thinking, and offered the kind of support that made difficult decisions feel manageable rather than overwhelming.

Nathan typed back, *Can I stop by the bookshop? I'll bring lunch. Need to talk about something important.*

Her response came within minutes: *Of course!*

Nathan closed the budget spreadsheet and shut down his computer, but the superintendent position document remained open in another browser window. He printed it, folding the pages carefully before sliding them into his coat pocket. This conversation with Emma would require more than just his scattered thoughts—she'd want details, specific information about what the opportunity actually entailed.

As he gathered his keys and wallet, Nathan caught sight of his reflection in the small mirror he'd hung behind his office door. The face looking back at him was the same one that had started the day focused on textbook budgets and maintenance schedules, but something had shifted. There was a tension around his eyes that spoke of major life decisions suddenly demanding attention.

Superintendent. The possibility felt surreal and thrilling and terrifying all at once. Three years ago, when he'd moved to Mistletoe Falls to escape the wreckage of his first marriage, Nathan had been grateful just to find a principal position where he could rebuild his confidence and focus on doing meaningful work without the complications of personal relationships.

Now everything was different. He'd found his footing professionally, earned the respect of his staff and community, and built something solid and successful at Mistletoe Falls Elementary. More importantly, he'd found Emma—the woman who made him believe in love again.

The superintendent opportunity represented the career pinnacle he'd never dared to dream about. But it also represented change at precisely the moment when his personal life had found its perfect rhythm. The timing felt both providential and problematic, a gift wrapped in complications he wasn't sure how to navigate.

Nathan locked his office and walked through the empty hallways of Mistletoe Falls Elementary, his footsteps echoing off lockers decorated with holiday artwork and bulletin boards celebrating the Christmas holiday. This building had become more than just his workplace over the past three years—it was where he'd rediscovered his passion for educational leadership, where he'd learned to trust his instincts again, and where he'd first worked alongside Emma on the Christmas play that had changed everything.

The thought of leaving felt both exciting and like losing something precious he'd worked hard to build.

Chapter 29

Emma saved the final words of her manuscript with a click that felt like releasing a breath she'd been holding for months. The cursor blinked at the end of the last sentence—*and sometimes the greatest magic of all is simply believing you deserve to be loved exactly as you are*—and she leaned back in her desk chair with something approaching wonder.

She'd done it. After months of struggling with words that felt lifeless, after deadline anxiety that had made her stomach churn every morning, she'd written something good. The story of Princess Buttercup's journey through the Valley of Lost Dreams had become, somehow, Emma's own story of finding hope after devastating loss. Every page hummed with the kind of authentic emotion she'd thought she'd lost forever when her mother died.

The bookshop beyond her office door bustled with its usual Monday afternoon energy—Molly's cheerful voice helping a customer find the perfect cookbook and Anna's patient explanation of various children's series to a harried grandmother. But Emma felt wrapped in a tight hug of creative satisfaction, finally understanding what writers meant when they talked about stories that wrote themselves.

A gentle knock on her open office door made her look up to find Nathan standing in the doorway, two takeout bags from the Pickle Barrel Deli in his hands and that smile that never failed to make her pulse quicken. He wore dark jeans and a navy sweater that brought out his eyes.

"Delivery service," he said, stepping into her office and setting the bags on the corner of her desk. "Lisa insisted on adding extra pickles when I mentioned I was bringing lunch to my favorite author."

Emma rose from her chair and moved around the desk to greet him properly, standing on her toes to press a quick kiss to his lips. "You're exactly what I need right now. I've been editing for three hours straight; the book is finished, and I'm absolutely starving."

Nathan's arms settled around her waist, holding her close for a moment. "How does it feel? Having the whole manuscript finished and polished?"

"Incredible," Emma said, meaning it completely. "For the first time since Mom died, I've written something I'm genuinely proud of. Something that feels like it came from my heart instead of just my deadline anxiety."

Nathan's expression grew tender as he released her to unpack their lunch. "I always had faith in you. Your gift for storytelling was never gone—it was just waiting for the right moment to speak again."

"You know... you were right about community-inspiring stories. This book is so much better because of everything I've experienced these past few weeks. The Christmas play, working with the children, and finding my place again in life."

"And finding us," Nathan added softly, handing her a wrapped sandwich.

"Definitely finding us," Emma agreed, settling back into her desk chair while Nathan pulled over the small reading chair she kept for visitors. "Which reminds me—I want to read you the final scene. It's about courage and love and choosing to believe in happy endings even when you're scared."

They unwrapped their sandwiches and settled into the comfortable ritual of shared lunch, conversation flowing as easily as always. Emma described her favorite moments from the final chapters while Nathan listened with the focused attention that made her feel like the most fascinating person in his world. She told him about Princess Buttercup's confrontation with the Shadow Dragon, about the revelation that courage didn't mean not being afraid but choosing love despite fear.

"It sounds like you wrote yourself into the story," Nathan observed, taking a bite of his turkey club. "Princess Buttercup finding her courage again after losing someone she loved."

"I did," Emma admitted.

Nathan smiled, but something in his expression seemed distracted, as if part of his attention was focused on something beyond their conversation. Emma noticed the slight tension around his eyes, the way his fingers drummed absently against his knee between bites of sandwich.

"Nathan," she said, setting down her sandwich, "what's going on? You seem worried about something."

Nathan paused, his sandwich halfway to his mouth, and Emma saw him weigh whether to share whatever was on his mind. The hesitation was so unlike him—Nathan was usually direct about his thoughts and feelings, part of what made their communication so easy and honest.

"There is something," he said finally, wrapping up the remainder of his sandwich with careful precision. "I got a phone call this morning from Dr. Hendricks at the county school board."

Emma felt a flutter of unease. "Oh? About the superintendent's retirement."

"Yes, they've asked me to interview for his replacement."

The words hit Emma like cold mountain air, stealing her breath and making the cozy warmth of her office suddenly feel inadequate. Superintendent. The top educational position in the county, overseeing dozens of schools and thousands of students. The kind of opportunity that comes along once in a career, if at all. Mrs. Benson had been right last week, as if she had sensed what was coming.

"Nathan," she breathed, her mind racing to process the implications. "That's... that's incredible. What an honor."

But even as the supportive words left her mouth, Emma's thoughts were spiraling in directions she didn't want to examine.

"I haven't said yes to anything yet," Nathan said quickly, as if reading the worry in her expression. "It's just a preliminary conversation next Wednesday. Nothing official."

Emma forced herself to focus on what this meant for Nathan rather than what it might mean for her. This was about his career and his dreams.

"Nathan, this is wonderful," she said, putting genuine enthusiasm into her voice. "They obviously see what I see—that you're an exceptional leader with exactly the vision and integrity they need."

Nathan's eyebrows rose slightly, as if her immediate support surprised him. "You think I should seriously consider it?"

"Of course you should consider it," Emma said, even as her stomach twisted with anxiety. "Think about everything you could accomplish on that scale. The outdoor education programs you've dreamed about, the funding advocacy for rural schools, and policy changes that could benefit thousands of children."

She watched Nathan's expression shift as he considered her words and saw the spark of professional excitement that he was trying to contain. This was what ambition looked like on a man who'd spent his career focused on serving others rather than advancing himself—tentative but real, waiting for permission to want something bigger.

"It would be a significant change," Nathan said carefully. "Different responsibilities, longer hours, a lot more politics and bureaucracy. I'm not even sure I'm ready for that level of leadership... or even if I want it."

Emma interpreted his uncertainty as modesty rather than genuine doubt. Nathan had always been more comfortable talking about his students' achievements than his own capabilities.

"You're absolutely ready," she said firmly.

Nathan was quiet for a moment, studying her face with an expression she couldn't quite interpret. "Emma, this could affect us. The job's based in Gatlinburg, which would mean either a long commute or..."

"Or relocating," Emma finished when he trailed off. "I understand that."

But did she? Emma's mind reeled as she tried to imagine what superintendent-level demands would mean for their relationship. They'd built something beautiful around quiet dinners, weekend adventures, and the gentle rhythm of supporting each other's work while carving out time for the personal connection that had become the center of both their worlds.

How would that survive evening school board meetings and district travel and the kind of public scrutiny that came with high-level positions? Would they become a weekend-only couple, stealing time between his professional obligations? Would she find herself competing with an entire county of schools for Nathan's attention and emotional energy?

"It's only an hour's drive," Emma heard herself saying, as if geography was the only concern. "People manage longer commutes than that all the time."

"True. And it would be an opportunity to influence educational policy on a much broader scale."

Emma watched the excitement building in Nathan's voice and felt her chest tighten with a complex mixture of pride and fear. She loved his dedication to education and loved the way his eyes lit up when he talked about programs that could help children discover their potential. How could she be anything but supportive of an opportunity that would let him serve that calling at the highest possible level?

But she also remembered her father's restlessness, the way bigger opportunities had eventually pulled him away from everything that should have mattered more. She remembered her mother's brave smiles and patient understanding until the day understanding wasn't enough anymore.

"What does your gut tell you?" Emma asked, pushing aside her own thoughts to focus on Nathan's needs. "When Dr. Hendricks first mentioned it, what was your immediate reaction?"

Nathan was quiet for a long moment, his fingers drumming against his knee again. "Honestly? Part of me was thrilled. The possibility of implementing changes that could affect thousands of students instead of just a few hundred... it's exactly the kind of impact I've always hoped to have someday."

"And the other part?"

"The other part wondered if I'd be crazy to leave what I've built here in this town," Nathan said, his gaze meeting hers across the small space between their chairs. "I love my job at Mistletoe Falls Elementary. I love this community and the life I've created here."

Emma's pulse quickened at the way Nathan's voice softened on those last words. But she also heard the longing when he talked about broader impact, the pull of professional dreams he'd perhaps never allowed himself to fully acknowledge.

"Nathan," she said gently, "you can't base a career decision on fear of change. If this is an opportunity that excites you professionally, you owe it to yourself to explore it seriously."

Nathan studied her face with that intense focus she'd grown to love, as if he was trying to read something in her expression that her words weren't revealing. "And what about us? How do you feel about the possibility of everything changing just as we've found our rhythm together?"

The direct question made Emma pause. She could be honest about her fears—tell Nathan that the thought of his attention being divided among multiple schools instead of one made her stomach clench with anxiety reminiscent of watching her father pack his suitcase for longer and longer business trips. She could admit that she'd been looking forward to a quiet future of shared dinners and weekend hikes and the kind of relationship that thrived on daily proximity and consistent availability.

But Nathan's professional dreams weren't her father's restless ambition. Nathan wasn't looking for escape, excitement, or validation from external success. He was considering an opportunity to serve more children, to influence policy in ways that could make education better for thousands of families.

How could she ask him to limit that vision for her comfort?

"I think," Emma said carefully, "that the right relationship should support both people's dreams, not constrain them. If the superintendent position is something you want to pursue, then we'll figure out how to make that work for us."

"You make it sound simple."

"Maybe it is simple," Emma said, though nothing about this felt simple at all. "You interview for the position and see if it's genuinely the right fit for what you want professionally. If they offer it to you and you want to accept, we'll deal with the logistics."

"Logistics like living an hour apart? Like my schedule being even more demanding than it already is? Like the possibility that county-level politics might require social obligations and public appearances that affect both of us?"

With each question, it felt like Nathan was listing reasons why the opportunity might be impossible, but Emma heard them as challenges they needed to overcome rather than barriers. Her own needs seemed selfish compared to the possibility of Nathan influencing educational policy across an entire county.

"We're both adults," she said, surprised by how steady her voice sounded. "We both managed demanding careers before we met each other. If we care about this relationship as much as I think we do, we'll find ways to make it work regardless of where your office and possibly even your home happen to be located."

Nathan was quiet for several heartbeats, and Emma held her breath as she waited for his response. Outside her office, the normal sounds of the bookshop continued—a customer asking about special orders, the soft chime of the register, Cora's voice explaining return policies—but Emma felt suspended in this moment of potential life-changing decision.

"You're right," Nathan said finally. "I shouldn't let logistics determine whether I pursue something this significant professionally."

Emma felt a stab of something that might have been loss or victory—she couldn't tell which. "So you're going to the meeting next Wednesday?"

"I should. I owe it to myself to understand what they're offering." Nathan reached across the space between their chairs to take her hand, his thumb tracing gentle patterns across her knuckles. "I appreciate your being so supportive. I wasn't sure how you'd really feel about the possibility of everything changing."

Emma squeezed his fingers, hoping her smile looked more confident than it felt. "I want you to be happy and fulfilled professionally. If that means adapting to some changes, then that's what we'll do."

Nathan lifted their joined hands to press a soft kiss to her knuckles, the gesture so tender it made her chest ache with love and fear in equal measure. "I don't know what I did to deserve you."

You didn't do anything, Emma thought as she watched Nathan's expression clear with what looked like relief and growing excitement. *You're just the kind of person who attracts opportunities like this because you've devoted your entire career to serving others. And I'm the woman who loves you enough to encourage you to chase dreams even when they scare me.*

"So what happens next?" She asked, proud of how genuine her interest sounded. "What's the timeline for this whole process?"

"Wednesday's meeting is just preliminary—a chance for them to explain the position in detail and for me to ask questions about expectations, challenges, that sort of thing. If we're both still interested after that conversation, they'd want to schedule formal interviews in early January."

Emma nodded. "And if they offered you the position?"

"I'd need to give Morrison plenty of notice for transition planning. I probably wouldn't start the job formally until the end of May, I imagine." Nathan paused, his expression growing more serious. "Emma, I need you to know that I wouldn't make a decision like this without talking it through with you completely. This affects both of us."

The consideration in his voice made Emma's throat tighten with emotion. Nathan wasn't just informing her about a career opportunity—he was treating her like a true partner in major life decisions. It was undoubtedly the kind of respect and inclusion she'd always hoped for in a relationship.

Which made it even more important that she not let her own thoughts influence his professional choices.

"I appreciate that," she said softly. "And I want you to know that whatever you decide, you have my complete support. This is your career, your calling. I trust your judgment about what's right for your future."

Nathan's smile was radiant as he squeezed her hand. "Our future."

Our future. The words should have filled Emma with warmth and certainty. Instead, she felt the first whisper of real fear as she imagined what "together" might look like if Nathan's professional life expanded to county-wide responsibilities.

Could they maintain the relationship they'd built around shared dinners and quiet evenings if Nathan was managing crisis calls from twelve different schools? Would their weekend adventures survive if Saturday mornings were consumed by school board meetings and budget reviews? Would she find herself dating a position rather than a person, competing with hundreds of staff members and thousands of students for Nathan's attention and emotional energy?

The questions felt dangerous even to think, much less voice. Emma had watched her mother support her father's advancing career with grace and patience until the day grace and patience weren't enough anymore. She'd promised herself she'd never be the woman who asked a man to choose between love and ambition.

But she'd also never imagined falling this deeply in love with someone whose ambitions might require fundamental changes to everything they'd built together so far.

"I should let you get back to your day," Nathan said, releasing her hand to gather the remains of their lunch. "We need to plan something to celebrate your finishing your manuscript."

Emma nodded, though part of her wanted to ask him to stay, to spend the rest of the afternoon talking through every possible implication of this opportunity until they'd covered all the scenarios that were making her stomach clench with anxiety.

But Nathan looked lighter than when he'd arrived, the worried tension around his eyes replaced by the kind of focused energy she recognized from his most productive planning sessions. Her support had given him permission to want this opportunity, to pursue it without guilt about how it might affect their relationship.

Which was precisely what a good partner should do, Emma reminded herself. *Even when that support felt like encouraging someone you loved to walk toward something that might take them away from you.*

"I'm proud of you, Nathan," she said, standing to walk him to the door.

Nathan paused in the doorway of her office, turning to cup her face gently in his hands. "I'm so fortunate to have found you. I hope you know that."

His kiss was soft and full of gratitude. Emma kissed him back with all the love and support she could pour into the gesture, even as her heart whispered questions she was determined not to voice.

"I'll call you tonight," Nathan said against her lips.

"I look forward to it," she said, meaning it despite the knot of anxiety tightening in her chest.

She watched from her office doorway as Nathan made his way through the bookshop. He moved with the easy confidence she'd fallen in love with, but there was something different in his posture now—a sense of possibility, of professional excitement that hadn't been there an hour ago.

Emma had given him that. Her immediate support, her encouragement to pursue the opportunity, and her assurance that their relationship was strong enough to weather whatever changes might come. She'd been the partner he needed her to be.

So why did she feel like she was standing at the edge of losing everything that mattered most?

Emma returned to her desk and stared at the computer screen where her completed manuscript waited, the story of Princess Buttercup's journey to find courage after devastating loss. She'd written about choosing love despite fear, about believing in happy endings even when you couldn't see how they might unfold.

But sitting in her quiet office, surrounded by the familiar comfort of books and the gentle sounds of her business thriving, Emma wondered if she'd just encouraged the man she loved to pursue a dream that would fundamentally change everything they had together.

The rational part of her mind insisted this was an overreaction. People managed relationships across professional challenges all the time. An hour's commute wasn't the end of the world. Nathan's dedication to education was one of the things she loved most about him—how could she not support an opportunity for him to serve that calling at the highest level?

But the part of her heart that remembered watching her mother's patient smile grow strained over months of increasing business travel whispered different concerns. What if county-level responsibilities consumed Nathan the way her father's ambitions had consumed him? What if the relationship that felt so solid and precious right now became collateral damage to professional advancement?

Emma grabbed her phone and scrolled to Aunt Lily's number, then hesitated. What would she say? That she was afraid Nathan might get a promotion that would require some adjustments to their relationship? That she was scared of changes that might affect their still-new partnership?

Her fears sounded selfish even in her own mind.

Instead, Emma set down her phone and opened the completed manuscript file and read through the ending one more time. She focused on Princess Buttercup's moment of choosing trust over fear, love over safety, and hope over the protection of keeping her heart hidden away.

Sometimes the greatest magic of all is simply believing you deserve to be loved exactly as you are.

But what happened, Emma wondered as afternoon light slanted through her office windows, when believing in love meant encouraging the person you loved most to walk toward something that might change everything?

Outside her office, the bookstore hummed with its usual peaceful energy. Customers browsed among familiar shelves, children laughed over picture books, and the coffee pot gurgled with a fresh brew that would comfort afternoon readers. Everything felt exactly as it should—except for the growing certainty that her world was about to shift in ways she couldn't control or predict.

Emma closed her laptop and picked up her phone, typing a message to Nathan: *So proud of you for being open to this opportunity. Can't wait to see how Wednesday goes for you.*

The response came quickly: *Couldn't do any of this without your support. Love you.*

Love you too, Emma typed back and meant it completely.

<h1 style="text-align:center">Chapter 30</h1>

Nathan set the printed email on Aaron's desk and slumped back in the chair, watching his closest friend scan the formal letterhead from the county school board. The choir room felt cavernous without children's voices filling it, nothing but the tick of the wall clock and the distant hum of the heating system breaking the Tuesday morning quiet.

Aaron's eyebrows climbed higher with each paragraph he read. "Well," he said finally, setting the paper down with deliberate care. "That's quite an honor. Though I have to say, the timing's interesting—I heard some chatter in the teacher's lounge last week about Morrison's retirement creating opportunities."

"You heard about this?" Nathan asked, straightening slightly.

"Not specifically about you being considered, but there was definitely speculation about who might throw their hat in the ring." Aaron leaned back in his chair, studying Nathan's face with the careful attention he usually reserved for students struggling with difficult harmonies. "So why do you look like someone just told you your favorite restaurant is closing down forever?"

Nathan managed a weak laugh, running his hands through his hair. "That's the problem. I should be thrilled, right? This is the kind of opportunity most principals only dream about."

"But?"

"But I can't stop thinking about what I'd be giving up." Nathan gestured around the familiar space—Aaron's piano covered with sheet music, the risers where children stood during concerts, and the bulletin board displaying photos from last month's Thanksgiving program. "Three years ago, I came to Mistletoe Falls because I needed to remember why I became an educator in the first place. This school, this community—they gave that back to me."

Aaron nodded slowly. "And now?"

"Now I finally have everything I thought I wanted. A job I love, a community that feels like home, Emma..." Nathan's voice caught slightly on her name. "Yesterday when Dr. Hendricks called, my first thought wasn't excitement about the opportunity. It was panic about losing what I've built here."

"What did Emma say when you told her?"

Nathan shifted uncomfortably, remembering yesterday's conversation in Emma's office. "She was incredibly supportive. Immediately started talking about what an honor it was, how I could influence educational policy on a larger scale, and how we'd figure out the logistics of it all."

"That sounds positive."

"It was. Too positive, maybe." Nathan stood and walked to the window overlooking the empty schoolyard. "She didn't hesitate for a second before encouraging me to pursue it. The idea of everything changing didn't faze her at all."

"And that bothers you?"

"It confuses me," Nathan admitted. "Part of me wanted her to say she'd miss having me close by, that she'd hate for my schedule to become even more demanding than it already is. Instead, she immediately started problem-solving, talking about adapting to changes and supporting each other's dreams."

Aaron was quiet for a moment, his fingers absently picking out a melody on the edge of his desk. "Nathan, can I ask you something?"

"Of course."

"What do you actually want? Not what you think you should want, not what would look impressive on a resume. What does your gut tell you about this opportunity?"

The question made Nathan pause. He'd been so focused on analyzing the pros and cons, on being responsible and considering all angles, that he hadn't simply listened to his instincts closely enough.

"I don't want it," he said, the words coming out in a rush of honesty. "The superintendent position—it's an incredible honor, and I'm grateful they are even considering me, but I don't want it. Not right now."

"Okay," Aaron said simply. "Tell me why."

Nathan returned to his chair, leaning forward with his elbows on his knees. "I love what I do here. I know every student's name, I understand their families, and I can walk through these hallways and see the direct impact of decisions I make. As superintendent, I'd be managing larger budgets and attending board meetings and dealing with district politics instead of helping kids tie their shoes and celebrating when they finally master long division."

"Those are good reasons."

"There's more." Nathan's voice grew stronger as he continued. "I hate politics, Aaron. The maneuvering and diplomacy and having to smile while people make decisions that hurt children because it looks good on paper. Morrison spends half his time in meetings that have nothing to do with education and the other half dealing with parents who want to complain to the highest authority about playground policies."

Aaron chuckled. "So why are you even considering it?"

"Because this is a massive opportunity," Nathan admitted. "This is something that could change my entire future."

"But?"

Nathan was quiet for several heartbeats, processing his thoughts. "But... I love the work I'm doing here. I'm at a good point in my life, and I don't feel my work here at this school is finished. I honestly believe that success doesn't always mean climbing the ladder and wanting more—sometimes it means finding exactly where you belong and committing to excellence there."

"That's pretty wise for a guy who was having an identity crisis twenty minutes ago," Aaron said with a grin.

"I'm a work in progress." Nathan smiled for the first time since entering the choir room. "But I know what I want my life to look like, and it doesn't include managing a dozen schools from an office in Gatlinburg."

"So what are you going to tell the board?"

"That I'm honored by their consideration but not interested in pursuing the position." Nathan felt another wave of relief in saying the words. "I'll recommend some excellent candidates from other districts who would actually want the job."

Aaron studied his friend's face, noting the tension that had eased from around Nathan's eyes. "You look better already. More like yourself."

"I feel better. Like I've been holding my breath since yesterday and can finally exhale." Nathan paused, considering his next words. "There's something else, though. Something about Emma's reaction yesterday has been bothering me."

"What about it?"

Nathan struggled to articulate the unease that had been nagging at him since leaving the bookshop. "She was so quick to encourage me to pursue it. So ready to adapt and make sacrifices to support what she thought was best for my career. It reminded me of..."

"Of what?"

"Of my mom. She spent thirty years encouraging Dad to take every promotion, take every transfer, and take every opportunity that came along. She packed up our lives and moved us across the state multiple times because she believed supporting his ambitions was what good wives did."

"That doesn't sound terrible."

"It wasn't until I realized she never once said what she actually wanted for her life or for our family. She never admitted that she might have preferred staying in one place long enough to build lasting friendships or that constantly adapting to Dad's career meant she never got to pursue her own interests." Nathan's voice grew thoughtful. "Emma's response yesterday felt familiar in a way that made me uncomfortable."

Aaron leaned forward, his expression growing more serious. "What are you saying?"

"I'm saying I want a partner who tells me when my dreams might conflict with hers. Who's honest about how changes would affect her, not just immediately supportive of whatever I think might advance my career." Nathan ran his hands through his hair again. "Emma's been through enough loss and disruption. If part of her was worried about how the superintendent job would affect our relationship, I wanted her to feel safe enough to say so."

"Maybe she genuinely wasn't worried."

"Maybe. Or maybe she's learned to be supportive at the expense of being honest about her own needs." Nathan stood again, pacing to the piano where sheet music lay scattered across the bench.

"That sounds like something you need to talk to Emma about. I have no good words to help you figure that out... or help you work through your thoughts. I'm happy to listen, though; I hope you know that. But... you're going to call Dr. Hendricks today, right?"

"This morning. Before I can second-guess myself or start over-thinking the decision again." Nathan turned back to Aaron with a rueful smile. "Thanks for listening to me work through this. I needed someone to help me sort through what I actually wanted versus what I thought I should want."

"That's what friends are for. Besides, I have selfish reasons for wanting you to stay. Who else am I going to complain to about parent conference scheduling conflicts?"

Nathan laughed, feeling lighter than he had since Dr. Hendricks' phone call. "Just because I'm staying doesn't mean you get unlimited venting privileges."

"We'll see about that," Aaron said with a grin. "So what's your plan for the rest of winter break? Besides calling the board office and disappointing them terribly?"

"Honestly? I want to spend as much time as possible with Emma. Maybe plan a day trip somewhere nearby; take advantage of having time off together." Nathan collected the printed email from Aaron's desk, folding it carefully. "I want to focus on what I have instead of worrying about opportunities that I'm confident I don't want."

"That sounds like a man who knows what makes him happy."

"I'm learning," Nathan said. "Slowly, but I'm learning."

He made it to the door before Aaron's voice stopped him.

"Nathan?"

"Yeah?"

"For what it's worth, I think you're making the right choice. You belong here, and not just professionally. You've found your place in this community in a way that matters. That's not something to walk away from lightly."

Nathan felt warmth spread through his chest at his friend's words. "Thanks, Aaron. That means a lot."

"Just promise me something."

"What's that?"

"When you talk to Emma about this, make sure you're having an honest conversation. Not just telling her what you've decided, but exploring why she responded the way she did yesterday. If you're going to build something lasting together, you both need to feel safe being completely truthful about your concerns and fears."

Nathan nodded slowly, recognizing the wisdom in Aaron's advice. "You're right. Thanks, Doctor Aaron... you may want to consider a career switch... you give good advice."

Aaron chuckled. "Good luck with that conversation with Emma. And with the phone call to Dr. Hendricks."

"Thanks. I'll probably need it for both."

Chapter 31

Emma stared at the chicken noodle soup growing cold in the bowl before her, the steam having long since stopped rising from its surface. She'd driven to Aunt Lily's house on autopilot, needing the comfort of familiar walls and the kind of unconditional listening that only family could provide. The sandwich beside her soup remained untouched, though Aunt Lily had made it exactly the way Emma had loved since childhood—thick slices of roasted turkey with sharp cheddar on homemade bread.

"You're going to wear a hole in that spoon if you keep stirring without eating," Aunt Lily observed from her position at the kitchen sink, where she was washing her lunch dishes.

Emma looked down to find she'd indeed been stirring the soup in endless circles, watching carrot and celery pieces chase each other around the bowl. "Sorry. I'm not very good company today."

Lily dried her hands on a kitchen towel embroidered with cheerful sunflowers, then settled into the chair across from Emma, her hazel eyes sharp with the kind of concern that missed nothing. "Now, what's got you so twisted up that you can't even enjoy my homemade chicken noodle soup?"

Emma set down her spoon, meeting her aunt's gaze. The surrounding kitchen held decades of family history—the same yellow walls Emma remembered from childhood visits, the worn wooden table where she and her mother had enjoyed countless meals, and the window above the sink that looked out over Lily's carefully tended winter garden.

"Nathan got a phone call yesterday from the county school board. They want to interview him for the superintendent position."

Lily's eyebrows rose slightly.

"It's an incredible opportunity," Emma continued, the words tumbling out faster now that she'd started. "The kind of position that comes along once in a career, if ever."

"How does Nathan feel about it?"

Emma picked up her spoon again, then set it down without taking a bite. "He was excited but nervous. Honored that they'd consider him but worried about what it would mean for the life he's built here in Mistletoe Falls."

"And how do you feel about it?"

The simple question made Emma's chest tighten with emotions she'd been trying to ignore since yesterday's conversation in her office. "I told him it was wonderful, that he should seriously consider it. What else could I say?"

Lily leaned forward slightly, her expression growing more intent. "What did you want to say?"

The question hit Emma like cold mountain air, stealing her breath and forcing her to confront thoughts she'd been pushing away for twenty-four hours. Her hands trembled as she reached for her water glass, taking a sip to buy time while her mind raced.

"I wanted to beg him not to take it," Emma said finally, the words coming out in a rush of honesty that surprised her with its intensity. "I wanted to tell him that the thought of his attention being divided among twelve schools instead of one makes my stomach clench with anxiety. That I was looking forward to many more quiet dinners and impromptu adventures and the kind of relationship that thrives on seeing each other daily and focusing on one another."

Lily nodded encouragingly.

"I wanted him to seriously consider what the changes would mean—not just for logistics, but for who he is as an educator. Nathan was made for the job he has now, Aunt Lily. He knows every student's name, understands their families, and can walk through those hallways and see the direct impact of his decisions. As superintendent, he'd be managing several schools and larger budgets and attending board meetings and other required events instead of helping kids one-on-one and interacting daily with them."

Emma's voice grew stronger as she articulated fears she'd barely acknowledged to herself. "And I wanted him to consider me in all this. The fact that we've found something beautiful around shared meals and easy conversations and the gentle rhythm of supporting each other's work. How would that survive evening school board meetings and district travel and the kind of public scrutiny that comes with high-level positions?"

She paused, taking a shaky breath. "But that would be selfish, wouldn't it? We've only been dating for a little over a month. Everything has happened so fast, but Aunt Lily... I've found my person. I know it with my whole heart. I don't want to hold him back if this is what he wants. That just seems wrong. I want to support him."

Lily was quiet for several heartbeats, studying Emma's face with the careful attention she'd always given to important moments.

"Emma, honey," Lily said finally, her voice gentle but firm, "can I tell you a story I promised your mother I'd never share?"

Emma's pulse quickened at the unexpected shift in conversation. "Mom?"

"Your mother faced a choice very similar to the one you're wrestling with now." Lily folded her hands on the table, her expression growing distant with memory. "I think she'd forgive me for breaking my promise, considering what's happening in your life."

Emma set down her water glass, giving Lily her complete attention. Stories about her mother always fascinated her, but Lily's tone suggested this was something significant, something that had been kept deliberately hidden.

"Your mother was twenty-four, just finished with her nursing degree, when she fell in love with a man named Lewis Hartwell," Lily began, her voice taking on the cadence of a carefully preserved memory. "He was a research scientist—brilliant, kind, and completely devoted to your mother. They'd been dating for about six months when he was offered a position with a medical research facility in Washington state."

Emma felt her breath catch. She'd never heard this story, had never known about a man named Lewis in her mother's life before her father.

"Lewis wanted her to come with him," Lily continued. "Wanted to marry her and start their life together in Seattle. Your mother was head over heels in love with him, Emma. I'd never seen her so happy, and so alive with possibility."

"What happened?"

"Our mama—your grandmother—was in the final stages of Lou Gehrig's disease. The doctors said she had maybe six months, and the care she needed was more than one person could manage alone.

Your mother had to choose between following Lewis to Washington or staying here to help me care for Mama until she passed."

Emma's throat tightened as she began to understand the parallel Lily was drawing. "She stayed."

"She stayed. She ended things with Lewis, even though every part of her wanted to beg him to wait. She dreamed of a long-distance relationship while we cared for Mama, dreamed of marrying him one day. But she assumed he wouldn't wait. She assumed he couldn't understand why she had to remain here, why caring for Mama had to come first. Back then, women didn't always feel they had the right to ask for what they wanted. We were raised to be quiet, to sacrifice, and to keep our needs tucked away. Your mom carried that silence with her—she made me promise never to breathe a word about Lewis to anyone, not even you. She said it was her choice, her burden to bear, and she didn't want anyone carrying guilt for the path she had taken."

The kitchen felt smaller suddenly, as if the weight of this long-held secret was changing the very air around them. Emma tried to imagine her mother at twenty-four, torn between love and duty, making a choice that would reshape her entire future.

"Did she ever regret it?" Emma asked softly.

Lily's expression grew sad, tinged with the kind of regret that came from watching someone she loved make choices that brought pain. "She never said so directly. Your mother was too loyal, too committed to the decisions she'd made. But I saw her sometimes, especially during difficult times with your father, staring out windows with a distant look in her eyes. Like she was wondering about a different life, a different choice. I can say with complete confidence that she always regretted not making the relationship work with Lewis. She lost part of herself when she let him go."

Emma felt tears prick at the corners of her eyes as she thought about her mother's marriage—the way her father's restlessness had eventually pulled him away from their family entirely, leaving behind a woman who'd already sacrificed one great love for duty and then lost the man she'd settled for to his own selfish ambitions.

"Lewis wrote her letters," Lily continued, her voice growing quieter. "I know because I was the one who collected the mail. She never opened them, but she never threw them away either. After Mama passed and your mother met your father, the letters stopped coming."

"Why are you telling me this now?" Emma asked.

"Because I watched my sister make a choice based on duty and fear rather than love and possibility. She convinced herself that supporting our family was more important than fighting for her own happiness, and that sacrifice colored every relationship she had afterward." Lily reached across the table to cover Emma's hand with her own. "Your mother's biggest regret was the chances she didn't take with a man she loved with her whole heart. It was the feelings and words she didn't express. She settled for less in life because she was afraid to ask for what she really wanted."

Emma stared down at their joined hands, seeing her mother's gentle strength reflected in Lily's weathered fingers. "But what if Nathan really wants this opportunity? What if expressing my concerns holds him back from something that could fulfill him professionally?"

"Then you'll have honored him by being honest about your feelings, and he'll have made his decision with complete information rather than assumptions about what you want." Lily's voice carried the conviction of someone who'd learned hard lessons through observation. "Emma, honey, love isn't about protecting someone from your honest thoughts and feelings. It's about trusting them enough to share those feelings and work through them together."

The simple truth of it made Emma's chest ache.

"I was trying to be like you," Emma said, the realization hitting her with sudden clarity. "Patient and supportive and endlessly adaptable. But that's not actually what good partnerships look like, is it?"

"Good partnerships look like two people who care enough about each other to tell the truth, even when it's complicated or scary." Lily squeezed Emma's hand gently. "Your mom learned too late that supporting someone doesn't mean staying silent about your needs. It means trusting them with your whole heart—including the parts that are worried or uncertain or hoping for specific outcomes."

Emma thought about Nathan's expression yesterday when she'd immediately encouraged him to pursue the superintendent position. Had there been disappointment in his eyes? Had he wanted her to express some concern about how the opportunity might affect their relationship?

"Your mom would want you to fight for love," Lily said without hesitation. "To speak your wants and thoughts clearly. To trust that the right person will want to work through challenges with you rather than being protected from your honest feelings. And most importantly, she'd want you never to have the regret of wondering, 'What if I'd been brave enough to say what I really want?'"

They sat in comfortable quiet for several minutes, the kitchen clock ticking steadily while Emma absorbed everything she had just been told. Outside, winter clouds were gathering, promising snow before evening.

"I need to talk to Nathan," Emma said finally, her voice stronger than it had been all afternoon. "Really talk to him."

"That sounds like the right next step," Lily agreed. "And Emma? Whatever happens with his decision about this job opportunity, at least you'll both know where you stand. That's worth something, even if the outcome isn't what you're hoping for."

Emma finally took a spoonful of soup, surprised to find she had an appetite again. The familiar flavors of her childhood brought comfort, but more than that, they brought clarity. This kitchen, this woman who'd helped raise her, this family history of choices made and regrets carried—all of it was reminding her that love required courage, not just support.

"Will you keep me in your thoughts?" Emma asked as she gathered her coat and purse, soup forgotten now. "I'm not sure how this conversation with Nathan is going to go."

"Honey, you'll be in my prayers every minute until you call and tell me how it went," Lily assured her, walking Emma to the front door. "And remember—whatever he decides, you deserve to have your feelings heard and considered. Never settle for anything less."

Emma hugged her aunt tightly, breathing in her familiar, comforting scent and the indefinable comfort that seemed to emanate from Lily's very presence. "Thank you. For the story about Mom, for the advice, for always knowing what I need to hear."

"That's what family is for, sweetheart. Now go and find your man and speak your mind."

Emma drove back toward Mistletoe Falls with her aunt's words echoing in her mind, the story of her mother's choice with Lewis weighing heavily on her heart. The parallels weren't exact—Nathan wasn't asking her to follow him anywhere, and she wasn't facing a family crisis that required her to stay. But the core issue remained the same: Would she be honest about her feelings, or would she convince herself that love meant staying silent about her own needs and desires?

The irony wasn't lost on her as she navigated the winding mountain roads. She spent her professional life crafting words and creating dialogue for fictional characters who always seemed to know exactly what to say in moments of crisis. Yet here she was, struggling to find the courage to tell the man she loved how she really felt about a decision that could change everything between them.

But maybe that was the point. Love wasn't a story she could control or edit until it reached the perfect conclusion. It was real and messy and required the kind of vulnerability that couldn't be revised or polished before delivery. Nathan deserved her honesty, and she deserved a relationship built on truth rather than careful diplomacy.

Chapter 32

Emma turned into the alley behind the Once Upon a Time Bookshop, her mind still processing everything Aunt Lily had shared about her mother's choice with Lewis. The familiar sight of her parking space came into view, but what made her pulse quicken wasn't the promise of her cozy apartment—it was the sight of Nathan's black truck already parked beside her usual spot, exhaust visible in the cold air as if he'd just arrived.

Emma's hands tightened on the steering wheel as she pulled in beside him. Through his passenger window, she could see his profile, his expression serious as he stared straight ahead.

She turned off her Honda and gathered her purse, her aunt's words still echoing in her mind: *Love isn't about protecting someone from your honest thoughts and feelings. It's about trusting them enough to share those feelings and work through them together.*

Nathan was already stepping out of his truck, his breath creating small clouds in the crisp December air. Emma walked toward him, her boots crunching on the thin layer of snow that had accumulated on the pavement.

"Hi," she said, reaching for his hands without hesitation. The familiar warmth of his fingers closing around hers should have been comforting, but the tension in his grip suggested they were both carrying a weight that needed to be shared.

"Emma. I was hoping we could talk. I tried calling, but it went straight to voicemail."

"We need to talk," Emma said simultaneously, their words overlapping in a way that would have made them laugh under different circumstances.

"Come upstairs," Emma said, tugging gently on his hands.

They climbed the wooden stairs to her apartment in silence, the only sounds their footsteps on the snow-dusted treads and the distant hum of traffic on Mistletoe Lane. Emma fumbled with her keys, acutely aware of Nathan's presence behind her, the warmth radiating from his body in the narrow space of her small back porch.

Inside her apartment, Emma hung up their coats while Nathan stood in her living room, hands shoved deep in his pockets.

"Nathan," Emma began, then stopped, turning to face him fully. "Before you say anything, I need to speak first. Please. I've been thinking about yesterday, about our conversation in my office, and there are things I need to tell you. Things I should have said then but didn't."

Nathan's eyebrows rose slightly, but he nodded, settling into her armchair.

Emma remained standing, needing the movement to process the rush of emotions fighting for expression. She walked to her front window, looking out at the town square where the Victorian gazebo was draped in snow, then turned back to Nathan with her hands clasped in front of her.

"When you told me about the superintendent opportunity yester-day, I said all the right things about how wonderful it was and how you should pursue it." Emma's voice was steady, but her pulse was racing. "I encouraged you to consider it seriously, talked about adapting to changes, and assured you that we'd figure out the logistics together."

Nathan watched her intently, his dark eyes reflecting something that might have been recognition.

"But Nathan," Emma continued, her voice growing stronger, "none of that was what I was actually thinking or feeling in the moment. I was so focused on being the supportive partner I thought you needed that I completely ignored my own honest reaction to what you were telling me."

She began pacing, energy building as she found the courage to voice thoughts she'd been suppressing.

"The truth is, when you described the superintendent position, my first thought wasn't excitement for your career. It was panic about losing what we have so far." Emma paused, meeting Nathan's gaze directly. "I was terrified that county-level responsibilities would consume you the way my father's increasing business demands consumed him. That our quiet dinners would be interrupted by crisis calls from colleagues, that our time together would disappear under budget meetings and board obligations."

Nathan started to speak, but Emma held up a gentle hand.

"Please let me finish. I need to say all of this." She took a breath. "I was afraid that our relationship and seeing each other daily and focusing on one another would become collateral damage to your career. That I'd find myself competing with hundreds of staff members and thousands of students for your attention and emotional energy."

Emma's voice caught slightly as she continued. "And I was scared that supporting your career ambitions meant I'd eventually might lose you entirely, just like my mother and I lost my father to opportunities that seemed more important than the family he had."

She moved to the couch, finally sitting down so she could look at Nathan without the physical distance her pacing had created. "But instead of being honest about any of those fears, I immediately started problem-solving. Talking about adapting and making sacrifices and supporting each other's dreams, as if my concerns didn't matter."

Nathan's expression had grown increasingly tender as she spoke, and Emma saw understanding rather than hurt in his eyes.

"I realize now that I was trying to be the perfect supportive partner instead of being your actual partner." Emma's hands were trembling now, but her voice remained clear. "I was protecting you from my honest thoughts and feelings instead of trusting you enough to work through them together."

She leaned forward slightly, her eyes never leaving Nathan's face. "Nathan, I want you to be happy and fulfilled professionally. I want you to pursue opportunities that excite you and challenge you and let you serve children at the highest possible level. But I also want you to make those decisions knowing how I really feel about the potential changes, not just what I think you want to hear."

Emma took a shaky breath, feeling tears prick at the corners of her eyes. "I want us to build something together where we're both brave enough to say what we actually want, even when it's complicated or scary. Where love means honesty, not just endless accommodation."

The apartment fell quiet except for the soft tick of the mantel clock. Nathan was studying her face with an intensity she had never witnessed before.

Nathan leaned forward in his chair, mirroring her posture. "First, I'm proud of you for trusting me with all of that. For being honest about your fears."

He ran his hands through his hair. "Emma, yesterday when you immediately encouraged me to pursue the superintendent position, part of me was grateful for your support. But another part of me was disappointed."

Emma's breath caught. "Disappointed?"

"I wanted you to tell me you'd miss having me close by all the time," Nathan admitted, his voice growing quiet. "I wanted you to say you were worried about how the changes might affect us, or even that you hoped I'd choose you over career advancement. Not because I needed you to talk me out of pursuing it, but because I wanted to know your honest feelings were part of my decision-making process."

Nathan stood and walked to the windows, looking out at the snow-covered town square where they'd shared their first kiss under the Christmas lights. "Your immediate support reminded me of my mother, actually. She has spent almost her entire married life encouraging my father to take every promotion and transfer that came along, never once admitting what she might have preferred. I realized I don't want a partner who protects me from her honest thoughts—I want someone who trusts me enough to share them."

He turned back to face Emma, his expression earnest. "I spent this morning talking with Aaron, trying to figure out why the superintendent opportunity felt more like a burden than a blessing. And I realized something important."

Emma held her breath, waiting.

"I don't want the job," Nathan said simply. "Not because of logistics or fear of change, but because I genuinely love what I do here. I take pride in knowing every student's name and understanding their families. I enjoy walking through the hallways of my school and seeing the direct impact of my decisions. As superintendent, I'd lose all of that, and the politics... well, let's not even go there."

Relief flooded Emma's chest, so powerful it made her slightly dizzy. "You don't want it?"

"I don't want it," Nathan confirmed, moving to sit beside her on the couch. "I called Dr. Hendricks this morning and declined to interview for the position. I told her I was honored by their consideration but that I'd found exactly where I belong professionally and personally."

Emma felt tears start to flow—not from sadness, but from the overwhelming rightness of Nathan's decision and the honesty they'd finally shared. "Nathan..."

"I choose you," he said, reaching for her hands. "I choose us. I choose this life we're building in Mistletoe Falls, with work I love and a community that feels like home and a woman who makes me want to be the best version of myself."

Emma couldn't speak for a moment, overwhelmed by the simple perfection of his words.

"But Emma," Nathan continued, his voice growing more serious, "I need you to promise me something."

"Anything."

"Promise me that from now on, we'll tell each other the truth about what we're thinking and feeling, even when it's uncomfortable or complicated." Nathan's gaze was steady and sure. "I want a partnership where we trust each other enough to work through difficulties together rather than trying to protect each other from our honest concerns."

Emma nodded emphatically, fresh tears spilling down her cheeks. "I promise. And Nathan, I need you to promise me the same thing. That you'll tell me when you're considering major changes, when you're worried about something, when you need support or space or anything else."

"Promise," Nathan said without hesitation.

They sat for several moments, hands intertwined, both processing the weight of what they'd just shared. The snow continued to fall outside Emma's windows, transforming Mistletoe Falls into a winter wonderland that seemed to celebrate their newfound honesty.

"I'm proud of you," Emma said finally, "for making the decision that felt right for your life rather than just taking an opportunity because it seemed impressive or because others expected you to."

"I'm proud of us," Nathan replied, "for figuring out how to have this conversation instead of letting fear and assumptions drive our choices."

Emma leaned against Nathan's shoulder, feeling more settled than she had since yesterday. "I love you for choosing us. But I also love that you made the choice for yourself, because you genuinely prefer the work you're doing here."

"Both things can be true," Nathan agreed, pressing a gentle kiss to the top of her head. "I can love my current job and also want to build a life with you. They're not competing priorities—they're complementary parts of the same happy life."

Emma was about to respond when her stomach gave an unmistakably loud growl, the sound echoing in the quiet apartment with embarrassing clarity. She pressed a hand to her midsection, suddenly remembering that she'd barely touched her soup at Aunt Lily's house and had been too nervous to eat properly for the past day and a half.

Nathan's laughter was warm and infectious. "When did you last eat?"

Emma's cheeks flushed with embarrassment. "I had a few bites of some soup at Aunt Lily's, but I was too anxious to eat much. And yesterday I just picked at dinner. I've been too wound up about all of this to have much appetite."

"Well, that settles it," Nathan said, standing and extending his hand to help her up from the couch. "We need to get some food into you before you waste away entirely."

"Nathan, you've seen my cooking attempts. And I've seen yours. Neither of us is exactly equipped to create culinary masterpieces."

"True," Nathan agreed with a grin. "But between the two of us, we should be able to manage something edible. What do you have in your kitchen?"

Emma led him toward her small kitchen, mentally inventorying her sparse grocery supplies. "Pasta, I think. Some canned sauce, maybe cheese if it hasn't gone bad."

Nathan began opening cabinets and peering into her refrigerator with the systematic approach he brought to most tasks. "Okay, we've got spaghetti noodles, a jar of marinara sauce that expires next month, parmesan cheese that smells acceptable, and..." He held up a bag of pre-made salad with only slight wilting around the edges. "This might work if we're not too picky about presentation."

"Care to attempt to make a decent meal together?" Emma asked, pulling out a large pot for the pasta water. "Fair warning—my track record suggests we might end up ordering takeout as backup."

"I'm willing to risk it," Nathan said, already filling the pot with water. "Besides, even if we completely fail at cooking, we've already succeeded at the important stuff today."

Emma felt warmth spread through her chest as they fell into the familiar rhythm of working together, Nathan handling the practical elements while she managed what few creative touches their limited ingredients allowed. The conversation that had felt so overwhelming an hour ago now seemed like exactly what they'd both needed—the foundation for something stronger and more honest.

"Thank you," Emma said as Nathan stirred the bubbling pasta, "for being someone I can tell the truth to. For wanting honesty instead of just support."

"I'm happy you were brave enough to trust me with your real feelings. For wanting a partner instead of just a cheerleader."

Emma stepped closer to him in the small kitchen, rising on her toes to press a soft kiss to his lips. The gesture was sweet and uncomplicated, full of gratitude and love and the promise of more honest conversations in their future.

Nathan's smile was radiant when the kiss ended. "I think we're going to be just fine."

"Better than fine," Emma agreed, watching steam rise from the pasta pot while snow continued to fall outside her kitchen window. "I think we're going to be extraordinary."

Chapter 33

Emma stirred the cream of mushroom soup with the concentration of someone defusing a bomb, while Aunt Lily stood beside her at Nathan's granite countertop, shaking her head with theatrical despair.

"Honey, you're stirring that like it owes you money," Lily said, gently taking the wooden spoon from Emma's grip. "The soup's not going anywhere. It just needs to be smooth, not beaten into submission."

Nathan looked up from where he was attempting to cube chicken breasts at the kitchen island, his knife work resembling more of a hacking motion than the precise cuts Lily had demonstrated. "I think I'm supposed to make these pieces smaller?"

"Lord have mercy," Lily muttered, moving to inspect his progress. She picked up one of his irregularly shaped chunks, holding it up to the light like a jeweler examining a flawed diamond. "Nathan, dear, this isn't firewood. We're making chicken casserole, not building a cabin."

Emma burst into laughter at the sight of Nathan's wounded expression, her worries over the perfect Christmas Eve dinner dissolving into the kind of joy that made her cheeks ache from smiling. The three of them had been attempting Lily's "foolproof" chicken and rice casserole for the past hour, with results that could generously be described as educational.

"Maybe we should order pizza," Emma suggested, wiping tears from her eyes as she watched Nathan attempt to salvage his chicken chunks into more uniform pieces.

"Absolutely not," Lily declared, rolling up her sleeves with renewed determination. "No niece of mine is getting married someday without knowing how to make at least one decent meal. And you, Nathan Reid, are a grown man who owns power tools. Surely you can manage a kitchen knife."

Nathan paused mid-chop, his eyebrows rising. "Getting married someday?"

Lily's cheeks pinked slightly, but her chin lifted with characteristic stubbornness. "Well, you two aren't exactly being subtle about where this relationship is headed. I've got eyes in my head, you know."

Emma felt warmth bloom across her face as Nathan's gaze found hers across the kitchen island. They'd been together for just over two months, but Lily was right—there was nothing casual about the way they'd built their lives around each other, the way they'd weathered the superintendent opportunity together, or the way that they spent every spare minute together.

"Back to the chicken," Lily announced, apparently deciding she'd said enough on that particular subject. She moved beside Nathan, her weathered hands guiding his as he attempted to create more uniform pieces. "Think of it like measuring lumber for one of your woodworking projects. Precision matters."

"I can do precision… well, maybe," Nathan said. "I feel like I need a tape measure."

"That's what your eyes are for, sweetheart. Here, watch—" Lily demonstrated a proper cutting motion, the blade moving through the meat with efficient strokes that created perfect bite-sized cubes. "See? Smooth, even cuts. Like slicing through butter."

Emma returned her attention to the soup mixture, following Lily's earlier instructions about incorporating the ingredients without creating lumps. The kitchen smelled wonderful—savory and warm, with hints of the herbs Lily had insisted they add for "proper flavor development."

"Now, Emma, add the rice slowly while you stir," Lily directed, moving to supervise this crucial step. "We don't want it to clump together like concrete."

Emma measured the long-grain rice carefully, pouring it into the soup mixture in gradual additions while maintaining her stirring motion. Under Lily's watchful eye, the ingredients began to come together into something that actually resembled the casserole they'd been attempting to create.

"There!" Lily said with satisfaction as Emma incorporated the last of the rice. "Now we add Nathan's beautifully cubed chicken—don't give me that look, young man, they turned out just fine—and we'll have something fit for a Christmas Eve dinner."

Nathan scraped his cutting board contents into the mixture, the chicken pieces disappearing into the creamy rice base. "I have to admit, this looks more promising than I expected when we started."

"Ye of little faith," Lily chided, though her tone was fond. "Cooking isn't rocket science. It just requires patience and following directions, two skills I know you both possess in abundance."

Emma stirred the complete mixture, marveling at how the simple ingredients had transformed into something that looked genuinely appetizing. "What's next?"

"Into the casserole dish, then into that beautiful oven of Nathan's for exactly forty-five minutes." Lily handed Emma the prepared baking dish—a ceramic piece Nathan had purchased specifically for this Christmas Eve dinner experiment. "And while it cooks, we can sit by that gorgeous fireplace and pretend we're civilized people instead of kitchen disasters."

Nathan preheated the oven while Emma transferred the casserole mixture into the dish, smoothing the top with careful attention to Lily's earlier instructions about even distribution for proper cooking.

"There," Emma announced, sliding the dish into the heated oven and setting the timer. "Forty-five minutes to prove whether we've created a masterpiece or a science experiment."

"Either way, we're eating it," Lily declared, hanging up her apron and smoothing her silver hair back into place. "I didn't spend two hours teaching you two the fundamentals of casserole construction just to watch you order takeout."

Nathan's living room had been transformed for Christmas Eve. The tree they'd selected together two days ago stood in the corner by the large windows, decorated with a mixture of ornaments Nathan had collected over the years and new additions Emma had contributed. White lights twinkled among the branches, casting a gentle illumination across the room, while the stone fireplace crackled with the fire Nathan had started.

Emma settled onto the leather sofa beside Lily, pulling her legs up under her.

Nathan remained standing near the fireplace, his hands clasped behind his back. "There's something I want to do before dinner... I can't wait any longer."

Emma felt her pulse quicken at his tone. "What kind of something?"

Instead of answering, Nathan moved toward the Christmas tree, kneeling beside its base to reach for something hidden among the wrapped presents they'd arranged there earlier. Emma watched with growing curiosity as he retrieved a small package wrapped in elegant silver paper with a simple white ribbon.

"Nathan?"

"I know we said we'd wait until after dinner to exchange gifts," Nathan said, settling into the chair across from where she and Lily sat. "But this particular present... well, it can't wait. I can't wait."

Lily's eyes had grown bright with interest, her gaze moving between Nathan's serious expression and the carefully wrapped package. A knowing smile played at the corners of her mouth, as if she'd suddenly understood something.

"Emma," Nathan continued, extending the silver package toward her with hands that trembled slightly, "open this now... please?"

Emma accepted the gift. "Nathan, what—"

"Just open it," he said gently, though his voice carried an undertone of nervous energy that made Emma's chest tighten with anticipation.

Emma glanced at Lily, who was practically vibrating with suppressed excitement, then back at Nathan's face. His expression was tender, anxious, and hopeful all at once, the look of a man standing at the edge of a moment that would change everything.

Emma untied the white ribbon and peeled away the silver wrapping paper. Beneath was a small velvet box in deep navy blue, the kind of container that could only hold one type of gift.

Emma's breath caught in her throat as the implication hit her. Her hands stilled on the velvet surface, her mind racing to catch up with what Nathan was offering her.

"Emma," Nathan said softly, and when she looked up, he was no longer sitting in his chair.

He was on one knee in front of her, his dark eyes fixed on her face with an intensity that made the rest of the room fade away. The firelight played across his features, illuminating the love and determination and barely contained nervousness that transformed his face into something transcendent.

"Open it," he whispered, his voice rough with emotion.

Emma's fingers trembled as she lifted the lid of the velvet box, and what she found inside stole her breath completely. Nestled in ivory silk was a ring that belonged in fairy tales—a round diamond that caught the firelight and threw it back in brilliant flashes, set in vintage platinum with delicate filigree work that spoke of timeless elegance.

"Nathan," she breathed, unable to form any other words as she stared at the most beautiful ring she'd ever seen.

"Emma Sullivan," Nathan said, his voice stronger now, filled with the conviction of a man who'd found his certainty, "I love you with everything I am. You've given me back my faith in love, in partnership, and in the possibility of building something beautiful with another person."

Emma felt tears begin to blur her vision as Nathan continued, his words washing over her like a benediction.

"You've made me a better man, a better educator, and a better human being. You've given me the courage to be honest about my feelings and to trust in something bigger than my fears."

Emma was dimly aware of Lily's soft sniffle beside her, but her attention was completely captured by Nathan's face, by the raw love and hope she could see in his expression.

"I don't want to spend another day without knowing you'll be my partner for all the days that follow," Nathan said, reaching for the ring with careful fingers. "Emma, marry me? Will you let me love you for the rest of my life?"

"Yes," Emma whispered, then stronger, "Yes, Nathan, yes."

Nathan's smile was radiant as he slipped the ring onto her finger, the diamond settling into place as if it had always belonged there. The fit was near perfect.

"Yes?" Nathan asked, as if he needed confirmation that he'd heard correctly.

"Yes," Emma repeated, laughing through tears as she admired the way the ring caught the firelight. "A thousand times yes."

Nathan surged upward from his kneeling position, gathering Emma into his arms for a kiss that tasted of joy and promise and the sweet certainty of forever. Beside them, Lily's delighted laughter mixed with the crackle of the fire.

"Well," Lily announced, wiping tears from her cheeks as Nathan and Emma broke apart, "I'd say this calls for champagne."

Nathan kept his arms around Emma, both of them still marveling at the ring that sparkled on her finger. "I may have picked up a bottle of champagne when I bought the groceries for tonight."

"You planned all of this," Emma accused, though her tone was filled with wonder rather than complaint. "The cooking lesson, having Aunt Lily here, the perfect ring..."

"I've been planning this since the Mistletoe Ball," Nathan admitted, pressing a soft kiss to her temple. "I knew that night that I wanted to spend my life dancing with you, building traditions with you, and creating the kind of family we've both been hoping for."

Emma turned in his arms to face Lily, who was beaming at them both with the satisfaction of someone who'd witnessed exactly the outcome she'd been hoping for.

"Aunt Lily," Emma said, extending her hand to display the engagement ring, "what do you think?"

Lily rose from the sofa to examine the ring more closely, her weathered fingers gentle as she lifted Emma's hand toward the light. "I think I'm witnessing the most beautiful moment I've seen since your uncle proposed to me," she said slowly. "I think that your mother would be absolutely thrilled. This is exactly the kind of love story she always dreamed you'd find."

The statement made Emma's throat tighten with emotion. Her mother's absence had been a quiet ache throughout the evening, and the awareness that she wasn't there to witness this milestone in Emma's life. But Lily's words brought comfort and assurance that love transcended physical presence.

"She would have loved Nathan," Emma said softly, leaning back against his chest as he held her close.

"She would have seen what I see," Lily agreed, her eyes moving between the newly engaged couple with deep satisfaction. "Two people who make each other better, who have something real and lasting, and who understand that love isn't just a feeling—it's a choice you make every day to put each other first."

The kitchen timer chose that moment to chime, reminding them that their casserole had finished cooking and was waiting for their attention.

"Well," Nathan said, his arms still wrapped around Emma, "our first meal as an engaged couple is ready."

"And it only took three adults to prepare it," Lily added with a chuckle.

Emma admired her ring one more time in the firelight. "I love you," she said, rising on her toes to press another kiss to Nathan's lips.

"I love you too, future Mrs. Reid," Nathan replied, his smile wide enough to rival the Christmas lights twinkling on the tree.

As they moved toward the kitchen to enjoy their carefully prepared Christmas Eve dinner, Emma felt the profound satisfaction of a story finding its perfect ending. Outside, snow was falling, blanketing Mistletoe Falls in the kind of pristine beauty that made ordinary moments feel touched with magic. Inside Nathan's warm home, surrounded by the man she loved and the woman who remained a constant positive in her life, Emma understood that this wasn't really an ending at all.

It was the most beautiful beginning she could have imagined.

Leave A Review

If you enjoyed this book, please consider leaving an honest review on Amazon

Visit Our Website:

www.tarabaisden.com

Visit Our Amazon Author Page HERE

Find Us On Social Media:

Facebook

Facebook Author Page

Instagram

Also by Tara Baisden

<u>Laurel Ridge Series</u>

#1. Season of Hope

#2. Finding Grace

#3. His Perfect Plan

#4. Love Redeemed

#5 Snowbound Blessings

#6 Sheltered Hearts

#7 Restoring Faith

#8 Love Rekindled

#9 Where She Belongs

#10 Shelter in His Arms

#11 Where Love Stands

#12 The Pieces We Mend

#13 Where Love Grows

#14 Where Hearts Heal

#15 Threads of Grace

<u>**Riverbend Valley Series**</u>

#1 A Cowboy's Second Chance

#2 Wanderlust & Wild Horses

#3 Heartstrings on the Horizon

#4 Runaway in Riverbend Valley

#5 Mended Hearts

#6 Healing Hearts

#7 Home to Lost Creek

<u>**Mistletoe Falls Series**</u>

#1 Whisk Me Under the Mistletoe

#2 Once Upon a Christmas

#3 The Mistletoe Express

#4 Candy Canes & Sweet Dreams

#5 Wrapped Up in Christmas

#6 Jingle All the Way Home

About The Author

Tara Baisden writes the kind of sweet, wholesome romances that feel cozy, comforting, and full of heart. She's the author of the beloved *Laurel Ridge* and *Riverbend Valley* inspirational series, as well as the *Mistletoe Falls* series, where Christmas magic and small-town charm are always on the menu.

A proud West Virginian, Tara makes her home on a peaceful stretch of mountain land where deer wander past her windows, the garden never quite weeds itself, and her pets supervise her writing schedule with great dedication. When she's not dreaming up stories of love, faith, and second chances, you'll likely find her quilting, digging in the dirt (sometimes successfully), hiking in the mountains, or curled up with a good book.

Family means everything to Tara, and some of her favorite moments are spent on the porch with loved ones—sharing stories, laughter, and maybe a slice of pie (because every good gathering needs pie). She also loves exploring the rich history of her home state and can't resist stopping at any bookstore she comes across.

Tara's readers often say her characters feel like family and her fictional towns like places they'd love to visit. Through every story, she hopes to inspire faith, celebrate love, and remind readers of the beauty found in life's simple joys.

You can connect with Tara at www.tarabaisden.com or follow her on social media for new releases, behind-the-scenes peeks, and the occasional glimpse of country life.

About Mistletoe Falls

Welcome to the fictional town of Mistletoe Falls, Tennessee!

Where Christmas Magic Lives Year-Round

*H*igh *in the Tennessee mountains, where winter lingers longer and Christmas spirit fills the air year-round, lies a town that feels almost too perfect to be real and looks like it stepped straight out of a holiday postcard.*

The winding mountain road to Mistletoe Falls tells you this isn't just any destination. Scenic Route 265 climbs higher into the Smoky Mountains with each breathtaking curve, past ancient trees heavy with snow that arch over the road like nature's own cathedral. But it's the final approach that steals your breath—crossing the enchanting Snowbell Covered Bridge, draped in evergreen garland and twinkling lights, as it spans the crystal waters of Mistletoe Creek below.

Beyond the bridge, the Welcome Pavilion greets every arrival with a hand-carved wooden sign: *"Welcome to Mistletoe Falls—Home of the Christmas Spirit."* The cheerful red pavilion, complete with candy cane striping and an archway of year-round twinkle lights, promises that something wonderful awaits just around the bend.

Mistletoe Falls (population 6,200) nestles in a perfect valley where the musical sound of cascading waterfalls mingles with church bells and children's laughter. The town spreads gracefully along Mistletoe Creek, whose series of waterfalls create the melodic backdrop to daily life.

This is Tennessee's beloved Christmas Town—because Christmas simply lives here. From the gas lamp streetlights wrapped in evergreen garland to the horse-drawn carriages clip-clopping down brick streets, every detail whispers of simpler times and sweeter moments.

The town square draws everyone like a magnet, centered around a Victorian gazebo where carols drift through the air and community life unfolds. Ancient oak trees frame the square, their branches creating natural shelter for the wooden benches below—each dedicated to a beloved neighbor who helped shape this special place. Thousands of lights transform the square into pure magic.

Mistletoe Lane curves gently around the town square before branching into charming side streets lined with century-old brick buildings. Each storefront tells a story through hand-carved details and cheerful striped awnings in hunter green, burgundy, and cream. Wide brick sidewalks invite leisurely strolls, while cozy benches appear just when you need them most.

The architecture whispers of careful love—original stonework preserved alongside modern conveniences, ensuring comfort while honoring the past. Three-story buildings house everything from the town bakery to the bookshop, with apartments above where business owners live.

From November through February, Mistletoe Falls transforms into a living snow globe. The special mountain microclimate ensures gentle snowfall that blankets everything in pristine white, while temperatures hover between 15 and 45 degrees—perfect for outdoor adventures and cozy indoor moments.

The partially frozen waterfalls become nature's chandeliers, catching winter light like thousands of diamonds. Snow-covered trails wind through frosted forests where the only sounds are your footsteps and the distant laughter from the town below. Long winter evenings mean crackling fireplaces, hot cider, and the kind of conversations that matter.

The Mistletoe Lodge stands as the town's crown jewel—a century-old mountain lodge with wraparound porches and stone fireplaces where love stories begin over morning coffee and evening wine. Its guest rooms blend historic charm with modern comfort, creating the perfect retreat for visitors who never quite want to leave.

The Snowbell Covered Bridge serves as more than transportation; it's where proposals happen and first kisses are shared, sheltered from mountain weather while framing perfect views of the approaching town.

The Mistletoe Christmas Tree Farm spreads across rolling hills on the town's outskirts, where families create memories among rows of Fraser firs and the air smells like pine and possibility.

What makes Mistletoe Falls magical isn't just its picture-perfect setting—it's the people who call it home. Three generations often work side by side in family businesses, while newcomers quickly discover they're not visitors but neighbors-in-waiting.

Local business owners coordinate holiday decorations and community events with the kind of collaboration that creates the seamless magic visitors remember long after they've returned home. This isn't performed charm—it's the real thing, preserved and protected by people who understand what they have.

In Mistletoe Falls, Christmas isn't a season—it's a way of life. The town square's gazebo hosts summer concerts alongside winter caroling. Local shops maintain touches of holiday magic through every season, because visitors quickly learn that any time is the right time to discover this special place.

The waterfalls provide cooling mists in summer and ice sculptures in winter. Mountain trails offer wildflower walks in spring and dramatic vistas in fall. But somehow, every season here feels like it's building toward December's grand celebration.